ETHOS

RICHARD A. GREYSON

To Carter—
I hope you enjoy
the ride!!

Richard A. Greyson

Ethos
Richard A. Greyson

ISBN 978-1-956197-00-6 paperback
ISBN 978-1-956197-01-3 ebook

It is sad that often, in order to be a good patriot, one must become the enemy of the rest of mankind.

Voltaire, 1764
Dictionnaire philosophique, "Patrie", iii

———

It is sometimes said that 'common sense is very rare'. What does this sentence mean? It means that in many men, the reasoning ability that had begun to develop was arrested in its progress by prejudices. Such men may judge very soundly in one matter and then always be grossly mistaken in another.

Voltaire, 1764
Dictionnaire philosophique, "Sens Commun"

———

Surely, whoever is able to make you believe absurdities can make you commit atrocities. If you do not use your God given intelligence to oppose orders from others to believe the impossible, then you will not oppose orders to do wrong despite the righteousness that God put in your heart. Once one part of your soul has been tyrannized then all other parts must follow. This is how religious crimes have inundated the earth.

Voltaire 1765
Questions sur les miracles

(All quotes loosely translated by the author)

Il est triste que souvent, pour être bon patriote, on soit l'ennemi du reste des hommes.

Voltaire, 1764
Dictionnaire philosophique, "Patrie", iii

———

On dit quelquefois, le sens commun est fort rare; que signifie cette phrase? que dans plusieurs hommes la raison commencée est arrêtée dans ses progrès par quelques préjugés, que tel homme qui juge très-sainement dans une affaire se trompera toujours grossièrement dans une autre.

Voltaire, 1764
Dictionnaire philosophique, "Sens Commun"

———

Certainement qui est en droit de vous rendre absurde est en droit de vous rendre injuste. Si vous n'opposez point aux ordres de croire l'impossible l'intelligence que Dieu a mise dans votre esprit, vous ne devez point opposer aux ordres de malfaire la justice que Dieu a mise dans votre coeur. Une faculté de votre âme étant une fois tyrannisée, toutes les autres facultés doivent l'être également. Et c'est là ce qui a produit tous les crimes religieux dont la terre a été inondée.

Voltaire 1765
Questions sur les miracles

CONTENTS

PREFACE

ETHOS is a compendium of thoughts based upon experiences lived, observed, and studied; however, despite its concrete origins, it is clearly a work of fiction and any resemblance to actual specific events or persons living or dead is entirely coincidental. As we simultaneously are and are not the simple equal part sum of our progenitor parents' DNA, the essences of this book's progenitors were smashed into fragments of various shapes, sizes, and hues and then reassembled like DNA into mosaics of character offspring that, while no single one ever existed, are comprised of the genetic shards and qualities of characters who indeed have.

Fundamental historical events and scientific facts in the book are all of course very real and references to government documents, peer reviewed literature, and contemporaneous reporting and writings are provided in order to accurately represent and support their objective foundations and present the reader with further reading on topics of interest. The characters in the book are of course free to be subjective regarding the meaning and significance of these events.

ONE

THE BEGINNING OF THE END

I don't have many possessions, but what I have is meaningful to me, is of good quality, and I retain these items with a sense of respect and devotion. When I was nine years old my parents gave me a prism for Christmas. I still have it. It sits on my bookshelf in front of *Cat's Cradle* by Kurt Vonnegut, and I look through it from time to time, as I have done since I first unwrapped it in front of the wood stove that gray snowy morning so many years ago. It is cut polished glass, nine inches in length, its base four and three-quarters inches in width and its cross section a one hundred twenty-degree isosceles triangle. Except for several pinky nail sized conchoidal chips and some minor scratches, its optical properties have remained essentially unchanged for more than the half-century that we have been together. Although temperature, pressure, stress, and impurities all affect the transmission of light through my prism, those effects are trivial. The engineered geometry at its creation and current orientation with respect to incident light are the prime determinants in defining how that light will be affected.

My prism can simply deflect light it encounters, or it can

accept and disperse it into discrete constituent wavelengths during its passage, splitting the incoming white light into bands of red, orange, yellow, green, blue, indigo, and violet. Following light through a prism is a bit like chasing Alice's White Rabbit through doorways of twisted perception. Some orientations make things larger or smaller, while others have the ability to bend the world into a rainbow-colored hallucination. Simply put, a prism never does nothing to that which passes through it. There is always an effect arising from the synergy of the inherent intelligent design and applied orientation of the device. I can observe as my prism twists, peels, and projects, and while what is projected is comprised of the constituent parts of the original thing, the projection often bears little physical resemblance.

Perhaps because I have spent so much time with my prism, the physics of these optical phenomena led me to create an analogous conceptual model for the metaphysics of human perception. I may also have been influenced a bit by something a friend once suggested long ago right after he killed someone in front of me, but that is another story. Of course, this model may not be accurate, but it helps me understand how one person's nightmare can be another's Nirvana. How sentient witnesses to a crime can provide such disparate descriptions of the perpetrator. How anyone could actually enjoy the smell of patchouli, the taste of tuna fish casserole, the appearance of huge plastic ear tunnel plugs, or be entertained by Garrison Keillor's Prairie Home Companion. In my model we are all prisms. We bend, split, and project what we sense according to our specific inherent internal properties and our current orientation, which are shaped respectively by nature (DNA) and nurture (experience). This prism paradigm explains the pathologically negative attractions and actions of others and perhaps allows me to navigate my life more positively around these human distortions. I am not interested in modifying anyone's optics. I just don't want to be around them.

Today, when I walk the streets of Austin, Texas, I see physical manifestations of these refractions and projections in graffiti tagged on walls and on streets and in the shallow aphorisms and symbols tattooed on young Trustafarians— you know, those wealthy trust fund kids who don't bathe or shave, wear designer Indian print clothing multiple nose piercings and dreadlocks, work infrequently for not-for-profit groups when they are not playing barefoot Frisbee or Hacky Sack, and spend more on their *ahimsa* and four elements tattoos than most people spend on a car. As I walk through Zilker Park, I watch as the older generations, faces largely hidden behind blue surgical masks, project fear and loathing through their nervous shifting eyes. They desperately two-step social distances between themselves and other humans, their hands outstretched and spinning invisible vinyl, while gleeful, hairy, maskless simians streak by in pursuit of Frisbees. One world. Two projections. Two perceptions.

I navigate physically through these disparate projections, and despite the heat I ease down onto my bench out on Lou Neff Point in what has now become a familiar incongruous cold sweat. I try breathing in the deep and controlled manner in which I have been instructed but instead gasp and wheeze in the uncontrolled manner to which I am becoming accustomed. I am uncomfortably enveloped by the diffuse sounds of revelry from the park behind me. The year is 2020 and it is summer, and the drumming of the hipster bongos synchronized with the beating of my feeble heart pounds my head with a sickening resonance.

It's almost ninety degrees Fahrenheit already and, as it is so often here in Texas, too hot for me to wear a mask. I have to take my chances. Even after dieting and bypass surgery I am still almost one hundred pounds overweight and as I sit alone on this bench of mine I feel the sweat collect within and then trickle down the folds of skin beneath my arms and pool, well, for lack of a better word, under my moobs. I stare out at the confluence of the Colorado River oozing by on my left, with Barton Creek on my right. I let my chin drop and contemplate my massive surgical scar. Like a purple worm crawling down my sternum, the scar is like an inanimate annelid notary stamp, certifying a new lease on an old life. Or perhaps it's more of an active parasite, slowly consuming the meager life remaining within me and leaving nothing in its place. I don't feel well and am partial to the parasite paradigm, which makes me wonder out loud.

"If nature abhors a vacuum, then what fills the emptiness the parasite leaves behind as it burrows through me? Shit?"

I moved to the Republic of Texas from the Commonwealth of Massachusetts in 1990 and I'm still not sure exactly why. I had a good job as an electrical engineer doing defense work at Raytheon outside Boston. I was happy living at home with my parents. I guess I thought a life change might be a growth opportunity for me and Texas sounded challenging at the time. I had no physical attachments, no house, no girlfriend, no real friends, and no real reason to stay except for work.

Maybe I thought I might meet some people who were more like me. Sometimes I think it had to do with the Berlin Wall and the collapse of a clear conceptual model of who our friends and enemies were and how everything that had fit together now seemed askew. Its fall confused much of what had previously appeared structured and predictable, despite the potential for violent conflict embedded within that defined structure, and it made me uneasy and left me a bit untethered. What would a post-Cold War defense industry look like?

For the time being, Texas Instruments was still in the

weapons business and therefore so was I. I made the move to Austin not knowing this small city was a haven for every liberal weirdo in the state. I also did not and could not know that seven years later in 1997, Texas Instruments would sell out my end of their business to my old employer Raytheon and they would clean house, leaving me here in Texas and out of a job. Look, I'm not crying over spilled milk. I didn't even have to go looking for the new job—it came to me. A couple of the guys in the office who knew about my international work back in Massachusetts and my interest in small arms approached me about joining them in a consulting group. They aimed to provide broad high quality security services to millionaires and billionaires, some of them with significant interpersonal baggage. These were often people with highly advanced security needs who already had at least one dedicated security professional on their premises. Domestically, our expertise in infrared and radar had frequent applications, while abroad, light and heavy weapons would likely play a more significant role.

I was forty years old by that time and I read somewhere once that a transition from engineering to sales around that age is a good career move. Maybe it is for some, but for me it was excruciating, and I should have seen it coming. Mingling with suppliers and onsite security professionals on the golf course, a fraternity of green, yellow, or pink khaki pants paired with a complementary colored polo shirt, collar upturned, sucking tasteless ultra light beer from cans. This became my reality. I feigned comfort and ease in crowds over raucous lunches with open collars and light blazers, studying the sports page beforehand like a textbook and pretending to be interested in who might make it to the Super Bowl. I was equally uncomfortable at our company team-building events, fishing off Galveston's offshore oil platforms, all of us dressed the same in our tan khakis and white or dark blue crew neck polo t-shirts. I courted some of our domestic clients directly from time to time, tightly buttoned up and focused like a tightrope walker over formal dinner describing our unique value proposition between laughing on cue as my client and his wife told racist jokes, sneered at the poor, and mocked the northern elite.

Despite my origins being precisely from the elite northeast, my aversion to racism, and proclivity for facts and solitude, I really loved designing security systems and putting together weapons packages, and so I accepted and was somehow successful in the associated theater. I crafted scripted communions and superficial rituals, and probably so did many of my clients to a certain extent, and we fed off each other with a wink and a nod to our success. There was plenty of insecurity to go around. I stayed in Austin and kept at it, and my act worked. I actually grew comfortable with these saccharine substitutes for relationships, despite the unnatural effort required to maintain them.

Overseas clients often preferred meeting outside the United States and I happily obliged. I met with African clients on their far west coast in the relatively safe and liberal Kingdom of Morocco, an easy commute for me and accessible to my clients by Royal Air Maroc from many major cities in Africa. The United Arab Emirates served as my business hub for the Middle East and Asia. Terminal 3 at Dubai International Airport was the largest building in the world when it was completed in 2008 and was a physical reflection of the burgeoning business in the region. These clients were different, and I looked forward to our meetings, as they were always interesting. I think because there was a language barrier, trivial conversation was minimized and that focus on honest, simple, direct conversation worked to draw us closer together. We didn't talk about sports, unless it was a World Cup year, and nobody wore polo shirts with the collar turned up. Many of my international clients were Muslim and didn't drink alcohol, and those that did tended towards good wine – none of them drank light beer. Unlike my domestic clients, these relationships were quite meaningful to me and over the years they grew along with the skylines of both Casablanca and Dubai.

Outside of work I developed no close friends, never connected with anyone, and never really tried. Even now I don't inspire even trivial recognition from my regular barista at Starbucks. The absence of inter-human responsibilities afforded me time to unplug from work. Strangely enough, I used this time for a busman's holiday of sorts, purchasing firearms and working on my marksmanship. I am personally partial to Heckler and Koch (H&K) and Fabrique Nationale (FN), and I sell elements of both product lines. I own an H&K MR556A1 in 5.56 mm and a FN SCAR 17S in 7.62 mm. Both are high quality reliable rifles that are enjoyable to shoot, but recently I have become more focused on pistols. I carry a small 9 mm Walther PPK and practice tactical shooting with it. I own a Colt 1911 45 ACP for when I feel I have to work out some particular kinks in my life. I also have a 22-caliber Smith & Wesson Model 41 competitive semiautomatic target pistol that has the same grip angle as the Colt 1911 but because of its smaller caliber is much easier on the wrist and the wallet to shoot. Texas is a Mecca for shooting enthusiasts and, like many others, I have a neighborhood indoor air-conditioned range where I go to work on my marksmanship, which as a result has become quite good. I keep to myself at the range, avoiding the blockheads with large biceps and low self-esteem shooting at human targets depicting African Americans and Arabs. I am at my most relaxed when I am in my own enclosed firing lane, insulated with my electronic noise cancelling muffs, looking down the sights of my rifle or pistol, slowly releasing my breath and fluidly squeezing the trigger.

Now, after 25 years of successful courting, conjuring, and selling, my neglected body is almost spent. I sometimes wonder about my soul, if such a thing exists. In dark retrospection, I see myself sleepwalking through the night terrors of much of that time as if in a Halcion haze, hiding behind thick drapes within the comforting darkness of my book-filled condominium after work, existing in order to awaken one day in retirement. Now I am retired, and I see the sum total of my life's work singularly reflected in my 401K, with which I am supposed to buy myself some time. I wipe the sweat from my brow, look down at my swollen ankles and sneaker-clad feet, and laugh out loud.

Time for what?

Although my mind remains sharp, my body retired me early, leaving me limping toward 70 and most likely a premature death alone, in Austin, sweating on a park bench surrounded by bongos, vapid coeds, democratic socialism and hipster stink. Consequently, I spend a significant portion of my waking time these days thinking about death and what is in store for me. You might think this is morbid, but I consider it to be appropriate. Some wait until they are on their deathbed to contemplate what might have been before, what might be after, and what just happened. These are the big questions, anyway. Where were we before we arrived in this life? Where will we go when we finally shuffle off this mortal coil? And while here, what is the nature of the reality we experience and what is the purpose of our existence? We cannot know the pre and post boundary conditions, but we can certainly dream about them while we work to observe and understand what occurs in between.

Sometimes I daydream about what a white evangelical Christian afterlife in their Paradise might look like. It is a beautiful sight: the sky a spectrum from robin's egg blue at the horizon to indigo set with shining stars and planets as a ceiling above, and a gossamer carpet of the softest bright white clouds below. Grinning white people wander aimlessly across the shifting terrain. Nobody wears a white robe or for that matter any clothes at all. Neither the men nor women have chins, just as in life, but strangely enough, many of the women have little penises and most of the men have brass testicles the size of cantaloupes. I ask a fellow standing next to me about these anatomical anomalies.

He replies, "Brother, this is heaven and up here you get what you wished for most during your life on earth."

The cries of men, women, and children rise up from somewhere below us and I peer over the edge of the cloud to a smoldering ring below. The inferno. The thirteenth century writer and philosopher Dante Alighieri wrote in The Divine Comedy of the inferno's nine rings, eternal homes to those who in life rejected spiritual values, yielded to bestial appetites and violence, and perverted their intellect to commit fraud or malice against others. In the first ring, decent pagans reside in a castle with seven gates symbolizing the seven virtues. The lustful, who in life threw reason to the wind, are buffeted by endless punishing gales in the second ring. The third ring is reserved for the gluttons, who wallow and fart in an icy slush. The fourth ring contains the hoarders and spendthrifts, who throw broken kitchen appliances and boom boxes at each other. The fifth ring is comprised of a deep water filled moat, where the angry curse and struggle to strike and slash at each other on the surface, while the sullen drown slowly and deliberately in the murky waters below. The smoldering tanning beds of the sixth ring are reserved for heretics. In the seventh ring, murderers, suicides, drunks, homosexuals, and blasphemers are rained upon by burning sand, torn apart by harpies, and then boiled in blood. The eighth ring houses liars, hypocrites, and politicians, who are forced to march around wearing lead clothes while they are beaten and disfigured by various means, and then submerged in a river of filth. The ninth ring is a frozen lake reserved for those guilty of betrayal, and is home to the most treacherous of all, Lucifer.

I turn to the gentleman, still close by my side. "I thought there were supposed to be nine rings below, but I only see one."

"Oh yeah, I heard there used to be nine rings years ago, but heaven would be pretty empty these days if we kept out all the drunk, angry, depressed, morbidly obese, lying, porn-addicted hoarders."

I nod my head in agreement. "So who are the people down there in that one ring now?"

"Those are the elites: you know, the educated liberal snobs, along with the Jews, Catholics, pretty much anyone who doesn't subscribe to our particular evangelical view of politics or Christianity."

Nearby, a large cluster of men and women pump their right fists in the air, chanting, spitting, and taunting those below.

JE-SUS-CHRIST! JE-SUS-CHRIST! JE-SUS-CHRIST! JE-SUS-CHRIST!

Other smaller groups huddle together, arms around each other's shoulders, swaying as they sing to the tune of Queen's "We are the Champions."

We are the Christians, my friends
And we'll keep on fighting 'til the end
We are the Christians
We are the Christians

No time for Catholics
No time for Muslims
No time for Hinduus
No time for Jew-ews
'Cause we are the champions
Of eternity!

I ask my companion about these cliques: "I thought in a Christian afterlife there would be more of a focus on loving one's neighbor, maybe an eternal existence guided by the prince of peace, you know."

He looks at me and frowns. "Hey, we're not just Christians here, we're evangelical Christians and we're white. You know buddy, you're starting to sound like an elite asshole. Look, why don't you just shut up, sit down, eat some fish and drink some wine and chant like everybody else?"

Other days, I imagine the *Olam Haba*, the Jewish world to come. I picture it as a celestial university. It's an excellent school. I study in silence, slowly rocking back and forth, for several millennia. They have a buffet with nova, borscht, bagels, potato salad, and celery soda. The food is not bad. Instead of earning a Ph.D., I graduate with a higher consciousness. With this credential, the food gets better, and I can now get ice-cold cream soda. I keep studying here for eternity, because you can never be too knowledgeable.

My Hindu daydream follows a different path. I stand on a bank of the Ganges River and watch as a group of people light the sandalwood pyre upon which my brightly colored cloth-wrapped body lies. The Lord of death and time and the destroyer of worlds, Kala, stands silently beside me. The pyre ignites, and my withered body, with all of its worldly blemishes, spirals into the twilight of the dawn sky and the grand illusion that has been my latest life comes to a close. My liberated soul now stands at the crossroads of the sun and moon. Although I look to Kala to learn my fate, I understand I have not used this last life to shake off the illusory attachments of existence - I have collected a lot of books, firearms, and furniture.

Kala taps his wrist, points toward the moon, and says with a wink: "It's time. Get it?"

My destiny, once again, is to follow the ancestral path to the south, become food for the gods until it is time for me to be rained down upon the earth, thus returning to the grand illusion, in search of the perfection that has managed to elude me since time began.

Absent an established religion, and therefore an associated religious conceptual model for the afterlife, I am instead left with a simple vision I often return to. I picture myself walking down a rural dirt road edged by mature hardwood trees, much like the one that leads to my childhood home in Massachusetts. The leaves are changing color, with reds, oranges, and yellows speckled throughout the maples, but many remain green, and few have fallen. The air is still and contains that sweet, earthy scent I associate with fall. It is always early morning, and the light is a diffuse yellow gray. There are no animals, insects, or other spirits. I am alone. I have no apparent destination. I walk. I am calm. I am satisfied. I am at peace.

I am unsure of my fate after death, as I believe any sane person is, but I hope I am not reborn to another life cycle through Texas, because while there are thankfully less woke hippies with their bongos outside Austin, things are intellectually worse. That other Texas is home to unwoke conspiracies. From the Kennedy assassination to Jade Helm 15, Texas seems to feed on uncertainty, breed disinformation and cultivate madness. These are people whose heads are stuck somewhere between the Dark Ages and Sean Hannity's asshole and want us to join them as they eat their musty turds. And it's not just Texas—did you know that only twenty-five percent of Americans today are able to name the three branches of government? And despite—or as a result of—that lack of fundamental knowledge, only seventeen percent trust that un-understandable government in Washington to do what is right? I mean, seriously, you only have to remember three things: legislative, executive, and judicial and have a rough idea of what each one does. How can these people know what their favorite sports hero eats for breakfast and yet not know something so fundamental and integral to being part of what Jefferson called a trusted informed electorate?

While crime continues to decline since 1993,[1] hate crime murders keep increasing, mostly directed at African Americans, Hispanics, and Jews.[2] Domestic violent extremists today cause more deaths than international terrorists, and they target those they believe—not even "know" or "understand"—promote multiculturalism and globalization at the expense of their white supremacist extremist identity. These people are the most persistent and lethal threat in our Homeland, yet they call themselves patriots and don't know the three branches of our government. They have neatly replaced the lunatic twelfth century belief that cabals of Jews engaged in ritual murder and cannibalism of Christian children,[3] with the ritual murder and cannibalism of children by a cabal of democrats in the twenty-first century.[4]

So Texas is not alone in this cognitive descent. Americans in general have steadily devolved from consciously informed, to consciously uninformed, to unintentionally misinformed, to deliberately and aggressively misinformed and unwilling to learn. They are overfed and undernourished. Accompanying this mental decline is the net decay of roads, bridges, airports, hospitals and schools, physical symbols of the internal intellectual rot. It is as if the country is afflicted with

Alzheimers. It has latched on to a mythic past that never was, is unable to understand the present, and lacks the imagination to imagine a future. I love my country, but it seems no longer capable of caring for itself and I no longer recognize it.

I fight this national entropy alone, at home within my bubble, with bookshelves supporting a collection of antique scientific instruments and over two thousand books spanning multiple topics within science, technology, and society: The King James Bible is bounded by the Koran and the Bhagavad Gita, *The Quark and the Jaguar* by *The Case Against Reality* and *Phantoms in the Brain*, *The Honored Dead* by *Tales from the Arabian Nights* and *Leo Africanus*. Outside my bubble strut squawking throngs of ersatz intellectuals at both ends of the political spectrum, lacking interest in objective knowledge of any kind, shouting to be heard and demanding to be respected. Connected to the world exclusively through television sets and computer monitors, they reject actual experience and high veracity information that does not immediately dovetail with preexisting belief structures they have conjured from trash. And the acquisition and consumption of trash is substantial. The average American watches three hours of television every day, which equates to almost a decade of 24-hour-a-day television watching over a 79-year lifetime. They burn half of their leisure hours each day connected to television sets, sedentarily ingesting the emitted predigested muck. I don't want to know how the other half is spent but I have my suspicions. The numbers are even worse if you consider time spent interacting with media in general.[5]

My observation is that, during my lifetime, observable and significant damage has occurred. Each year more and more of these subjectively knowledgeable idiots insist their opinions, no matter how substantively uninformed and absurd, be treated with the same serious respect as that of informed experts. Charles Darwin said - "ignorance more frequently begets confidence than does knowledge".[6] These are people who, as Dunning and Kruger might say, don't even know enough to know what they don't know.[7] Everybody seems messed up these days except for me, which is in itself a pretty cliché observation and suggests that perhaps I am actually the one with the problem. Maybe I am—maybe I am the one that has latched on to a mythic past— I'm not sure. What I am sure of is that I am painfully alone, yet I want nothing to do with these other human beings.

My present is wretched and the future appears at best limited and bleak, but it wasn't always like this. Before three decades of takeout burritos, enchiladas, and queso wrecked my heart, before work wrecked my soul, before cable TV and twenty four hour news and the Worldwide Web drained the pool and began the lobotomizations, before we added the last one hundred million people and all of their whiny superficial needs and desires to our nation, before the collapse of the familiar geopolitical structures that supported my worldview, for a while, when everything was simpler, I was trim and fit and found order and meaning and comfort and inspiration in the world and the people around me. The world was probably messier then than it is now, but at least I was not a passive observer. I moved through that messy world, and one could observe the perturbations and quantify the effects that I had upon the systems I touched. I was real, I was physical, I was significant, and I made a difference.

There was a fundamental clarity then that is gone now. It was a time of pragmatic pessimism because we knew our enemies and they were very dangerous, and they wanted to kill us just like we wanted to kill them. It was also a time of boundless optimism born of the confluence of youth and serendipity, and there were real people with whom I could share these experiences. But time killed those days, polluted my heart, and separated me from those I loved. I search the mirror now for clues to my existence when I floss at night. My eyes, like smooth beach stones set in empty sockets, have no depth, yet I continue to look to them for recognition, meaning, or understanding in their nothingness. Do four billion years of DNA peer out with me through these dark windows into this world? Are my ancestors saddened by what they see? Are they disappointed that we are so alone and that our communal strand ends with me? Or is it all just nothingness?

The intent of the surgery was to correct a physically damaged heart, and my physicians assure me their observations confirm this has been accomplished. What they cannot see, however, are the inner knock-on effects of this surgery: a swirling spiritual meteorological system, spawning high- and low-pressure subsystems of reality. Just as winter storms uncover old shipwrecks on the beach, these metaphysical storms expose elements of the past, many of which had rested in peace for decades. These are not all personal memories, as some events I experience belong directly to the lives of others I am connected to that I did not participate in. How is that possible? I think it's a bit like a quaking aspen forest. Above ground one sees thousands of individual trees. Look below ground and they all share a common root structure. Peer into their genetic sequence and they are in fact all identical organisms. Or maybe it's a case of quantum entanglement: multiple humans remote from each other yet inextricably linked across space and time like electrons.[8] For lack of a better word I refer to these things as recollections, emphasis on the "re", with me retrieving and collecting this information from the past of my entangled human aspen forest through beyond-space-time tendrils.

These connections are complicated. I never know if I will arrive in my lived past, someone else's lived past, an alternate past, or here in the present in beyond-space-time; or am I in some alternate present, or maybe just simply dreaming? As far as recollections go, these are neither skeletal nor pedestrian. They are physical, vividly leveraging all five senses and, like the skin of an unripe avocado, not easily separated from the flesh of reality. Some leave me squinting in shame. Others straighten my posture and may even evoke a smile. My relationship with these recollections is emotionally complex but simple in that they all make me feel again. Given I am associated with their birth it seems I should embrace their corpses, and given I exhumed them, then perhaps it is also my responsibility to reinter them. Although some recollections are easier to embrace than others, I find it remarkable that, when the accounting is complete, how such a small fraction of one's life is associated with the powerful emotions accompanying the quest to fulfill dreams and aspirations—and how that small fraction tends to reside within our youth. Maybe that is why so many of us live in the past, because the present is so vapid and the future promises nothing but emptiness?

The palpable nature of these recollections, if that is in fact what they are, has reintroduced me to the simple flaws associated with our Newtonian view of absolute time and space—a conceptual model that works fine for everyday activities—and shoved me back, past even the discomfort of Einstein's space-time with its curvatures and black holes, a conceptual model that most physicists today will tell you is itself overly simplistic and in fact doomed.[9] While string theory and the land beyond-space-time are outside my ability to truly comprehend, like Einstein, I am confident that our simple linear conception of time, our daily practical reality framework, is flawed. This confidence does not arise from quantum mechanics and special relativity, but because my mother could predict the future, not all the time but sometimes and specifically, and if time is linear then this is impossible, and we probably wouldn't have the term déjà vu in our lexicon. Yet somehow, she was able to tap into the non-linearity of time for a glimpse of things both meaningful and mundane that were not yet. Without listening to the traffic report on the radio, she always seemed to know when my father would be late from work because of an accident on Route 2 and would adjust dinner accordingly. She packed her bags the day before getting a call that my grandfather had unexpectedly passed away. And she bundled me into the car one day and swiftly drove me to the hospital even though I insisted I was feeling fine; my appendix ruptured as we pulled into the circular drive at Emerson Hospital in Concord.

Einstein wrote that time and space are human constructs, not objective realities.[10] They are simply modes by which we think and not conditions within which we live. The fourteenth century alchemist Paracelsus wrote that the superficial observer sees only that which exists for his senses, but the interior sight, or conceptual framework, discovers the things of the future.[11] Einstein was a quiet thoughtful genius and Paracelsus a raging alcoholic madman, yet both seem to agree that the model through which one views reality defines the constraints of what is possible to see and that model arises in part through the gift of free will and the power of imagination.

The Nobel laureate physicist Richard Feynman's self-esteem was not wounded by his inability to understand quantum mechanics because he recognized that nobody possessed a true understanding;[12] the important thing for him was to imagine and remain entranced by the possibilities and to have fun. But despite my intellectual and imaginative capabilities—or perhaps because of my disabilities in these areas—I still lack a single clear conceptual model of what my vision of beyond-space-time looks like that satisfies, much less delights me.

Is it like the predestined world of the Arabs, a fuse of finite length that was manufactured, lit fourteen billion years ago at the big bang and is now burning towards the end of time—or maybe another big bang? A world where the most trivial occurrences are already woven within the fuse of time, and everything is *maktub*—already written?

Maybe it's buried somewhere deep within our two-dimensional computer interface approach to defining reality, images and experiences appearing real to us when viewed superficially through our eyes from our specific focal distance, but when examined at a quantum level are no longer holistically meaningful and instead pure pixels of deep information. Take a pixelated look at another human being and 99.9999 percent of that person becomes a massless sky filled with beautiful clouds of gauzy dynamic electrons.

Then again, maybe we are just like Schrödinger's cat, hiding in a land beyond-space-time with an equal probability of being dead and alive in our unseen existence. Or maybe like the snake Ouroboros eating its own tail, beyond-space-time flows like the cosmic River Tao, descending in tall roaring mountain cascades to lazy coastal meanders and then into the sea, only to be resurrected as a cloud and fly back to the mountain cascades and begin the journey back into the sea again in an endless cycle of rebirth?[13]

Recollections of singular events regularly differ between collocated observers, opening the door to a reality Venn diagram, complete with overlaps and exclusion zones. Some-times, a shared contemporary reality contains elements discordant with the constitutive elements of a previous reality shared by the same observers. Some call this the Mandela effect because so many people (not me) recall Nelson Mandela dying in prison back in the 1980s, with great mourning across the world and rioting in Johannesburg; but Mandela did not die until 2013, long after he left prison. As kids we watched the evil Queen in Disney's Snow White say, "mirror, mirror on the wall, who's the fairest of them all", when in fact she does not say this if you watch the movie now. Ask one hundred people to describe Frankenstein, and very few will offer that he is a young, handsome, Swiss scientist. It seems we all (including me) recall Humphrey Bogart saying "Play it again Sam" in Casablanca and Darth Vader saying, "Luke, I am your father" in Star Wars, even though neither line is spoken if you watch these movies now. So where did those elements in our collective memory come from or go to, or were they ever really there to begin with? Are we part of an extraterrestrial virtual reality game where these discrepancies represent flaws in the game's code? When we sleep, are our disconnected dreamtime dramas simply our reality sold at a lower price to multiple other game players?

While it is imprudent for someone like me to attempt to reconcile all of these conceptual models within a single unified framework for others, there's nothing wrong with developing a user-friendly amalgamation for myself. I like the River Tao as a big picture beyond-space-time model, but it doesn't work very well on my first-person singular I-AM scale. I slip back and forth these days between the past and the present, which means the river must be frozen and I am wearing metaphysical ice skates. This seems like a bit of a stretch.

If I begin with a conceptual model of consciousness fixed in time and space, I favor the elephant rider analogy, where the elephant represents my autonomic system and the rider my higher consciousness, my I-AM.[14] To reconcile my recent slipping in time and space with the clumsiness of the ice skate analogy, I have decided to adopt a simple Newtonian approach, where my I-AM becomes a block on the inclined plane of beyond-space-time. When the tilt of the plane becomes great enough that the metaphysical static frictional force of what we think of as reality that holds my consciousness to this place and time is exceeded by whatever metaphysical gravity-equivalent force is tugging at me, I begin to slip down the beyond-space-time slope until I hit a patch of beyond-space-time where the metaphysical equivalent kinetic frictional coefficient becomes great enough such that I come to a stop. I have no idea how the plane gets tilted one way or another. I exist throughout this process but, like a quantum particle, I don't have a fixed position of existence until I stop and ascertain my position. If I am indeed following some quantum rules, depending upon whether I am introspective or not, I might exist in a single location or, like a wave, be distributed across several places simultaneously. It can be a bit confusing.

So far, I have been slipping backwards, down the slope, usually to a known time and space and then back to Austin again. Sometimes I find myself in a previously unknown time and space, but I have never, like Billy Pilgrim, slipped to another planet to fall in love and have supernatural sex with my very own beyond-space-time version of Montana Wild-hack, however appealing that may sound. I rarely slip back to the recent past and I have never found myself golfing with clients in Texas. It is as if some of my past has no texture, and I slide right by. Since I began slipping, much of the available past is that which occurred before I came to Texas or occurred someplace other than Texas. I'm not sure why. It's not that nothing happened, and I have no past in Texas, it's perhaps that so much of my life here never really meaning-fully happened. The meaningful past to which I slip is often a bit rough, like an uncomfortable plunge into the dark cold waters of a murky forest pond. But often I find myself cradled within a warm bath of recollection that relaxes with familiarity and cleanses with introspection.

My first slip beyond-space-time occurred as the anesthetist placed the mask over my face on the operating table. Or perhaps it occurred a bit later, when the surgeon reached in and touched my heart with his hands. I can't be sure, but when I landed and opened my eyes it was May 12, 1979 and I was with my friends in Amherst on the University of Massachusetts stadium field and I instantly felt a familiar joy that had long since gone dormant within me.

Despite the familiarity of place and feeling though, the experience of arriving there on that field via this first slip was complicated. I was there, in my body, looking through my eyes, just as I had in 1979—that was simple. I was, however, also omnisciently observing myself being there, which added a significant layer of peculiarity to the experience. How is it possible to be both participant and observer? Well, it was sort of like when you walk into a store and look up to simultaneously see yourself walking into that store on a closed circuit video monitor hanging from the ceiling in the doorway; but, absent the clunky physical technology gap, the duality of my metaphysical experience was seamless.

To make things even more confusing, I was tripping on acid that day while listening to Patti Smith and waiting in a light rain for the Grateful Dead to come on stage. I had tried acid only once before; it was Mad Hatter blotter and I found it controllably enjoyable, with nice trails, breathing tree leaves, crystalline air, and all that sort of lovely tripping stuff. But today I had taken a very thick piece of aquamarine blue windowpane and as a result, during Smith's set both her nose and wide brimmed floppy Panama hat grew progressively, and impossibly, larger until eventually I stood in the deep shade of this swelling pavilion peering uncomfortably up her dark cavernous nostrils. Circling—not very high above her head it seemed—a red biplane left a rainbow colored trail through the pudding-thick air as it performed graceful aerial acrobatics in time to the music.

Then suddenly the Grateful Dead appeared out of nowhere, replacing Smith's discordance with their familiar quavering folky strains, the crowd's upraised arms gyrating in time to the music. The song sounded like Jack Straw, which I love but I couldn't be sure, as it was about this time that I lost my ability to discern words from sound. Voices became smudged and indistinct with everyone, except me, sounding like the teacher in a Charlie Brown cartoon. Bwa maw maw wa shwah wah thwah waw. This loss was disconcerting and I wondered if the LSD had permanently fried a circuit in my auditory cortex.

Before I had a chance to enter a full-blown freak-out, a torrential roar like the storm carrying Wagner's Valkyrie distracted me. I turned to look in its direction as the crowd on the field parted, like the Red Sea before Moses' staff, and a corpulent Hell's Angel seated upon a gigantic black Harley Davidson motorcycle, sporting swastikas and an iron cross, emerged from the gap. Gunning his engine and working the clutch, this filthy Norse troll made his way slowly through the tightly packed crowd, shutting the bike down with a backfire right in front of the stage. Ho jo to ho! The crowd roared, the sun broke through the clouds, and as if a healer's hand had passed over me I regained my hearing and the world was right again. I smiled, looked up, closed my eyes and took a deep relaxing breath. Then I opened my other eyes. The sterile white walls and sheets, and the cool, dry, solitary silence of my hospital room a visceral dichotomy to the warm drizzly air thick with tie-dyed bodies, the smell of weed and the sounds of psychedelic music I had just left. I closed my eyes again and embraced the simple darkness, smiling the smile of the truly blessed, grateful for a chance to relive the past and never considering that brief slip beyond-space-time to be anything more than a one-off aberration. Since then, I have come to slip more easily—without anesthesia or surgery—and lately I find myself slipping quite often.

TWO

THE END OF THE CENTURY

The 1970s neatly contain all of my formative teen and college years and perhaps it is the associated frictions within that decade that frequently bring my slips to a stop there. When that decade ended so too did many of the simple foundations of my childhood, destroying my heretofore school-centric universe and ushering me smoothly into a linear work chute leading to old age and death that I am sure Temple Grandin would find cruel and offensive. 1979 cracked open the door to a nascent maturity for which I was only somewhat prepared yet clearly doomed to accept. Arriving concurrent with that forced maturity were a rapid series of global events that stretched the boundaries of sanity and encouraged one towards a greater consumption of cannabis with which to dull the jagged edges of reality. Sometimes, I close my eyes and begin to smell sewer gas, dog shit, and diesel exhaust from worn out city buses mixing with the pungent odors of old urine and marijuana, then I hear the staccato strains of rebellious punk rock escaping from a musty Bowery basement and I let myself go. The Ramones sang that 1979 was not just the end of the 70s but instead the end of the century. Chronologically, there is no sane argument to be made against 1979 being the end of the 70s or to be made for it being the end of the century. But perhaps those talented glue-sniffing cretins were right about the 20th century coming to a figurative end. The zeitgeist of 1979, a very messed up year in and of itself, christened the launch of the titanic 1980s, which more resemble the twenty-first century than the twentieth. Maybe that is why I slip so often to that particular interface year between the old and the new.

1979 was the year McDonalds first offered the Happy Meal, Sony launched the Walkman, and the first American cinematic reflection of Vietnam—*The Deer Hunter*—won an Academy Award for best picture. Brenda Ann Spencer got the blues one Monday and opened fire at a middle school, inspiring the Boomtown Rats song: "I Don't Like Mondays." Eleven fans were stampeded to death when the doors opened to The Who's general admission concert in Cincinnati. Pink Floyd opened *The Wall* live in Los Angeles. The Who opened *Quadrophenia* live in London. Some were following the trial of Sid Vicious for killing Nancy and listening to the Talking Heads and the Clash. Others were grooving to the top 40 hits, with new songs like Rod Stewart's "Do Ya Think I'm Sexy", "My Sharona" by the Knack, Donna Summers "Bad Girls", "YMCA" by the Village People, and the piña colada song by Rupert Holmes. The anti-disco song "Dancin' Fool" by Frank Zappa only hit number 45 on the charts, a reflection of how many disco ducks still remained on the dance floor.

In January the North Vietnamese invaded Cambodia, driving out Pol Pot and his genocidal Khmer Rouge and uncovering the skulls of millions of intellectuals executed in places like Choeung Ek. In February, Iranian anti-nationalists overthrew America's friend the Shah of Iran and Sid Vicious died in New York City of a heroin overdose. By spring, Iran had become a New Republic, with Ray-Bans replaced by veils and leather jackets by robes; in late summer the book burnings began.

In early spring, the movie *China Syndrome* was released and an eerily similar problem at the Three Mile Island nuclear power plant in Pennsylvania arrived immediately at its heels, serving to amplify and make "China Syndrome" a household term. Industry experts, who had never heard of the Soviet town of Chernobyl, ascertained the danger from radiation in Pennsylvania was insignificant and this type of accident would not happen again in the next one thousand years. In Pakistan, the deposed Prime Minister, Zulfikar Bhutto, was hanged in April. In Uganda the gluttonous cannibal Idi Amin waddled out the back door, leaving behind nothing but human bones picked clean of flesh. Just down the road the Marxist Mugabe's Zimbabwe was gestating with serious birth defects. On the Caribbean island of Grenada, a coup installed Maurice Bishop as the new pro-Soviet leader of another brilliant communist nation right in our backyard.

In early June, the Gulf of Mexico experienced its largest oilfield catastrophe to date when the Ixtoc 1 well exploded, spewing hundreds of millions of gallons of oil into the sea. In late June, sixty-two sheiks were murdered in Syria by the fundamentalist Islamic group The Muslim Brotherhood and in July, Iraqi President Hasan Al-Bakr resigned and was replaced by his handsome mustachioed Vice President Saddam Hussein. One month later, Saddam dispatched twenty-two of his liberal political opponents and began a close relationship with America to fight totalitarianism in the region as brothers in arms. In July, President Carter secretly authorized direct aid to mujahideen fighters challenging the pro-Soviet regime in Afghanistan. In Nicaragua, pro-Soviet leftists who called themselves Sandinistas overthrew America's friend Generalissimo Somoza. In August, a swamp rabbit attacked President Carter while he was canoeing in Georgia.

In a September coup supported by the Soviet Union, another Amin, this one in Afghanistan, overthrew Taraki to become president. And at the small liberal arts Occidental College, a young African American freshman from Hawaii named Barry Obama arrived wearing bellbottoms and a wide brimmed hat, shaking shakas, and beginning to carve his patriotic path in life.

In October, the Director of the South Korean CIA assassinated President Park Chung-hee on a whim, a freak EF4 tornado demolished Windsor Locks in Connecticut, and a more freakish tsunami killed 23 people on the Mediterranean beaches of Nice in France.

In November, the President of Bolivia was deposed in a coup allowing the leftist Lidia Gueiler Tejada to become the first female President of Bolivia. In Texas, the Burmah Agate lost almost 11 million gallons of oil off Galveston in what, at the time, was America's worst oil spill. A group of several hundred fundamental Islamic militants occupied the Grand Mosque in Mecca, demanding that one of their members be recognized as the messiah. The militants were eventually all killed or captured by French commandos invited into the Kingdom by the House of Saud, but not before thousands of Islamic fundamentalist students at Quaid-I-Azam University in Islamabad, Pakistan, convinced that in fact America had invaded the Grand Mosque, attacked and set fire to the American embassy. The embassy was destroyed, and four employees killed. Thousands of young Koran-waving fanatics from Iran's universities attacked the American embassy in Tehran and took ninety hostages. America watched these kids posturing every night on the news for the next four hundred and forty-four days. On the thirteenth day of the month,

Ronald Reagan announced his candidacy for President with a platform built upon his vision for a free trade agreement between the United States and Mexico that would, under the tutelage of George H.W. Bush, eventually become NAFTA.[1]

On Christmas Eve, the Soviet Union invaded Afghanistan and overthrew Amin. Two days later, on December 27th, the Soviet Red Army assassinated Amin in Afghanistan and the Soviet Red Army hockey team assassinated the New York Rangers 5-2 at Madison Square Garden. To add insult to injury, on December 29th the Soviets terminated the Islanders 3-2 at the Nassau Coliseum.

America was living on the edge in 1979, and was dealing with that existential angst by conjuring images of exactly what the day after nuclear annihilation would look like. We were always at the brink of war with the Soviet Union and at Pease Air Force Base on the New Hampshire seacoast, nuclear-armed FB-111s from the 509th Bomb Wing cycled out over the ocean to practice for the end of days. In 1979, General Dynamics produced seventy-six of these planes; one of them crashed in downtown Portsmouth in 1981 and eleven others met equally violent fates in the quiet forests of Maine and Vermont before they could deliver their deadly packages.

I started college in 1976, one year after Saigon fell to the communists, and graduated in 1980, the year Ronald Reagan was elected President and the world changed, but it seems my whole life is tinted by 1979. It is a critical inflection point for me, and the events of each subsequent year were set at least in part within its twisted context. As a college freshman, I arrived on campus like a human pupa. Over the next four years, I slowly emerged from my chrysalis—aided by those who would be my first real human friends. By 1979, my wings—while still fragile—were dry, my nascent relationships mature, and now the prime influences on the nature and boundaries of my super-ego instead of my parents. It was as if the path of my life had led upslope to scale the heights of 1979 just in time for my first independent comprehensive view of the world. The absence of opacity and the elegance of simplicity of that view were appealing and it would have been easy to stay on that summit with its unchanging view of the surrounding madness, and many like me did. Instead, I scaled more mountains, gaining additional perspectives that have contributed to my current sexagenarian conceptual model of the world. But those multiple subsequent perspectives and that formative view from 1979 are not mutually exclusive so much as complementary, and that first breath-taking panorama of the mad world we live in has not escaped me.

So, I agree with the Ramones: 1979 was the end of the century. It was also the beginning of the end of my time in college, the beginning of the end of the friendships I had made there, the beginning of the end of how I looked at the world, and the beginning of the end of who I had become in those critical years.

THREE

ROOTS

I try to reconcile my current situation in this space and time, here on this bench in Texas, with that of my origins. How does one willingly trade cool clean air, a clear blue sea, and an enlightened history for the converse? I sound like Roger Waters, having exchanged uncertainty and change for cold comfort and safety within this cage I created for myself. And nobody got me to do it—I did it to myself. I gaze up at the sky as the oppressive heat that is my life now continues its punishment, and feel the shame that accompanies the irresponsible loss of something precious. I close my eyes, grimace, and slip.

The summer sun, embedded within an azure sky loosely punctuated by cumulus clouds, sits high and hot over a broad field of emerald and amethyst clover, rimmed by crumbling stone walls and tall red oaks. The fragrant wind is subtle, and a lone asynchronous cicada shatters the quiet from his tree as the clover silently sequesters nitrogen from the warm breeze in the field below. A kid in worn Levis, porcelain white t-shirt, and battered blue Keds kneels hunched mid-field as if in prayer. But he is not praying, because he needs neither guidance nor help. He finishes packing the parachute in the nose cone, and then expertly loads the Estes C rocket engine into the body of the rocket. Gently removing the nichrome wire igniter clenched between his teeth, he folds, then inserts it into the engine, splays the two ends, and then slides the rocket down the launch rod and onto the launch pad. He attaches alligator clips, whose wires lead to the motorcycle battery he has placed five paces away, to each end of the igniter. Siting upright now and balancing back on his heels, he stretches his arms high up into the air then lets them fall slowly to his sides like a yogi. The stage is set. He stands and walks serenely back to where he has set the battery, a pair of binoculars, and a box of rocket engines and igniters. He connects the positive cable to the terminal, checks that the launch switch on the ground cable is set to pre-launch, then connects the ground cable. It is T minus almost any time now to launch. He sets the binoculars next to him, brushes a deer fly from his forearm, picks up the launch switch, and begins the countdown out loud: "10, 9, 8, 7, 6, 5, 4, 3, 2, 1 and ignition!"

With a fluid motion the boy flips the switch, the engine ignites immediately and the rocket streaks skyward with a loud hiss. He reaches quickly for the binoculars and tracks the rocket's ascent. It climbs up through the sky 500 feet, 1000 feet, 1500 feet, and reaches apogee. The engine cuts out, backfires, and the delicate parachute unfurls like a flower, gently returning the rocket back to earth. The boy smiles, having moved once again through the familiar well-defined multi-stage process that, if followed fastidiously, rewards with comforting predictability.

My name is Christopher LeBlanc, and I am that kid. I grew up outside of Boston in rural Stow, Massachusetts. Everybody called me Christopher back then—not Chris, not

Topher—and they still do now. My father James was an Army war hero in Korea who returned to work for the government, and my mother Elizabeth a registered nurse who went on to become a nurse practitioner after I had successfully completed elementary school. They were an unusual couple for the times in which they lived because they loved each other very much and, while strict, were considerate of me. They played classical music on the stereo each morning, relying on their collection of thick vinyl records that leaned heavily towards Vivaldi and Dvořák, and jazz in the afternoons dominated by Thelonius Monk and John Coltrane. I was encouraged to listen to modern music, on thinner vinyl, in my bedroom at a reasonable volume.

Although both my parents had been raised as Catholics, we didn't follow any particular religion. My father told me he had some experiences while in Korea—experiences he never shared— that opened his eyes and made him question our *raison d'etre* as described by the church. While he continued to seek an answer to this fundamental question, he had developed substantial clarity of thought regarding the genesis, form, function, and dysfunction of organized religion.

"Christopher, for most of human existence we existed freely under the sun and stars without a structured set of religious edicts and constraints. We respected that something greater than ourselves existed—something so wondrous it was indefinable—that we called the Great Spirit, or something of that nature. And because we understood it was indefinable, we didn't bother—we had other things to do like hunting, fishing, and enjoying life. We simply offered it respect, as we did with all life on earth. It was only when humans gave up freedom for security and began living clustered fearfully together in towns and cities that we started to define the indefinable and create complex religious frameworks that resembled our new fearful urban lives. We issued religious laws, rules, and regulations to keep all those people crammed into the city from misbehaving. As our new lives became progressively constrained and empty of the freedom and dignity we had previously enjoyed, we began to instead live for the promise of an afterlife, something resembling but better than this life we had created for ourselves. Centuries after Jesus the Jew walked the streets of Palestine, Christians concocted and aggressively marketed a celestial version of their earthly nightmare—a big white city in the sky surrounded by a gigantic wall with a single locked gate ruled by a jealous, wrathful king on a throne—replacing the mud walls of their reality with ormolu. And the evolutionary path to today's Christian normal is remarkable for its hypocrisy and violence. Let's look at Rome, December 25 in the year 274, Emperor Aurelian proclaims that the worship of Sol Invictus, the unconquered sun, will join the other fundamental religious cults as an official state sponsored religion. Sol Invictus, in fact, goes on to become the favored cult of Aurelian and, after his murder at the age of sixty-one by his own troops, by all his successors up to and including Constantine. Emperor Constantine has been happily sponsoring the torture and killing of Christians for not following pagan religious rituals and practices approved by the state and then, after a vivid hallucination, in the year 313 he issues the edict of Milan, which says, oops, sorry Christians about all that persecution. By the year 380, Christianity is the sole state-sanctioned religion, with all Christians required to follow the contents of the approved government Christian operations manual, also known as the Gospels of the New Testament. Those that don't follow the government manual are put to death. This Catholicism, a government religion created by a bunch of crafty politicians seventeen hundred years ago, also commanded that the annual festival of the birth of Christ, Christmas, be celebrated each year on December 25th, coincidentally the same day used to celebrate the most important cult festival of Dies Natalis, the birthday of the Sun god, Sol Invictus. Catholicism institutionalized the days of the week we still use: Monday for the goddess of the moon, Tuesday for Mars, the god of war; Wednesday for Mercury, the god of money; Thursday for Jupiter, the thunderous king of the gods; Friday for Venus the goddess of love; Saturday for Saturn, the god of agriculture; and of course Sunday for the Sun god himself. Now, they say if it looks like a duck, swims like a duck, and quacks like a duck, then it's probably a duck. It seems like a pretty transparent bait and switch to me, simply rebranding Sol Invictus as Jesus, eh? I find it a bit intellectually offensive, Christopher, don't you? It just smells gamy! Who knows, maybe that's why some Protestants call the Catholic Church the Whore of Babylon.[1]"

I couldn't help but nod in agreement whenever my father laid out the facts and set Roman Catholicism within a historical context. He wasn't easy on the Protestants, either.

"Then along comes Martin Luther in the sixteenth century, who takes up the exact same government operations manual and pagan associations, but he puts his own colorful colloquially eloquent spin on it. Do you know what Martin Luther's favorite word was? No idea? Shit! That's right, shit! Luther was habitually constipated and did most of his writing in a foul mood while sitting on the crapper. In his old age he wrote, 'I'm like a ripe stool and the world is like a gigantic anus, and so we're about to let go of each other.' If you think that's wild, well you should hear the kind of things he wrote to the buttoned-up Pope of the Corporation in Rome."

My father would then quickly leave the table, my mother

looking over at me smiling and rolling her eyes, and return with his reading glasses and a well-worn book.

"All right, you must listen to this letter Martin Luther wrote, because it exemplifies the crudeness that attracted the first of Luther's followers, and the tawdry carnival foundation upon which modern evangelical Christianity rests. I imagine the current practitioners haven't changed much, and I doubt many are cognizant of this historical reality or are even interested."

He would then clear his throat, adjust his glasses with his right forefinger, puff out his belly, purse his lips, and begin reading with a German accent in a bombastic, resonant voice.

"Most Hellish Father, Gently, dear Pauli, dear donkey, don't dance around! Oh, dearest little ass-pope, don't dance around—dearest, dearest little donkey, don't do it. For the ice is very solidly frozen this year because there was no wind— you might fall and break a leg. If a fart should escape you while you were falling, the whole world would laugh at you and say, 'ugh, the devil! How the ass pope has befouled himself!'" [2]

Upon which my father would smack the book shut and laugh hysterically. That "dearest little ass pope" thing got him every time, and me too.

"You know, Christopher, nobody knows if Martin Luther was emotionally unstable because he had been abused as a child, or if he simply lacked moral character, or if perhaps when he first began launching his tirades he was just a skinny little poser trying to look tougher than he actually was—and that act worked for a certain slice of the populous. Whatever the case, maybe all of them are true, but I think we can say with certainty that at the very least, this guy had a screw loose. And quite frankly, so do many of those who follow his teachings. Thomas Jefferson, when comparing the merits of atheism and demonism, not only preferred atheism, but also noted that many who consider themselves Christian are in fact demonists themselves.[3] I agree with Jefferson and frankly prefer atheists to most Christians, ethically, intellectually and socially."

Absent a recognizable theology, my parents emphasized ethics. Aristotle provided the framework for justice: treat equals equally and unequals unequally. Buddha and Epicurus for virtue: treat others as you would be treated. The *Udānavarga* and Immanuel Kant for duty: be a good person and act rationally. And Jeremy Bentham for consequences: embrace that which benefits and pleases the greatest number of people. And they worked to practice what they suggested to me, a high degree of moral character. They never lied to me about anything, no matter the cost of truth, but they were also creative people.

"Christopher, Mom and I have never personally seen Santa Claus but when we were kids, we both got presents that said 'from Santa' on them, and nobody knew where they came from, so who knows, it sure seems suspicious, like, yeah, somebody somewhere or something is maybe mysteriously delivering presents, don't you think?"

They took a similar approach with the Tooth Fairy, the Easter Bunny, and "the birds and the bees"—allowing me to grow into my own understanding, instead of catching them in a big fat lie. Likewise, if I asked a question they could not answer, they first admitted that they had no answer and then invited me to go discover the answer with them. I think this helped me in puberty. While I had the same physical anxieties as any teenager, I never cultivated that deep-seated disrespect that many of my classmates had for their parents. Parents that pretend to know everything eventually get caught, because omniscience is almighty, and parents are human. I believe when teenagers are old enough to catch their parents in this big lie of hubris, that's when their justifiably indignant rage arises. When kids rightfully explain to their parents why they are full of shit, parents call them incorrigible. I guess my parents thought: lie to your kid and tell him you know everything, and eventually he will grow up to see you as not just ignorant but as an ignorant liar.

My father James told people he was a government researcher and in a way he was. He worked for the Central Intelligence Agency—the CIA—as an analyst in the Boston office, reading news stories from around the world, seeking to make sense from chaos and divine hidden policy positions from seemingly featureless print. My mother Elizabeth, besides being a health care professional, was the archetypal New England homemaker, skilled at carpentry and tending our apple orchard while preserving order and serving nutritious meals in our two-hundred-year-old home at the end of a small dirt road. Growing up, I never heard my parents utter anything racist or anti-Semitic and was unaware of their politics. If they had an ideology, I didn't see it. They were highly engaged with the news and world events, but seemingly from a neutral observer's perspective, urging me, usually at dinnertime, to look at all sides of an argument. One night, my mother had grilled eggplant fresh from the garden, served with linguine *aglio e olio*, an arugula salad, and a long crisp fresh baked baguette, when my father began the familiar Socratic questioning that served as conversation in our house at dinner time.

"Christopher, eleventh grade, history, you are probably almost to the present day. I think they pace history in high school so that it runs out when you graduate, is that correct?"

My father took another substantial fork full of homegrown arugula, dredging the leaf in the fresh lemon dressing my mother had made and ensuring the adherence of a parmesan shaving before shutting his eyes and placing the payload in his mouth.

"Pretty much. We are talking about World War II now."

"Mmmmm. European theater or Pacific?"

"Both."

"Uh huh, and your thoughts are?"

"I don't understand how so many people in Germany and Japan could have eagerly supported such evil political and military agendas."

"Excellent. Let's talk about Germany. It's 1932, the banking system has collapsed, and unemployment is running at about twenty four percent. Herr Hitler had predicted this back in 1928. Pretty bright guy, huh? Maybe a guy smart enough to predict this depression could pull Germany out of it, hmmm?"

"Well, uh yeah, maybe."

"Of course he could, in fact that's the platform he ran on in 1932, he promised not just to lower unemployment, he promised he would abolish it. Unemployment is now forbidden! Sounds like Germany, eh, where everything is either required or forbidden, nothing in between. Pretty good huh?"

"Yeah, I guess."

"Hitler proceeded to ban many forms of mechanized manufacturing, awarded government contracts to firms that employed human labor-intensive manufacturing, formed voluntary labor forces, funded massive public works projects, and restored Germany's pride through rearmament. What a sensitive, human-centered, empathic, patriotic fellow, huh? And did that reduce the quality of what Germany built? Absolutely not! The Germans invented the pocket battleship, a highly effective heavy cruiser with innovations driven by compliance with the treaty of Versailles, and of course the autobahn, an amazing feat of massive manual labor built during this time period that allowed the rapid deployment of mechanized armaments and supplies across the country."

"Yeah, you bet, the autobahn is still amazing!"

"So, Herr Hitler predicts the collapse of the economy, and then when it collapses, he rides in on his white horse and saves the day. Before, you were a hungry and unemployed German with a family to support. Now, you have all the bratwurst and potatoes you can eat, all the beer you can drink, your kids have new clothes, you are proud of your country and your wife is smiling. For you Herr Hitler is a real hero."

"Yeah, a hero, I guess he is."

"But then the evil began, and no sane person can deny it occurred or that it was a significant low point in human history. Those people that supported him eagerly at first, then watched in horror as he lost his mind, then profoundly regretted their support later after the atrocities began, were those people evil, or had they made an honest mistake and were they simply human?"

"Yeah, pretty human, I guess."

"How about the others, those that supported him to the bitter end, despite the atrocities, despite the horrors, how about them?"

"Yeah, I would call them evil."

"Fair enough. Nobody's perfect but, as Erasmus used to say, we need to call a spade a spade. Someone that continues to support a flawed ethos or leader must live with whatever branding comes with that support. Like my grandmother always said, if you hang out in the pigsty with filthy pigs, you're going to smell like pig shit. Sometimes that brand or stink is called "evil". Christopher, would you pass me the pepper grinder please?"

"Sure, here you go Dad. So, what happened to those evil people after the war anyway?"

"Well, after World War II, the United States Office of Strategic Services, the OSS, engaged in a structured program of 'denazification' within Germany and the repatriation of what they called 'obnoxious' Germans from other countries.[4]"

"Obnoxious Germans?"

"Yes, the term was applied specifically to Nazi intelligence operatives, SS officers, and whatnot who had been creeping around other countries and causing mischief. The goal of the program was to remove or neuter all Nazi elements from the general population of the world."

"Well, that seems like a really good move, given the horror those people had just put the world through."

"You might think so. But people like General George Patton would disagree. In his position as the Military Governor of Bavaria, he opposed denazification. Patton said the Nazis and Anti-Nazis in Germany were comparable to Republicans and Democrats back in the United States and we should just leave them alone to duke it out.[5] The other major opposing force to denazification came from the Evangelical Christian Church."

"Evangelical Christians opposed denazification?"

"Yes, you bet they did. Heck, even during the last days of the war—after all that Hitler had put the world through—an Evangelical pastor wrote that The Führer was the epitome of Lutheran piety, a leader of God's grace, whose orders came directly from God and his commands were the same as those of God.[6]"

"Whoa!"

"Yes, Christopher, loony tunes. I mean, what do you call these people who stuck with Hitler to the very end and then protected Nazis after the war? They are not necessarily collaborators. Maybe they are sympathizers? Apologists? Associates? Guilty by their association? [7]

I am not sure. Some things are beyond the ability of a healthy mind to imagine, and this is one of those things. Elizabeth, that dinner was remarkable! Can we have the same thing again tomorrow night please? And Christopher, perhaps tomorrow night we can talk about something more lighthearted, how about the art that emerged from the war, allied art that is. Let's leave the Nazis alone for a while, OK?"

I was an only child, introverted, independent and often up to no good. If I was a child today, I might be diagnosed as a hyperactive Aspergers kid, if that is possible—who knows? In my teens my favorite pastime, in addition to launching model rockets, was smoking weed I grew out in the woods and building bombs. I loved explosions, and as the years progressed, my bomb-making skills moved from match head incendiary devices to pipe bombs with custom blended gunpowder and electric detonators. I would swipe the ingredients for the powder from the school chemistry lab: potassium nitrate, carbon, sulfur, and some powdered magnesium to spice things up a bit. The detonators ran the gamut from a nichrome wire igniter to more exotic capacitor arrangements. By the time I was thirteen, I knew exactly what I was going to study in college: electrical engineering. Those guys built missiles, bombs, and the systems that managed their direction and detonation, and that was totally cool.

Because I grew up in the boonies, I didn't really have any friends to hang out with outside of school. That helped my grade point average but added to my social retardation. My parents expected me to go to college the way they expected fall to follow summer, and I never thought twice about it. High school had taught me a bit about how the world worked, and I was eager to better understand why it worked the way it did. Although many of my classmates headed west to Zoo-Mass in Amherst, I went northeast up the coast to UNH, a smaller school with a quieter reputation. While some kids might have strategized that classes with fewer students would be more conducive to learning, I hoped the intimate size might be more social and help me make friends, something I had not come close to mastering in high school.

FOUR

BERG

A bead of sweat cascades down my nose and tickles me back into this uncomfortably corpulent old body on my park bench in the steadily increasing Texas heat. I open my eyes, and the unkind light of the sun is fluorescent white and punishing. Something is killing me. It could be the bongos and patchouli vapors, or simply my torn up old heart. Maybe there was a chemical spill upstream on the River Tao and the toxic fingers of the pollutant plume are tightening their grip on my bench and me. If only these Trustafarians would just stop beating their bongos. The throbbing is sliding towards a sickening resonance with my heartbeat, and I am concerned, because if the intercavity pressure goes up too much it could blow the temples out of my skull. I squeeze my eyes closed and mercifully the light dims, the pressure eases, and I slip away, down the beyond-space-time slope.

"It is poison power, man; evil incarnate, and everyone knows that."

The hippy takes a hit of the joint and passes it to the sleeveless patchouli paisley chick with hairy armpits standing next to him at the archetypal Friday-night party in a smelly 100-year-old mill house in Dover, New Hampshire. Bob Dylan is whining on the stereo about how the times are a-changin', and sandalwood incense fills the air. Berg slouches against the doorway between the kitchen and the living room. He is neither tall nor short; not heavy and not skinny; his hair is not long but it's definitely not well trimmed; he is wearing slightly faded Levis, unlaced newish Timberland boots, a brightly colored plaid flannel shirt over a white t-shirt and he wears a smirk on his face as he begins to lecture the hippy.

"It isn't poison, it's simply energy released by natural processes and harnessed by man. How can nature be evil?"

The hippy exhales with a confused look on his face. "You don't get it man; look at what just happened at Three Mile Island! And even if you could prevent accidents from happening, those wastes will be with us for thousands and thousands of years, slowly killing the planet."

The hippy nods sagely to the gathering crowd. They are eager to ease the boredom of the party by listening to the evolving debate while sipping warm cheap beer from their plastic cups.

"Three Mile Island is an excellent example of people getting their knickers in a knot for nothing—show me one fucking person who got hurt except for a dumbass Pennsyl-tucky rent-a-cop who wet his pants and stubbed a toe while running out the door. And look, I'm concerned about the wastes too. We should reprocess the shit, get the plutonium, and freshen our nuclear arsenal like the Russians, French and everybody else is doing. But apparently that flies in the face of reason for some people, which leaves us with entombing the shit out in the desert where, if like Houdini it manages to somehow get out, only a few lizards might get sick." Berg leans back and waits for the hippy's response.

"Nuclear nonproliferation begins at home, my friend. We must *be* the change we wish to *see* in the world—Gandhi said that. And lizards are part of the natural world too, man, we as humans have got to respect life." The hippy spreads his arms wide to embrace all of Buddha's creation while the crowd nods in agreement.

"Listen, I get trying to do no harm, and I get being fair, but I don't get why there is a problem with defending myself from people who clearly want to kill me, or harming some lizards I don't know in a shithole state filled with morons who desperately need the money from the disposal of these wastes so that they can continue living their subhuman existence in the desert with a bunch of mutant fucking lizards." Berg looks over at Laurie who had been staring at him from a frayed couch covered with a cheap tapestry, her jaw slightly agape. "Hey Laurie – it looks like you need a beer."

"Yeah, I do!" She jumps up from the couch.

"Awesome, get me one too while you're at the keg. And why doesn't someone put on some real music from this fucking decade!"

That was pure Berg. He had apparently been born this way; emerging from the womb iconoclastic and charmingly rude, he grew smoothly into deliberately incorrigible, much to his mother's chagrin.

"You will not use that derogatory word in this house, do you hear me Robert?"

"But that's what they are ma, they're niggiz, pure and simple. These baby black panthers walk north past our house every day then come riding back down south on shiny ten speeds. White America gives these jungle bunnies welfare to pay their bills so all they do is jive around on street corners and pay for their drugs by stealing white American kids' bikes."

"You don't *know* that Robert, so you can't *say* that."

"I don't know that they jive around on street corners? Come on ma, you know that too."

"Well, they are a musical race Robert, and dancing is a natural outlet for them. You need to appreciate their culture. After all, they did give us jazz."

"I appreciate their culture and their music, for sure. I also appreciate that they take our stuff and don't give nothing back. It's that simple, ma. It's what they do."

His parents named him Robert Michael Berg, but everyone just called him Berg. He was never addressed by his first name except by his parents. I don't know why. Berg's father Michael was a prominent attorney for a large national insurance company based in Manhattan. He rode the Long Island Railroad to work each day and created tools with which large corporations could evade paying their fair share of taxes. Berg's father and his clients believed paying taxes was un-American. One of their schemes went like this: a large corporation creates an insurance company in Bermuda or the Cayman Islands; this insurance company has no offices on the island, no furniture, only a mailbox. The large corporation pays its insurance company—in other words, itself—regular premiums, which it deducts as business expenses. If there is a loss, the big company pays itself for the loss from its insurance company. If there is no loss, then the money sits offshore in an account with the ability to come back to the business owner tax-free. It's kind of like having your cake and eating it too, except once in a while someone might ask you for a little bite. It was all very legal.[1] In addition to being a patriotic American, Berg's father was a very short, handsome, philanderer.

Berg's mother Sarah was a classic Long Island liberal. She was sympathetic to the poor and hated the inequality of American wealth creation, but she loved to spend money. Sarah was also an alcoholic, alternately melancholy and charming, punctuated by brief choleric episodes of extreme violence. During her charming periods she handled her alcohol well and wrote poetry and painted; watercolors, not oils; whimsical scenes, not still lifes. Berg's mother was also very short, like his father, and in her prime had been very attractive. She had a thin pointed significant nose, defined cheekbones, and long auburn hair. In the early 1960s she cultivated a Jackie Kennedy look and did it quite well, but by the mid-1970s the many years of Smirnoff and violence eventually took their toll. She knew of Berg's father's philandering, and this drove her progressively mad.

Berg, like me, was also an only child. Before college, he lived with these two very small people in a very large house in West Hempstead, Long Island. West Hempstead sits between Garden City to the north and Hempstead proper to the south. Berg used to tell us Garden City was so white back then that even Jews were not allowed to buy homes.[2] Telly Savalas, the Greek TV star that played Kojak, was about as ethnic as Garden City could stomach, and Telly had that big time cheap star appeal going for him. Joe Namath, (the Noxzema-selling quarterback for the Jets football team in their heyday) lived there too, as well as a handful of congressmen and senators. If Garden City was the WASP dream of pastoral England, then Hempstead was their nightmare of urban Nigeria. Hempstead was black as the ace of spades, and according to Berg filled with nothing but drug addicts and thieves.

Berg attended a private school during the day, played sports, and got decent grades despite his disinterest in learning. By night, he listened to the violent clashes of his parents. They seemed unashamed of what they screamed at night, perhaps believing they operated at a private frequency and only they could hear each other—like people in an airport with ear buds and a phone—breaking dishes and furniture, making sure to not cause any visible physical harm on each other's bodies in their well-rehearsed drama. They both had reputations to uphold. Periodically Berg's father would disappear, replacing his mother with another woman for a while. Some of the divorcees he shacked up with even had children, giving him an instant new happy family. When this happened, Berg's mother would go over the falls, but not miss a beat; the violence must go on. She always said Berg was just like his father, and when Berg's father left, she was left with Berg. As a child he slept with a hunting knife under his mattress in case she tried to kill him, just like she swore she would one day kill his father. Berg always said he was confident that if she had tried it, he would have killed her first.

Berg could have attended any number of fine private New England colleges, but chose UNH primarily because of its sub-percent level of black students and deep conservative roots. The state was white as snow, and the spirit of John Birch strode proudly through the granite mountain passes. Berg and I lived in the same dorm freshman year, and because Berg was studying civil engineering we overlapped on classes like physics, chemistry, and calculus—common to all engineering majors. My high school classes had covered most of the material we were assigned freshman year, so I did well on tests. Berg did not. One day, after our second chemistry quiz, he caught up with me outside the lecture hall.

"Hey man, how's it going?"

I looked around to see whom he could be talking to. There was only the two of us. "Uh, OK I guess."

He stuck out his hand. "My name's Berg."

"Yes, I know. I'm Christopher."

Berg smiled and clasped my hand. "Yeah, I know. Listen, we're in so many classes together maybe we should get together and study?"

"Uh yeah, I guess."

"And party. I know some cool people. You get high?"

"Uh yeah, I guess."

"Excellent, let's start this afternoon."

"Uh, studying? Partying?"

"Yes!"

As college progressed, Berg gradually lost the most caustic elements of his New York accent and flunked fewer classes as he assimilated to his surroundings and figured out how to get decent grades without learning too much. He wanted to have some fun, get that piece of paper, and get on with life. In Berg's perfect world, he would leave college after four years, intellectually untouched by the liberal lies of the faculty, which seemed a bit weird to me because most of his classes were objectively technical.

Unlike high school and unlike Berg, I loved learning in college and was fascinated by the first principles of engineering and how my courses logically evolved, calculus providing the tools with which to analyze Newtonian physics and differential equations allowing me to design and conceptually weld together advanced circuits. Although, like Berg, I didn't have many liberal arts electives, I managed to take one psychology course my junior year called Thinking About Thinking—that changed how I look at the world to this day. The core topic of the course, metacognition, helped me conceptualize my proactive thought processes as a kind of FORTRAN code. A structured algorithm for thinking, planning, and executing gives you a portable problem-solving strategy that you can transfer to any situation. Combining this with a retrospective concept I learned that same semester in a manufacturing class (where you ask the question "Why?" five times to discover the root cause of an existing problem), my eyes were opened to critical thinking skills in college that allowed me to better analyze the world, understand my failures, make corrective design changes, execute, and measure the effect.

As powerful as these tools were for me, I was surprised by Berg who, while clearly smart, worked with what seemed to me feral and not intellectual thought processes, rejecting structure and relying instead upon amygdala fight or flight strategies. I guess just like the benefits of diversity within systems, whether financial, biological, or sociological, these different ways of thinking by people like Berg and me must make for a better world. But at times I felt sorry as I watched him do physics problems where, instead of applying the simple structured problem-solving approach that we had been taught, and then pause to understand the physical meaning of the answer, he would intuitively attack each problem as a unique enemy to be dispatched with the greatest speed regardless of the veracity of the outcome. I tried reasoning with him, but he was uninterested in my advice, and instructed me as to where I could go and what I could do when I got there.

FIVE

LAURIE

I open my eyes and two lithe blonde coeds slide by my bench in bikini tops and tiny denim shorts, brilliant white tennis shoes, diamond tennis bracelets, and matching gold Rolex watches. Dressing down Texas style for a woman requires considerable tennis gear even if she doesn't play tennis. I can see the perfume vapors wafting off their necks and wrists in chartreuse, magenta, and violet hues, but I cannot smell them from my bench. I am having trouble smelling much of anything these days. God bless America, this humidity is kicking my ass today and no matter how I try, I just can't seem to stop sweating or catch my breath. Inhale, hold, and exhale. Mop the brow. Inhale, hold, and exhale. Mop the brow. Inhale, hold, and exhale. I close my eyes, my chin drops slowly to my chest, my anxiety eases, and I slip.

"No matter how cute and awesome you think he is right now, somewhere, some chick is sick of his shit."

"Phi Delts rule."

"Go Green. Recycle. Eat your shit."

She took her eyes off the magic marker graffiti on the

back of the toilet stall door, squinted and bore down, but her bowels were not having anything to do with collaboration today. Sometimes Laurie Harr would go a week without a bowel movement. This was a peculiar phenomenon for those of us guys on a daily shit-shower-and-shave routine, and reminded me a bit of what my father used to say over dinner about Martin Luther's constipation. Unlike Luther, however, she would eat regularly and as healthy as you can eat in college, wasn't overweight, and was not prone to inter-movement flatulence. She was in many ways like an efficient high-pressure chemical reactor: wastes drained once a week and the reactor placed back online again.

Laurie was the youngest of three children, her brothers Sven and Alexander five and six years older respectively. Laurie's parents had amicably and intellectually separated early in her childhood, understanding clinically how unsuited they were for each other. Divorce was not an option for these social conservatives. Both parents were tall, blond, and from well-moneyed backgrounds. Finances were not a problem, which made life easier to rearrange. Both were devotees of Ayn Rand and found beauty in the opaque emissions from the petrochemical smokestacks of their home state of New Jersey. Each kept a proper separate home on the same New Jersey street, and each led a carefully manicured life.

As a young child Laurie played games like other children, just not the same games. She was dissecting frogs by the age of four and actively engaged in the microscopy of everything by first grade. When other children learned how to spell "rock," Laurie already knew the difference between a rock and a mineral and could explain on an elemental level the difference between biotite and muscovite. But in her early childhood, when other children slept safely at night, Sven and Alexander alternately preyed upon her. This activity ended around the time Laurie turned six, but she never felt truly comfortable at home until both brothers had left the house for college.

In high school, Laurie took all advanced placement classes and excelled particularly at math and science. While her peers met with guidance counselors to gain insight into career paths, Laurie sought guidance from her parents and received it unsolicited from her now graduated high school football star brothers, both attending Ivy League schools. She would study chemical engineering and be part of America's chemical revolution. Laurie applied to UNH and gained early admission. She could have gone to school anywhere but chose UNH because she loved skiing and the seacoast; but most of all she loved the state motto: live free or die.

Like her parents, Laurie was tall, blonde, and athletic. She had milky blue eyes set in whites permanently riddled with red blood vessels, the combined pastel clouding suggesting a recent emotional event. She was very attractive but had never felt any type of sexual attraction for another human, either male or female. She was intelligent enough to realize that this asexuality made her different from the other kids and she used that understanding for her amusement.

In high school senior year, she walked up to Marvin Zimmer and invited him to the prom. Marvin was a nice kid who flew under the radar. He played no team sports and was not involved with band or debating or anything. He seemed to appear for school and then vaporize at the last bell. He was the perfect foil for Laurie. Marvin didn't drive, so she drove over to pick him up in her car, a silver Datsun 240Z with a black interior and air conditioning. Marvin's parents were watching out the window when Laurie pulled up, opened the door and, one stiletto heel at a time, slowly stretched her long limber legs out, revealing fishnet stockings leading up to a tiny leopard print mini skirt and a sheer flowing silk blouse that left little to the imagination whenever it lighted upon her body. They looked at each other, back out the window, and called up to Marvin—who was buttoning up his black suit—to let him know his date had arrived.

After arriving at the prom, Laurie quickly separated from Marvin and began the night's game, which was breaking up couples. Guys with wandering eyes dancing with girls in long shapeless prom dresses were her prime targets. They couldn't keep their eyes off Laurie: her outfit was screaming sexuality, her walk was broadcasting availability. Once a victim was unlucky enough to make eye contact with her, she would quickly alter course, tap the victims date on the shoulder and ask for a dance with her beau. The nice girls never refused and would walk off to help themselves to a fruit punch at the snack table. Then Laurie would begin her act, close dancing, grinding her hips, whispering in her victim's ear with quick flicks of her moist tongue. The act frequently ended with her victim ejaculating then running towards the exit to stop his sobbing date; sometimes it ended with her simply pushing him away in disgust and moving to her next target.

She caught up with Marvin later that night; they smoked a joint on the drive home, and when they arrived Laurie gave him a deep French kiss, then pushed him out of the passenger car door and onto the driveway. Watching from the window, Marvin's parents looked at each other and smiled contentedly in the knowledge that their son had made it through the dreaded high school prom—including a good night kiss from a beautiful girl.

Berg and Laurie each arrived freshman year with a clear ethos. Their beliefs had substance and they could elucidate them and the common culture they aspired to see become dominant, albeit using some rough language. While technically competent and confident, I was neither politically sophisticated nor philosophically anchored. That left me unattached and open to almost anything, especially when friendship was an associated outcome. Berg's conservatism had a bit of racism to it that, I admit, made me somewhat uncomfortable. But I knew he was a good guy at heart, and I wrote the racial slurs off to his urban upbringing. I had no experience with diversity, and he did. I accepted Laurie's anti-Semitism as being a component of her Protestant upbringing and, given Martin Luther's murderous stance on Jews, her simple prejudice was pretty liberal. So I listened quietly to my outspoken friends. I earnestly agreed when ideas like fiscal restraint and a strong defense resonated with me. I remained uncomfortably silent when they drifted towards white supremacy and anti-intellectualism.

Berg used to say that talking honestly about any significant topic with the left-wing nut-job chicks at the university would blow your cover and any real chance of getting laid. Most guys like Berg grew their hair a bit long and wore faded denim Levis and stylishly unlaced Timberland or L.L. Bean boots that always looked like they had just been purchased. They pretended to fit in, but felt as uncomfortable in those clothes as in the role they pretended to play. However, far from feeling the lesser for the charade, Berg seemed to feel greater. It was as if he was in on a cosmic joke that they did not get. He was better than those freaks: smarter, more powerful, on the outside looking in at something vile. Needing to be connected in some fashion to this dominant social system, Berg attached himself like a parasite attaches to a host. That may sound bad but look: a leech needs blood to eat, a virus needs a cell with which to self-replicate; parasitic symbiosis is natural and actually elevates the parasite to that of the dominator, the host giving and receiving nothing in return. Berg would have said, "fuck the host" and then slowly sucked the life out of it. He told me once that every hippy girl that he left weeping in the night made him understand the difference between us and them: we are strong and positive; they are weak and pessimistic. We have the real knowl-edge and knowledge is power and power is everything.

Say what you will about Berg's conservatism, at least it was a clearly articulated ethos, and most importantly it brought me into a circle of friends and made me feel better about myself. And for many, feeling better—or anything positive for that matter—was rare in those times. Those were the years when it was fashionable for Americans to feel bad about themselves, to feel bad about simply being Americans. The cheerleader for this American flu was President Carter, who invited America to join him in his crusade of Southern malaise. Berg said Carter was the perfect standard-bearer for depressing liberalism, and a gift to conservatism.

There weren't many who thought like Berg and Laurie, and most of them were under deep cover. Talking about the news over coffee in the student union building offered the opportunity to incrementally explore interpretations of events and gauge reactions and sniff people out. Sometimes, after a few beers, Berg and Laurie didn't care what the freaks thought, and would wage war against their liberal bullshit with sarcastic impunity. Berg and Laurie were culture warriors, and they were my friends. I listened intently to them as they dreamed about the time we would leave this left-wing incubator together and enter the real world and begin changing the culture and making a real difference.

In the fall of 1979, we were on the cusp of graduation and the world was a weird and exciting place. I had made two real friends in college and that made me feel good. Berg introduced me to a bunch of other people too and got me out of my shell a bit. But I felt most comfortable hanging out with just him and Laurie. The three of us did every-thing together in those days and the migration from moun-tains to beaches to concerts to parties created a rhythm that swept us peacefully along through the final years of school, lulling us into the belief that this life would never really end and that we would always be young, and everything would always be fresh and fun and we would be kings and queens forever.

The UNH fraternity row extends from Main Street in Durham up Madbury Road and the stately fraternity houses framed by expansive porches and lawns drift across Garrison Avenue to continue up Strafford Avenue. Fraternities were places for people who thought like us to cluster together. They were also convenient places to drink, since the university banned kegs from dorms in 1979 when the state drinking age increased from 18 to 20. Berg liked the guys who populated fraternities mostly because they shared his racist attitude and didn't think too much. But he thought they were pussies for hiding from the outside world in their filthy frat houses. Berg said he preferred to live amidst the enemy. He also wasn't much of a joiner and lived independently, as did Laurie and I.

One Saturday night in October 1979, the three of us attended a party at Pike, the large white clapboard three-story Pi Kappa Alpha frat house up on Strafford Avenue behind Stoke Hall. The party that night was typical. Cheap beer. Plastic cups. Top 40 music played at distortion volume. The house was packed, from the dimly lit basement where students danced zombie-like in the wet filth pooled on the cement floor to the third story where people mostly went to do drugs and have semi-consensual sex, and overflowed out onto the porches and grassy back yard.

Berg was off somewhere that night, probably getting stoned with the rugby players. Laurie was hanging by a bar on the first floor, and I was keeping an eye on her. She had been slugging down the cheap keg beer pretty hard and as a result was aggressively hitting on guys with the whitest teeth, shortest hair, and biggest biceps. She had landed on one especially large fellow, challenged him to a chugging contest, and won. That required a rematch, and so on and so forth.

I had consumed a few beers, and had to pee. That unfortunately involved entering the Pike bathroom, which was a bathtub in a large urine-soaked closet that the guys clustered around and peed into. The line for this latrine was long and aggressive, but once I made it inside the hideous closet with all the shoving and shouting, I simply could not relax enough to urinate. I finally zipped up my pants and left, with my bladder still crying for relief. I jogged through the maze of bodies and exited the back door of the less crowded kitchen into the sweet smell of the clear New Hampshire night. I looked around and spotted two dumpsters in the darkness along the tree line at the edge of the drive that afforded some privacy, and I carefully began making my way towards them, avoiding the sporadic piles of wet trash and vomit. I had almost reached the dumpsters when I heard a muffled cry and a slap of skin on skin. I hesitated for a moment, then continued. I really had to pee. I rounded the back of one of the chipped yellow dumpsters and froze. Laurie was pinned to the ground by Bicep Boy's large hulk, her head shaking from side to side like a metronome. He had one hand over her mouth and the other was tugging on her jeans, which he had succeeded in shifting enough to expose her panties. Lacking any forethought or planning, I pounced on his back screaming, my arms locked around his neck, yanking instinctively with all my might. I had surprised him, and he yelped, let go of Laurie and reared up quickly, throwing me off and onto my back in a pile of garbage. He turned, took two staggering steps toward me, and punched me in the face. His fist connected with my left jaw and the jarring impact sent me rolling onto my right side, seeing stars. I looked up, and as he came at me again, I covered my face with my hands and prepared for the beating. I heard a crack but didn't feel a thing. I let my hands drop and there was Laurie standing over me, the skin on her face taut, her hair a mess of leaf filled tangles, spittle and blood on her lips, blue jeans at her knees and claw marks on her thighs, holding a piece of two by four. Bicep Boy was on the ground next to me clutching his head and moaning.

"Christopher, are you all right?"

"Yeah, I think so, how about you?"

"Yeah, yeah, I'm good, but this fucker here is in bad shape."

"He doesn't look that bad."

"Oh, don't worry, he's gonna be."

Laurie turned and swung the board into Bicep's ribcage with a hard whack. He cried out and curled into a ball. She cocked back again and hit him in the back of the head. The board made a sickening thud and he stopped moving. She cocked back again but I reached her in time to interrupt her swing. She turned to me, her eyes flat and lifeless and shoved me hard in the sternum with the heel of her left hand.

"Fuck off, Christopher, he's mine!"

"Laurie, you have hurt him real bad and that's good, he deserved it. But I can't let you kill him, so please put the board down and let's get out of here."

Laurie paused, her eyes, which a moment before had shown no life, registering what I had said. She nodded, then looked down at Bicep Boy, grimaced, gave him one last crack on a knee and then dropped the board. She sniffed and looked at me with the hint of a tear at the corner of her right eye, then stepped forward and hugged me.

"I love you Christopher. You are my savior."

I didn't know what to do, so I hugged her back, then looked down at her pants and kneeled to pull them up. She slapped me in the face, then pulled me back up, hugged me again, then abruptly shoved me back.

"I got the pants, Christopher. Come on. Let's cruise."

Berg didn't ask us the next day where we had gone that night. It was not unusual for the three of us to fragment like that. And although Laurie and I never spoke afterward about the event, it had redefined our relationship and drawn us closer. The next week, she began what became a lifetime study and practice of Tae Kwon Do. I suspect she intended to never allow anyone to place her in such a vulnerable position again. Having watched the untrained version in action, I feel sorry for anyone who tried after that.

We made a diverse trio, sitting together in a fluorescent-lit basement room of the Memorial Union Building, attending a service of the New Church of Christ the Conservative that Sunday morning: Berg, in denim jeans, black T-shirt, slightly shaggy straight brown hair, his long slender nose outstretched like a fox wearing an expression somewhere between amusement and annoyance; Laurie, the picture of a Playboy bunny playing dress up in a business suit, designer eye glasses with non-prescription lenses that she said made people respect her more, her body language and expression that of one riding in an elevator with someone who has just farted. And then there was me: tall, skinny, buzz cut blond hair and a poor complexion, khakis, and wrinkled Oxford shirt, and my personal peculiar bodily aroma that people said was a subtle cross between skunk and lobster. I was also sporting a bruise on my jaw and worried that Berg would notice but he didn't.

"Let us read from the gospel of Matthew, 27:24-25: 'So when Pilate saw that he was gaining nothing, but rather that a riot was beginning, he took water and washed his hands before the crowd, saying "I am innocent of this man's blood; see to it yourselves." And all the people answered, "His blood be on us and on our children!"'"

The preacher paused and gazed out at the audience.

"These Jews who killed Jesus cried out that they were okay with his blood staining their children and grandchildren and on and on for eternity. They were okay that, just like the blood of Abel in Hebrews 12:24, that blood would cry out for vengeance and punishment. They just wanted him dead, didn't they? And they were willing to have their descendants pay for eternity."

Another significant pause accompanied by a deep breath.

"Brothers and sisters, is it a coincidence the Spanish drove the Jews out of Spain, across the sea and back into Africa? Is it a coincidence the Russians launched pogroms to cleanse their soil of the Jews? Is it a coincidence the Germans sought to tidy their country and relocate German Jews elsewhere? Is it a coincidence that all these things befell those who killed our God? And what now of this so-called nation of Israel? It's a mythology, it's a hoax! In history, Israel existed over three thousand years ago for only a brief three-hundred-year blink of the eye. Think about it. The Moors ruled the Spanish Andalus for almost eight hundred years—should they now have a historic right to that land? Of course not! So why do we respect this fictitious notion, this nation of god killers? Why do we allow America to be wagged by this despicable tail?"

The audience is listening closely now, and the preacher knows it. He licks his lips, lowers his voice and a smirk steals across his face. "Oh yes, and Martin Luther, the father of Evangelicals, wrote extensively on the Jew."

The preacher pauses, making eye contact around the room and arches his eyebrows and his next line is delivered dripping with sarcasm. "Luther wrote that the Jew is such a noble, precious jewel that God and all the angels dance when he farts!"

Eyes widen with the mention of farts, and some snicker. The preacher's voice rises.

"Oh yes, and Brother Luther had a clear solution for these god killers, to be performed in honor of our Lord and of Christendom, so that God might see that we are in fact true Christians. Perhaps Luther's greatest work titled *On the Jews and Their Lies* provides the blueprint. First, we set fire to their synagogues and schools and bury the foundations beneath soil so that nobody will ever have to look at them again. Second, we knock down and destroy all of their homes. Third, we take away all of their prayer books. Fourth, we forbid their rabbis from teaching and if they refuse, we kill them. Fifth, safe conduct on the highways is abolished for Jews because they have no business being in the countryside and should stay at home. Sixth, we take all their cash and property and we put it aside for 'safekeeping,' wink wink, nudge nudge. And finally, seventh, we put those lazy Jews to work—real work, instead of allowing them to just sit there behind the cash register, feasting and farting and bragging about how rich they have gotten off the sweat of our honest Christian brows.[1]"

Heads nod silently at these historical revelations. The preacher steps back, looks down and closes his eyes for a moment.

"The American Jew is no different from Luther's Jews. He is a money-hungry liberal Democrat who seeks to destroy the fabric of American values we hold so dear. This is not new behavior. Think about what Martin Luther wrote! Read *The Protocols of the Elders of Zion*! You can see for yourself! Henry Ford, one of our greatest American heroes, told us in no uncertain terms about the Jewish conspiracy against the world's fundamental social, economic, and government institutions.[2] I ask you now, knowing all this, don't we have a Christian duty to save America from these killers?"

Heads nod.

"I say let the American Jews go! Let them go back to

their so-called homeland. Their Muslim neighbors can deal with them as so many have dealt with them before, and tell me, with whom should we Christians find fellowship in that region anyway? Should we seek fellowship with those liberal thieves who killed our God—or with those who seek retribution for that blood curse?

"Ohhhhh, brothers and sisters, the Bible tells us our God is a vengeful God, and he spits out that which is lukewarm. Are you lukewarm about this, or are you righteously indignant? Will you join God in his work?"

More nods and smiles.

"And what of America without the Jew? I will tell you. With his filthy hands unloosed from our banks, an era of Christian affluence can finally be realized. And brothers and sisters, this will be a special time when, through righteous violence, we will have made our country great again and paved the way for the end times and the return of the Prince of Peace!"

The rich baloney smell of unwashed armpits, the acrid aroma of skid-marked underwear, the stale smell of pancake oil and bacon fat, permeated and recalcitrant within synthetic clothing, comingled and filled the air with its pungency. The room—and its aroma—was a reflection of its contents: a small cinderblock enclosure filled to the brim with cheap plastic chairs cradling mostly oversized evangelical Christians with poor complexions. Berg and Laurie were the physical exceptions to the parishioners. I fit in, sort of, except for my weight. But we were all gathered to hear the message of truth from Pastor Phil, a travelling evangelical preacher. After the service was over, we walked up the musty flight of stairs into the brightness of a clear fall morning.

Berg was ecstatic. "That was amazing! You know, our classes are taught by these same left-wing Jews that Pastor

Phil was talking about, and that's probably why we don't hear about any of this stuff in history classes."

I wanted to say we didn't hear about this stuff in history classes because we were engineering students and didn't have room in our schedule for history classes. I also wanted to say that I had already heard a bit about Martin Luther, and I thought he was goofy, not great. Instead, I bit my tongue.

Laurie glanced up from inspecting her fingernails. "Frankly, I thought that was a bit boring, and Jesus Christ, what a stink down there—no offence, Christopher. Breakfast at the Diner?"

As they walked down the gently sloping hill towards downtown, Berg and Laurie broke into spontaneous song.

"Oh, the Protestants hate the Catholics
And the Catholics hate the Protestants
And the Hindus hate the Muslims
And everybody hates the Jews
But during National Brotherhood Week
National Brotherhood Week
Its National everyone smile at one
another-hood week
Be nice to people who are inferior to you
It's only for a week so have no fear
Be grateful that it doesn't last all year[3]"

I went back to my apartment later that day, and reflected on the events of the weekend. I lived by myself in Newmarket, across the street from the Timberland shoe factory, in an old brick apartment building with eight units: four on the ground floor and four above. I had one of the single second floor units, and my apartment was furnished typically: a mattress and beanbag chair on the floor, milk crates and two by tens as bookshelves, and an ancient green velvet junk shop couch with a lobster trap for a coffee table. I grabbed a quart of milk from the fridge and sat on the couch. All this talk of Jews and Muslims was perplexing to me. I didn't know any Jews or Muslims, so I had no experience with which to even begin the most fundamental Bayesian analysis. My parents had taught me to question organized religion, reject hatred and seek to be inclusive. I guess from a Christian perspective, that preacher made sense and if I believed in their god, I might be angry, too, that those Jewish folks had killed him because that was clearly wrong. But what about other religious things, like it's wrong to work on Saturday, it's wrong to work on Sunday, it's wrong to drink alcohol, it's wrong to eat meat on Friday, it's wrong to ever eat pork, it's wrong to say certain words and think certain thoughts, it's wrong, it's wrong, it's wrong? They all seemed kind of crazy.

But this provoked a deeper question within me, one that had to do with right and wrong. I had been buying quarter pounds of weed for $120, selling three ounces for $40 each and getting a free ounce to smoke. What I was doing was against the law, but was it necessarily immoral or wrong? My parents would have asked the following ethical questions: Will my miniature dope dealing apparatus harm others? No. Would I be OK requiring everyone to deal dope like this? Yeah, I guess, but that would kill my business. Would I be OK seeing a story about my dope dealing in the newspaper? No, not really. Is my dope-dealing fair to others who don't deal dope? Yeah, but life treats unequals unequally, and if you snooze you lose.

I took a long swig of milk, pulled my bag of pot from under the couch cushion, and rolled and lit a joint to help with my thought process. The smoke curled from the burning tip in the fading fall daylight, and I thought about life, about death, and about marijuana. Was the living plant now a mere corpse of dead leaves interred within this plastic body bag, or was the essence of the plant now embodied within this pale ghost of smoke, drifting for a while in organized visibility and then fading into an entropic oblivion to live forever? Or is the plant's life force now embedded within its seeds, just waiting to be reincarnated? How might this model be applicable to people? I took another hit and closed my eyes to ponder this question some more. Life is not simple.

And then four years had somehow passed. For me, each one was rich in education, both formal and informal, and camaraderie. After four years, I was less ignorant and less alone—and that was good. But they say for everything there is a season. The ocean tide floods and recedes, the moon waxes and wanes and summer becomes fall. Eventually, they say, there comes a time to break down and refrain from embracing. With the three of us, it was not a sudden abrupt end as much as a slow disintegration, our bonds fraying and life courses branching into their inevitable and inexorable divergences. We began to refrain from embracing. While this nascent independence seemed to mature Berg and Laurie, I slipped back into my earlier introverted self, as it was the only skin readily available for me to crawl into. I had grown somewhat in those four years, but like an old suit, it still kind of fit, so I put it on.

We graduated just in time for the deepest recession since the Second World War. Unemployment was 7.5%, inflation 13.5%, and the prime interest rate hovered around 20%. 1980 made the 2008 bump look like the Renaissance. Because of the revolution in Iran and the diminished oil output, throughout 1979 we had been on an odd/even day rationing system for gasoline. This had battered the global economy and resulted in frustration for consumers with vehicles. But given the record high price for a barrel of crude, it had also created a boom in the oilfield and a high demand for offshore engineers looking for adventure. Berg had managed to squeak through college with a degree in civil engineering. His father had oil and gas connections and Berg had a job offshore in the Gulf of Mexico waiting for him. He was tired of always having to bug his father for money and was looking forward to having some real cash of his own in hand. Laurie, always with her act together, had quickly landed a job with Upland Chemical, a manufacturing leviathan with great pay and benefits, which was a rarity in 1980 America. My father had helped me get an entry-level electrical engineering job at Raytheon down in Andover, Massachusetts. I wasn't quite sure exactly what I would be doing, but Raytheon was in the weapons business, and that was good enough for me. Besides, Andover was close to my parents' house in Stow, so I could live at home and save some money. We all three promised to keep in touch and I never considered that we wouldn't. The shared experiences of four years of college are an indelible tattoo that, while perhaps dulled a bit by time, cannot be wiped away. Although it was unclear exactly what the future had in store, given my lack of supernatural powers and proclivity for a Bayesian view of probability, I had some rough ideas and looked forward to updating them as the years progressed.

SIX

WASTE OF 1980

I open my eyes and the coeds are gone, as is my beyond-space-time visit to 1979. It is 2020 again, and I am alone on my bench in this heat. Maybe seeing those two coeds walk by in their bikini tops and short shorts sent me back to Laurie. I'm not sure. While it's easy for me to slip these days, I have difficulty understanding the catalysts and nuances of the mechanics of this travel beyond my crude Newtonian conceptual model, which leaves the questions of "Why 1979?" and "Why Laurie?" unanswered. Back in those days, Berg sought me out to collaborate on homework because he needed help. Laurie, on the other hand, was a solitary studier. We speculated that she had a secret corner of the library that she retreated to, but nobody knew for sure. She always had her assignments completed on time, and graduated with a near perfect grade point average. I close my eyes and her face appears, her eyes hard and flat, her lips set in an asymmetrical sneer.

Laurie got her start at Upland visiting active manufacturing sites with her supervisor where chemical contamination from past disposal activities had been found. The first site she visited on her own was in rural New Jersey. So far, that site was shaping up to be fairly typical of what she had seen previously at other sites. Inside the plant, manufacturing was humming, filling today's orders and looking forward to tomorrow. But out behind the plant, like archaeologists in the summer sun and humid heat, teams in hard hats were busy extracting evidence of the past: chemical contamination. Instead of trowels, they used a mechanical device to push the equivalent of a steel straw into the earth; they would then withdraw the straw and recover the soil that remained within it. That column of soil would inform them about the physical and chemical properties in the layers of soil beneath the plant. The team worked their way down, foot-by-foot, collecting, retrieving, and cataloging soil samples from each borehole for subsequent subsurface mapping and chemical analyses. The mechanical coring device was driven by diesel-powered hydraulic pump mounted to a large red truck with oversized tires that the crew called The Goat. The tool pusher, a fellow with a hard hat that looked like a silver pith helmet, would rev up the diesel then push a lever sending a steel rod tipped with a three-and-one-half inch diameter sample barrel—the straw—smoothly down into the soil to the proscribed depth and then withdraw the straw back up again for the retrieval of its soil contents in a cacophonous mechanical dance. The diesel noise was deafening, especially when they were push-ing, and the crew communicated almost exclusively with hand signals consisting of pointed fingers and clenched fists.

Laurie liked getting outdoors and away from her desk to do fieldwork and would dress provocatively in tight jeans and T-shirt in order to distract the guys on the job. Stan Wilcox, a stout graying middle-aged engineer who was the plant's environmental manager and not easily distracted, guided her on the tour.

"We've been working on a grid pattern with some high-density sampling around potential source areas to characterize the back forty."

"How much have you sampled?"

"We've completed about sixty percent of our planned soil, shallow groundwater, and underlying aquifer samples to date."

"And?"

"Well, we have some results I think you should see. Let's head inside to the conference room and I'll show you the data."

They made their way back up the dirt path to the plant and inside the to the cool sickly sweet-smelling air. Wilcox opened several file folders and pulled select gas chromatograph mass spectrometer (GC/MS) analytical readouts of the chemicals they had found.

"We've got two problem hot spots so far. Concentrations of trichloroethylene, TCE, in the underlying groundwater are in excess of the regulatory maximum contaminant level, MCL."

Laurie looked at the GC/MS reports and the elevated concentrations in the aquifer. "It looks like we've got some migration heading off site and biotransformation of the TCE to vinyl chloride."

"Yep. The problem is, the aquifer is used as a drinking water source by some private homes a mile or so away."

Laurie already knew this. She had gotten the MLS data on the homes and properties, all below $25,000, and she had done a drive by and seen the doublewide trailers with trash smoldering in the backyards, pickup trucks, four-wheelers and American flags, and knew everything she needed to know about the potential liability. These properties were expendable.

"Are their wells impacted above the MCL?" She knew the answer.

"We don't know, but my guess is not yet."

"Well, we can't let those people worry about their drinking water if there's no problem with it and there might never be a problem with it, now, can we?"

"Uh, no I guess we can't."

"Good."

Laurie tore up the GC/MS reports. "These samples don't exist, so there's no problem, and those folks can continue to sleep soundly."

Wilcox blinked and looked down at his feet. He lived in the same community as these folks. But he also had a large mortgage on a new custom-built log home, two cars with notes, and a wife and three kids to support. Laurie was from corporate headquarters, corporate made the rules, and he was a good corporate soldier. In his complex world of hydrogeology, contaminant transport and risk assessment, in the end it was just that simple.

"Yes ma'am. No problem here."

Laurie smiled sweetly, extended her hand. "Great! Thanks so much for the tour, Mr. Wilcox. Oh, and please tell the boys to keep it up."

Laurie winked, turned on her heel and headed out to the parking lot for the drive back to the office in her new BMW 320i. Life was good.

The Saltville, Michigan facility was Laurie's first major solo project. The town got its name for a reason. Four hundred million years ago during the Silurian period, melting ice caps on the supercontinent Gondwanaland raised global ocean levels and flooded areas of the arid Laurentian continent, progenitor of modern Michigan. A poorly circulating shallow sea periodically spilled into the sinking Michigan basin, eventually leaving behind deposits, thousands of feet thick, of evaporated salt from the seawater. These ancient, desiccated deposits buried beneath the town of Saltville were reborn as chlorine for Upland Chemical's manufacturing processes. And there was a great demand for chlorine in 20th century America, given most industrial solvents, pesticides, plastics, and synthetic rubber all incorporated chlorine to some extent within their molecules. Upland had been in Business since 1900 and during this time had experimented with several chemical-manufacturing approaches, each one producing its own suite of toxic byproducts. The most recent chlorination process had relied upon mercury, and as a result had produced mercury-tainted wastewater. Upland sold some of the chlorine it produced, but used much of it to make the chlorinated hydrocarbon perchloroethylene (PCE), a solvent that dry-cleaned the suits of corporate America.

Behind Upland's Saltville plant was a broad expanse of grassy lawn, providing a pastoral dichotomy to the corroded reactor towers and the featureless concrete buildings that housed manufacturing until operations ceased in 1972. The lawn also provided a functional cover for two former ponds that had been used by Upland Chemical to dispose of wastewater. Waste tars from PCE manufacturing were placed neatly in barrels and shipped offsite for disposal. The disposal company was Joey Faloni's Trucking Service. Joey himself would pick up Upland's barrels, drive them a short distance out of town to his garage complex, and dump them in the most recent hole he had dug in his back forty acres. Upland knew this, but didn't know this. What Faloni charged for the disposal of their toxic waste was peanuts, so he clearly was not handling it with any special care. But once Upland handed the barrels off to Joey, they could wash their hands of the mess like Pontius Pilate and get back to the business of making money.

In Faolini's waste pits, the barrels of Upland's chlorinated tars were tipped in with hundreds of barrels of waste from other nearby manufacturing facilities. Once the hole was filled to the brim, Joey had his boys bring in the backhoe, skim a cover of dirt over the barrels, and move down the line to dig the next quarter-acre mass grave. It didn't take long for corrosion to eat through the barrels, and then, like water spilled at the top of a staircase, gravity pulled the liquid wastes down through the soil to the water table thirty feet below. Some of the wastes that dissolved in this groundwater migrated laterally towards the nearby river. But relatively insoluble globules of dense chemicals like PCE would continue to plummet through the sediments saturated with less dense water, trying their best to reach the center of the earth, but eventually being stopped by the fractured bedrock at the base of the aquifer. There, like dissolving toxic Tootsie Rolls, the PCE globules would sit and continue to bleed their pollution into the groundwater for the next several hundred years. The chemicals merely complied with the law of physics, as understood by Newton when the apple hit him on the head. Nothing more than compliance and nothing less: that's the dispassionate way physics goes. Likewise, by giving Faloni their wastes and allowing him to place them where they would pollute the groundwater, Upland was merely complying with the law of the nation as understood by industry at that time, because there was no federal law in the 1960s telling you that you were responsible for your wastes— cradle to grave—or that it was wrong to pollute a community's drinking water. Industry was given the freedom to do the right thing, which they saw as what was most cost effective. Such was the law of free enterprise that made America great.

Eventually the pollution party came to an end, and in 1976 Congress enacted the forward-looking Resource Conservation and Recovery Act (RCRA) that said industries were responsible—starting today—for all the waste they generated, from cradle to grave. Then in 1981 Congress enacted the retrospective Comprehensive Environmental Response Compensation and Liability Act (CERCLA), also known as Superfund, which dealt with the mess from hazardous wastes that had been dumped by chemical companies and their disposal minions in the past. To the chemical company patriots, paying good money to dispose of hazardous wastes had been looked at as un-American, and a law requiring them to manage disposal responsibly and pay lots of money to do so made them sick. Adding insult to injury, they were now being told to clean up the mess they had already made, which gave them only two choices: (1) admit their error, roll over like wimps, and pay to clean up the mess; (2) deny everything and fight like patriotic Minutemen to not clean anything up. Laurie was part of a group assigned to defend Upland from CERCLA, this new anti-American law cooked up in the waning days of the socialist Jimmy Carter's presidency. She was a determined warrior in Upland's new army and the mission was simple. Deny and fight.

By 1986, Upland and Laurie understood the magnitude of their potential liability in Saltville. The ponds at the facility were contaminated with mercury, and that was a problem, but the federal Environmental Protection Agency (EPA) didn't know that yet, so all was well for the time being. The big problem was the Faloni site. Upland had saved millions by allowing Faloni to indiscriminately dump their wastes in his pits. In economics this is called a negative externality, where you let someone else pay the price for your pollution. It is a great deal if you are a corporate stockholder, and a bad one for those who have to pay the price. In business, a penny saved is more than a penny earned if invested properly, and those millions in unspent responsible disposal costs had earned the company billions in returns. But now, the wastes had risen from their graves and been detected in the adjacent river, people in the community initially alarmed to the fact by the arrival of two-headed hermaphrodite frogs. If Upland were now required to pay for their share of the Faloni site cleanup, they might actually come out in the red on the deal. That is what infuriated the Upland warriors the most about this new liberal anti-business legislation more than anything else: losing the financial game.

But there are a number of ways to fight the EPA in this Superfund liability battle, and Laurie had experience with all of them. If you had dumped your waste in the back forty of a farmer's field with a bunch of other frugal chemical companies and somehow the EPA got wind you were one of the dumpers, say from your logo on a corroded barrel, they would send you a letter identifying you as a Potentially Responsible Party (PRP) and ask lots of uncomfortable questions about your past. At this point, you had two paths to choose from: admit or deny. Down the admission pathway you could provide the EPA the information they asked for, and agree to cooperate in the cleanup. Down the denial pathway you clam up and provide no information, let the EPA clean up the site, and then fight them when they sue you for reimbursement of their cleanup costs. Denial was the path to take if you gambled the EPA, and other PRPs lacked sufficient evidence to figure out exactly what you had done. Because CERCLA's joint and several liability provision does not discriminate between a PRP that dumped a teaspoon and a PRP that dumped a tanker truck, each PRP at the site is equally responsible for the cleanup—until, that is, they crack a back room deal with the other responsible parties, where the bill can be discretely apportioned a bit more equitably. It's understood that this back room deal is only possible if everyone pulls down their pants and slaps their dicks on the table. This dick slapping usually takes place in a dark smoky room under the premise that there is in fact honor among thieves. By slapping a fake dick on the table and denying how badly they had polluted the Faloni site, Laurie could maybe get a few sucker companies to pay for some of Upland's cleanup costs. Look, save a million here, a million there, it can add up. Survival of those with the least shame in American industry allows the craftiest to persevere. Although J.R. Upland was a creationist and railed against the teaching of evolution in schools, he loved to use it in the corporate environment where he felt it was absolutely applicable.[1]

If the EPA had the goods on them, then Upland would head strategically, not tragically, down the admission pathway. There would be embarrassed smiles, apologies, and faux contrition, and an agreement to voluntarily clean up the site. That agreement provided Upland with the ability to hijack the environmental investigation and control all the information coming from the site. Private consultants could be hired to collect unrepresentative samples, destroy data indicating the presence of serious contamination, submit samples of clean soil imported from offsite, and maybe even dump some one-headed frogs with only one set of reproductive organs back in the river. Once the site was suitably mischaracterized, a feasibility study comparing low-cost ineffective remedies could be proposed by Upland, and the EPA given the opportunity to select a remedy within the realm of these cost-effective alternatives. Given her engineering problem solving approach, ability to remain cool and smile under pressure, and feverish need to always win, admission and damage control had become Laurie's specialty. She had saved Upland millions so far, and she was on the road towards the billion-dollar mark and all that came with it.

SEVEN

STINGERS

(ZILKER PARK, AUGUST 11, 2020, 10:05 CST)

This bench on Lou Neff Point faces east, and since early spring I have offered my face and eyes to the morning sun for several hours here each day. For some reason, the sun today is more punishing than usual. Since the surgery, wearing sunglasses hurts the bridge of my nose and makes me feel claustrophobic. I am now willing to sacrifice my eyes and squint rather than suffer the alternative: pain and psychological discomfort. I don't wear commercial sunscreen either, and I never have. Research shows that the active ingredients in sunscreen—avobenzone, homosalate, octinoxate, octisalate, octocrylene and oxybenzone—are all absorbed through the skin and into the bloodstream, and while we don't know much about these chemicals, what we do know is not very comforting. I choose to formulate my own solar barrier. I call it So-Bar. I use eight dollar a pound titanium dioxide mixed with whatever inexpensive facial moisturizer is on sale the week I whip up a new batch. So-Bar works well and costs me pennies per application; however, it leaves a dull whitish film on my skin that is a poor complement to my naturally unhealthy pallor these days.

But I am not concerned about appearances. Times have changed and so have I, at least physically. My doctors have me on a strict diet, with light exercise. They tell me that, if all goes well, I can advance to a more strenuous exercise regime, but tragically I can never return to my former diet, which consisted primarily of deep fried Tex-Mex food and melted cheese. Sometimes I imagine myself in several years, residing in something that better resembles my twenty-something-year-old body. But I am unsure these days whether I am destined to last long enough to make these physical improvements that might also allow me psychologically to be open to new challenges, the way I was back in my twenties. I fear the last scintilla of the "me" of those days may already have been permanently uncoupled from this old train, leaving the current me rusting at the station siding, filled with nothing but crumbled, yellowed schedules from past runs. Jesus, morning in America takes on a hurtful character when you are sitting on a bench in the Texas summer sun.

Ha! Morning in America! Even though it was over thirty years ago, I find myself slipping smoothly into that lovely 1984 campaign commercial and then beyond.

It's morning again in America. Today, more men and women will go to work than ever before in our country's history. With interest rates at about half the record highs of 1980, nearly 2,000 families today will buy new homes —more than at any time in the past four years. This afternoon, 6,500 young men and women will be married, and with inflation at less than half of what it was just four years ago, they can look forward with confidence to the future. It's morning again in America, and under the leadership of President Reagan, our country is prouder and

stronger and better. Why would we ever want to return to
where we were less than four short years ago?

Ronald Reagan's election in 1980 brought a significant
sea change to the White House. Jimmy Carter's solar panels
were quickly torn down and disposed of with extreme prejudice, along with the quaint notion that assassinations and
strongmen dictators were distasteful. Reagan's CIA chief
William Casey was a self-made American millionaire who, as
a New York lawyer, had invented the corporate tax shelter.
For Casey, the world was very simple: he loved money and
the Catholic Church, and he hated the Soviet Union. His
hatred of the Soviets was strategically manifested through his
support of the mujahideen in Afghanistan and the Contras
in Central America, both of whom he likened to America's
founding fathers. Casey's struggle with the Evil Empire was
not so much about strategic global geopolitics as it was
simply part of the epic battle between good and evil
described in the Bible. Although Carter had initiated Operation Cyclone in 1979 to modestly support the mujahideen
in Afghanistan, by 1984 under Reagan, we were sending
over almost $500 million in covert aid annually. Strange
bedfellows arose. A thousand Tennessee mules were bought
at auction and sent to Pakistan to haul munitions and
medical supplies across the mountains into Afghanistan.
Charlie Wilson, the alcoholic Democrat Representative from
Texas, joined Casey in his Afghan obsession, and equally
strange bonds were forged in the frigid caves and on the hot
arid plains of Afghanistan between the CIA in Langley, the
Inter-Services Intelligence in Islamabad, the Saudi General
Intelligence Department in Riyadh, and the mujahideen.
The war against the godless communists was bringing
together unlikely brothers in arms, and in Afghanistan the
war against the Russians was about to be fought in earnest.

Casey and his American patriots were ready for their moment of glory.[1]

The young me glanced at my new Rolex Submariner as I pulled my slightly used Saab 99 into the Raytheon campus. I loved that Saab, the new car smell of polystyrene, the feel of the rack and pinion front end, the pull of almost two liters of engine displacement, and the Swedish fighter jet manufacturer that built it. I loved that watch too, a sapphire crystal face set within a stainless-steel case, the second hand making eight iterations each second. In my opinion, it was the finest of all Swiss chronometers, and I had bought the car and watch from the significant savings I had accumulated by living at home with my folks. It was midweek, midmonth: Wednesday, September 17 in 1985, exactly 15 minutes and ten seconds before eight, and the maple leaves in Massachusetts were already showing their colors.

In the years since college, I had lost my old lobster body odor and gained a greater sense of self. I began my tenure at Raytheon six years earlier working for my first two years on the Integrated Air Missile Defense product line with the Patriot Missile system, refining the phased array tracking radar of the company's bread-and-butter anti-missile missile that was finally operational and deployed last year in 1984. Working on the tracking system was interesting but not quite a dream job for a kid who cut his teeth on building home-made explosives and blowing things up.

In late 1982 I was moved from the Patriot to Raytheon's new Stinger missile program in the Land Combat product line. Earlier that year, six Stingers and a trained SAS operator from D Squadron had joined the fray in the Falkland Islands war. Despite the operator being killed before he could fire even one of these new hand-held surface-to-air missiles, his untrained mates were able to pick up the system because its operation was so simple, and score a hit with one of the six missiles they fired, knocking down an Argentinian Pucará turboprop. Even though the Pucará has a maximum speed of only five hundred kilometers per hour, the Stinger had still demonstrated some real promise, especially for deployment to areas with untrained guerrilla forces.

The system, ready to launch, weighed a mere 32 pounds, and delivered a 5-pound heat-seeking warhead containing a full pound of high explosives. It was a fire-and-forget weapon that could reach a target up to five miles away at an altitude of up to ten thousand feet. I was in love with the Stinger. To me, its warhead was phallic and its machine oil like pheromones, and because of its size I got to play with the whole package, not just the tracking. I guess I was still a bit of a pervert when it came to weapons and explosives. For me, going to work back then was a bit like a pornographer going to shoot a movie.

My boss had called an eight-thirty group meeting that day to discuss some recent market developments, and as people began to arrive, he was already settled into the conference room chair with a styrofoam cup of watery black coffee. The room was small but so was the Stinger group: me, and my co-workers Dana Flanders and Rob Gleason. My boss, John McIntyre, was an ex-Air Force Minuteman missile jockey who had spent much of his service time in the 1960s like a mole, deep down in a subterranean silo in Kansas. He seemed to live every day like his first day out of the silo, and he was overflowing with the hatred for the Soviets he had cultivated during those many underground years. Everyone at Raytheon understood the symbiotic relationship between our company and the government, and McIntyre was one of the primary corporate liaisons along that blurry line. The lights in the room were dimmed, the slide projector illuminated, and the projector fan the only sound. The image on the screen was of a massive rock mountain face, a valley, and a helicopter. The helicopter was fat, ugly, bristling with weapons, and wore a red star. It was a Soviet Hind. McIntyre began his nasal monotonic delivery as if he were in a large lecture hall.

"People, this is a Russian Mi-24 helicopter gunship. NATO reporting name: Hind. The Russian pet name for the Hind is 'Galina or 'Crocodile,' because of its paint job. Next slide.

"The Hind is a 'flying tank.' It carries a pilot and a weapons system officer, each with their own cockpit, and has additional capacity for up to 10 lightly equipped troops. Next slide.

"The top speed of this crocodile is around three hundred kilometers per hour—a lot slower than that Pucará the Brits shot down in the Falklands. Next slide.

"OK, weapons. A 12.7mm four-barrel Yak-B Gatling-gun, four 57mm rocket pods, and four Fleyta radio command anti-tank missiles, NATO reporting name Swatter. Next slide.

"The Hind has the capability of carrying a diversity of additional ordinance, like these one-hundred-kilogram and two-hundred-fifty-kilogram bombs with which to wreak unguided mayhem and murder on any poor bastards below. Next slide.

"These mountains are the Hindu Kush in Afghanistan, and those poor bastards below are our friends, the mujahideen, and the Hind is the tip of the Soviet spear that is currently killing our friends. Next slide.

"It's our job to snap this spear and drive these commie bastards back to Moscow and we're gonna do it with none other than our Raytheon Stinger missiles. OK, that's the end of the slide deck. Lights on.

"We are confident that our Stingers will lock on to the Hind's exhaust signal, not be fooled by countermeasure flares, and they will blow these sons of bitches out of the sky. So, we aim to deliver the first shipment of three hundred to our friends waiting for them in Pakistan. We are planning for that delivery in around 180 days and then see how things progress from there. Our Senator, Paul Tsongas, has been pushing for Raytheon to help turn the tide over there and of course bring those federal dollars in to the state of Mass-achusetts as well. The DoD has to stay out of this project for obvious reasons here in the U.S. and the CIA has to stay out for somewhat less obvious reasons over there—for some reason those Mujahedin don't trust our spooks—so we'll need someone from this group to babysit the cargo and provide onsite operational instruction. Be warned—I am looking for someone interested in some patriotic international travel. Thank you, that's all.[2]"

We all got up, and after shuffling out of the small confer-ence room door and into the fluorescent-lit hall I overheard Rob murmur to Dana in a low voice, "No way your gonna catch me going to Pakistan to get dysentery and maybe get shot at."

They smiled at each other and nodded. You would have to be a bit crazy to volunteer for a project like that.

EIGHT

OILFIELD TRASH

These days I spend on my park bench provide time in which to think—and I spend a considerable portion of it thinking about Berg and Laurie. I am not sure if this suffocating heat is an asset or a liability. It seems to help unstick me, and the forethought provides a trajectory for slipping beyond-space-time. But the heat also amplifies the lucidity and messes with my sense of where I physically am at any given moment. I have written off slipping up the slope to the future, so I am good with crossing out that dimensional possibility. While I believe I am getting better at framing my beyond-space-time travel, given the recalcitrant uncertainties, the act of slipping in general is no picnic.

Life in America in the early 1980s was no picnic either. The country was in a recession. They tried deregulating the banks, cutting taxes, increasing government spending on weapons, and increasing the national debt. But like a big ship that turns slowly, it took some time for the economy to begin to right itself. Life for Berg offshore in the Gulf of Mexico in the 1980s was not all it had been cracked up to be. After four years of rotations, primarily on derrick barges—three weeks on and two weeks off—Berg had managed to stash some cash, and he was ready to bolt. Sure, he had seen some cool stuff, like high-speed crew boat rides that rivaled scenes from *Apocalypse Now*, bumpy helicopter commutes, and death rushes on close call helideck landings. The food was perfect, and he feasted on the biggest grilled steaks and frog's legs in the world, and fresh deep-fried doughnuts at three in the morning that melted in your mouth.

The sheer violence of the job itself was a turn on for Berg, too. Like one day when a new guy decided to hop on the pipe he had been welding to get to the other side, like a bad chicken-crossing-the-road joke. Doing this maneuver saves about one, maybe two minutes of walking around the barge. All the old hands do it. It was unfortunately bad timing for the fucking new guy, or FNG. Berg was up in the anchor tower, spinning the tugs around the barge in an elegant Baroque dance, lifting and placing anchors, stretching and pulling anchor lines, and dragging the barge slowly across the bottom like a huge aquatic insect as welded pipe snaked off the stern and down to the bottom of the Gulf. He had just started walking the barge forward and as the FNG stepped on the pipe it began to move, dropping him on his ass with his feet pointed towards the stern. Mercifully, his dark welding glasses fell down into place over his eyes, visually shutting out what was about to happen to him. But Berg in the anchor tower had a bird's eye view, and couldn't take his eyes off the scene. The FNGs feet were headed directly into the tensioner, a powerful roller rig that keeps the 42-inch diameter steel pipe horizontal on deck while it is welded to another length and allows it to bend in a graceful arc from its rollers down to the ocean floor some 300 feet below. The FNG was about to be consumed by the tensioner. Berg heard the welder's screams as he entered the rollers and his toes, then his feet, then his ankles, began to be squeezed, crushed, flattened, and snapped. The large derrick barge was in motion and there was nothing anyone could do to stop it now, and nothing Berg could do but watch the scene unfold from above. As the pipe drew him deeper into the mouth of the beast, the FNG's screams grew deeper, his upper body growing larger as the blood from his extremities squeezed upwards into his torso. As his thighs were consumed, he pushed against the tensioner with his arms and with one last roar his head snapped back, and blood exploded from his ears and nose. The welding glasses caught his eyeballs, which had blown out of their sockets. When they bagged him, the FNG's corpse weighed only about 60 pounds, having been drained of most of its liquid weight. Berg saw other cool stuff like that happen, and some wicked meteor showers too, and shitloads of sunrises as he often drew the crappiest shift from midnight to noon.

Berg fiddled with the stereo while he drove. Rice University's KTRU had just segued from alternative rock to some boring talk topic. He popped in a cassette, and the reverberating first chords of Billy Idol's "White Wedding" emerged from the speakers. Berg cranked it up, settled back into the black Naugahyde seat of his federal gray 1982 Jeep Cherokee, and focused on the cigarette he had lit just before Rice University let him down. After three weeks at sea, and four hours on the road back from Port Aransas where the crew boat had dropped him off, he was anxious, and he was almost home. He had stopped briefly in Aransas Pass to gas up and grab a Whataburger and fries, which he quickly consumed, pitching the leftover fries and burger wrapper out the window on I-35 as he passed Holiday Beach, to keep the stink of the uneaten food from spoiling the ambiance of his drive home. His tires squealed as he made the final fast slalom turns through the palm tree-lined streets of his neighborhood, then smoothly flicked the burning butt of the Marlboro Medium through the sunroof and turned hard into his potholed oyster shell driveway. He quickly turned the key, shut down the engine, and glided silently up the drive, under the house and into the carport. He hopped out of the Jeep, the humid air a familiar contrast with the crisp air-conditioned bubble he had been locked in since he left Port Aransas. Despite experiencing this same thermodynamic phenomenon each time he left the anchor tower on a barge for a smoke or to grab some food in the mess, the contrast was never trivial and it physically focused his attention on exactly where he was.

Berg opened the back hatch and grabbed his grease-stained Atlantis sea bag and the one-inch rock-climbing webbing that lashed together the loops on his battered Redwing steel toed boots, swung them both over his left shoulder, and bounded up the broad wooden staircase at the front of the house. The door had an external combination padlock as well as a deadbolt, the added security giving him peace of mind but requiring additional work when he returned from an offshore hitch. He moved efficiently but anxiously through the procedure with his free right hand, kicked the humidity-swollen door open, dropped the gear on the floor, and headed to the kitchen. He opened a cabinet and took down a can of Bay Seasoning and a plate, pulled a credit card and a crisp twenty from his wallet, and folded one corner of the twenty up to the eleven-digit serial number. He then rolled the bill, tucking in the fold to make a rigid tube, opened the can of Bay Seasoning, dumped a small pile of white rocky powder onto the plate, crushed the rocks with the flat side of the credit card, then chopped the powder into four neat one-inch-long piles. He picked up the rolled twenty, stuck it up his right nostril and inhaled one of the piles, cocked his head back, grimaced and sniffed, then repeated the process with his left nostril. He set the bill down, turned to the refrigerator, opened a Coors, took a long satisfying pull, then let out an even more satisfying belch. Berg smiled, lit a cigarette, and looked approvingly around the house as the cocaine hit his brain and bowels, then headed to the bathroom for an even more satisfying shit. He was home.

Berg had rented this shack in Seabrook, Texas down by the water. Because of hurricanes, all the houses in this small muddy cluster were elevated at least ten feet up on pilings. Berg could either walk or ride his bike to the nearby bars. This was important because, although Berg was getting totally fucked up on a regular basis, he clearly understood that an arrest for drunk driving would cost him his job offshore and his excellent lifestyle. His house consisted of a single large room with a futon in one corner, a pile of stereo equipment on top of an old shipping crate in another, and a Yucatan hammock strung across the room. A king-sized mattress occupied the far corner of the room, but more often than not, unless Berg had some female company, he would find himself in the hammock come sunrise. The fridge was always filled with beer and the freezer with rum, and from the back deck you could see both Clear Lake and Galveston Bay. It was an excellent place to party. Down in the yard, Berg kept his twenty-five-foot Mako center console boat on a trailer when he was offshore. The ground around the boat was a hardened breccia of gumbo clay, sand, and broken oyster shells, punctuated by cigarette butts flicked from the porch that Berg raked into a large pile once a month and shoveled into the trashcan.

Life between offshore gigs was excellent: what with a fistful of cash and two weeks off, there was plenty of time for partying. There were also some clear partying rules for offshore work. Rule number one was: don't smoke pot.

Smoke a joint and the THC stays in your body for over a month and can be picked up in piss tests, which were administered randomly and regularly. LSD detection requires a spinal tap, but combining acid and offshore work was pretty fucking stupid, and some of those that did wound up contestants for the Darwin Awards. Cocaine, on the other hand, metabolized rapidly and, within a week, could not be picked up in urine. Because of this, and the nature of the beast, frosted flakes became Berg's breakfast of champions, and by 1985 this was not your garden-variety coke anymore, at least not down in Seabrook, Texas.

When Berg got onshore, he partied on NASA Road 1 where the three-mile stretch from Route 146 to the Hilton Hotel was speckled with Florida wannabe bars, complete with plastic pink flamingos, ice-filled buckets of Coronas, fried shrimp, blackened gator, and tons of dumb chicks with humongous silicone breasts. It was paradise. During the week, Berg would wander down to the Turtle Club, a floating bar at the end of a pier jutting out into Clear Lake that had opened recently. He would often arrive right before five o'clock to get a jump on the working crowd and stay into the darkest hours when the Cigarette boats that had been racing back and forth across the lake made their way to the docks for last call. On weekends, the level of his hangover dictated when he made the migration, usually starting with a breakfast of biscuits and gravy washed down with red hot bloodies at the Classic Cafe. After living on Long Island and then in New Hampshire, Berg had finally found his Promised Land in Seabrook. Jimmy Buffet was Moses, and cocaine was sweet manna sent from heaven to keep everyone running through the alcohol fog.

Berg had an established social scene, even though his offshore work made him an episodic character in the non-stop drama of NASA Road 1. One of the guys he worked with offshore, Geoff, a doodlebugger, lived down the road. Doodlebugging was looking for underwater oil and gas deposits with seismic surveying gear, and Geoff and Berg had met on one of the odd jobs Berg had done on seismic boats when the company got in a bind. This was the white-collar offshore world where everyone had a college degree and their own stateroom. As a regular barge monkey, where life was quite different, Berg always jumped at the opportunity to shoot a job on a big 3-D seismic boomer. Geoff and Berg had shot some shallow water surveys together off Louisiana, Berg on the gunboat creating the periodic explosions needed to transmit the seismic signal, and Geoff on the boat behind him dragging the hydrophones around platforms, peeking at the hydrocarbon reflections below. Geoff was from England and had an accent that made everything he said sound intelligent. Berg was a bit jealous of the air of sophistication that Geoff exuded and was convinced that his accent got him all the sweet jobs and cush chopper rides, while Berg's New York accent got him nothing but shit jobs riding crew boats to work. Geoff lived with his girlfriend Carol, a mousy insurance underwriter, and they all would hang out from time to time on shore. Carol was always trying to hook Berg up with one of her desperate friends, most of whom were dull as battleship paint, but every once in a while, Carol would deliver a real freak, so Berg never said no to her suggestions. Berg loved the gumbo down at the Classic Café, and the bartender there, Kinky, became a good friend. Kinky knew everyone. Everyone. Through Kinky, Berg got hooked up with Captain Jack and a fat, sweaty attorney named Tom Brewer, both of whom would soon change his life.

In 1985 the Saudis increased oil production, and the price per barrel began to crater. Berg did not get a promotion or a raise, and his mother committed suicide in their West Hempstead home with a bottle of sleeping pills she had been hoarding. Berg got the news offshore through a satellite phone call from his father. He let his son know that his mother had already been cremated and there would be no big, involved service or anything, so Berg didn't need to fly home. That was perfectly fine with him, and he caught the biggest redfish of his life off a platform that night. By December, Berg's father was engaged to Trixie from Jericho; she came complete with two enormous breasts and two teenage girls with terrible acne. She spoke like a charm school graduate and was a mental midget; so were her girls. Trixie immediately quit her job as a secretary and began living to shop. Berg began skipping holidays at home.

NINE

KARACHI

(ZILKER PARK, AUGUST 11, 2020, 10:13 CST)

I try to look around Zilker Park without turning my head, because that involves too much effort. It doesn't work. Oh well. Days like today are what make up a typical Texas summer, and each day feels like another nail driven into my coffin. The late morning air is already one hundred degrees. It is thick and still, heavy on pollution and light on oxygen. Days like today remind me of Karachi. I guess that's one positive thing about Texas.

The flat clouding eyes of the dead stare blankly at me as I sip my coffee, grinning clenched teeth, leering lolling tongues. Morning in Karachi is filled with the scent of donkey shit, diesel, dough frying in boiling oil, and coffee. This March day promised to be another ninety-degree scorcher. I left the hotel at sunrise to stretch my legs and jetlagged mind in the relatively cool early morning air, and had settled in at a café next to a butcher shop sporting a fine assortment of goats' heads. The Raytheon cargo had arrived by ship, and after the stevedores offloaded the five-ton load, we spent the next week in the warehouse carefully unpacking, unwrapping, checking, and repacking one hundred

Stingers back into their crates and onto our truck in the Port before starting out on the trip north. The Karachi sun rose each day like a filthy fist curling into the sky, tightening its grip as the day progressed, relaxing a bit with the coming of dusk. With each day that we worked in the port warehouse, our driver Waqas ripened. Given the customary infrequency of full body hygiene, it was inevitable. Waqas was my age, short and sinewy with dark skin and wavy black hair. He wore the same dark brown light pajama-style pants and a dark gray T-shirt every day. The heat and coastal humidity extracted sweat, filth and stink from us all, but particularly from Waqas and his recycled attire. In the short time we had known each other, I had come to look on him as a friend and interestingly—unlike the odor of a stranger on a bus or train —the aroma emanating from Waqas grew to not offend me. I had worked with him to crosscheck the manifests with the goods, and all we had left to do was put a meter across sensitive junctions on a final random sample of the launchers, and that phase of the job would be complete.

We got underway the next day before dawn, the sea mist mingling with smoke from early morning fires and diesel exhaust, creating a low ceiling of smog through which stars had no hope of penetrating. The plan was to depart Port Qasim and follow the brand-new N-55, tracking the Indus River north to our rendezvous in Peshawar almost 1,400 kilometers distant. Depending upon what happened along the way, the drive could take anywhere from nineteen hours to forever. From the Port, our truck rolled through the Dockyards Road then up West Wharf Road and into the city of Akbar Sadiqi. Turning left onto Nawab Mahabat Khanji Road, we passed the Hospital on the left, navigating through the feral cats and organic debris of the vegetable market. We veered right after the Police station, up Siddiq Wahab Road, across Jamila Street and the Teen Hatti Bridge, snaking at a crawl though the narrow streets of the slumbering city until we reached the N5, which would take us to Hyderabad and the genesis of the Indus Highway.

I had learned a bit of Arabic before leaving Massachusetts, and there was some crossover with the Urdu spoken in Pakistan. During our time in the port, Waqas had taught me a few Urdu words with Hindi roots, and I now had a lexicon of approximately twenty words that I managed to assemble and reassemble into multiple new combinations on the drive. With Waqas driving and me riding shotgun, we were able to sing and joke our way across Pakistan. Only by the grace of Allah did the four well-armed regular Pakistani Army—or Inter-Services Intelligence, ISI—babysitters in the back survive the circuit of the sun and lack of ventilation. And only because of the excessive starch in their uniforms did they continue to appear freshly creased, albeit more mottled and sienna-hued as time passed.

The trip up into the Pakistani-Afghan border region was pretty easy. Several years earlier, before the N55, we would have had to put up with kidney- and jaw-jarring roads and incessant dust. The load of Stingers I was accompanying was going to this guy Gulbuddin Hekmatyar, a Pashtun warlord with strong connections to the ISI. Hekmatyar had studied engineering at Kabul University and ran his mujahideen like a well-oiled machine. If a part malfunctioned it was swiftly removed, disposed of, and replaced. Hekmatyar's men ran sorties into Afghanistan, mostly from the Northern tribal regions of Pakistan. I had volunteered and been selected to accompany this load as a technical advisor for Raytheon. I assume my father's position with the Agency probably helped my selection—and possibly the fact that I was the only volunteer from my group. I thought my engineering expertise with the Stinger, physical stamina from years of hiking the White Mountains, and my patriotism made me the perfect candidate for the mission. I was also just dumb enough to want to go.

The valley scenery was monotonous, punctuated occasionally by random street vendors hawking Kleenex and inedible-looking food. At Dera Ismail Khan, the scenery began to change, and the air freshened and cooled a little as we left the river track and began our westward slide up into the barren hills. When we reached Dara Adamkhel, a pale green plateau in a sea of flinty rock and dust just south of Peshawar, we stopped at the Dana Bazaar for tea, to make phone calls and to part ways with our Army or ISI guests. They were skipping the Hotels of the Khyber Bazaar up the road, a favorite of NGO workers and spooks, and avoiding Peshawar in general, as there were eyes everywhere. They would proceed directly to their safe house in the Khyber Agency near Ali Masjid, on the road to the Khyber Pass and Afghanistan beyond. Waqas and I would continue to our destination, off the main road into the hinterlands past Landi Khotal and just shy of the Torkham border crossing.

We reached the Hekmatyar camp after dark. Waqas had wrestled the truck back and forth across switchbacks, endlessly downshifting to get us up the rugged faces of the mountains, the floor and cab of the truck heating up with the engine and emitting an odor of burning metal. With the help of some filthy urchins who appeared from the shadows of the house, Waqas began unloading our cargo under a thick blanket of brilliant stars set in a cloud free sky, while I was quickly directed to a basin where I could wash the patina from the road off me. The water was icy, and quickened my breath. I let it flow across my scalp and behind my ears, returning the dust to its home. There was no towel, but in the low humidity of the cold mountain air, the moisture quickly evaporated dry, adding to the cooling. Kerosene lamps glowed through the open windows of the low clay and brick building, and I had to stoop to enter the doorway where two pairs of leather sandals sat. Inside was a simple room with layers of wool carpets, mattresses, and pillows placed around the perimeter and a low large wooden table made from a shipping crate in the middle. The room was smoky with kerosene, tobacco, and a small wood fire. The lamps lent a warm flickering glow to the ochre walls. Hekmatyar was speaking with a tall, bearded, lean, and pleasant-looking mujahideen not much older than me. He wore a camouflage jacket, baggy black pajama pants, and a white turban. His dark brown eyes were large and welcoming as he smiled at me, touched his heart, and offered greetings in Arabic, "*salaamu alaykum, marhaba*, welcome."

"Hi, I'm Christopher LeBlanc!"

Hekmatyar, steely-eyed, spoke gruffly in simple heavily accented English and gestured abruptly. "We finish business now. You sit."

As the fighters concluded their discussion, I removed my boots and took a seat. Hekmatyar clapped his hands and barked out the window. A bucket of water and large plates of food appeared. There were baskets brimming with naan and a mountain of pilau and spicy mutton. The fighters washed their hands, gave thanks to Allah, and gestured for me, their guest, to begin eating. I took a piece of naan, tore off a fragment with my right hand and clumsily shoveled up a chunk of mutton and a small pile of spicy rice. The food was delicious, and during the meal while Hekmatyar was stiff and formal, his companion was warm and friendly, always smiling and encouraging me to eat more. His English vocabulary was broad and deep, and he spoke in a soft voice with a British accent complemented by the Middle Eastern rolling of the letter r.

The young mujahideen was a foreign fighter from Saudi Arabia named Osama. The son of a wealthy civil engineer, he had followed in his father's academic footsteps in college, but upon graduation, in that particularly peculiar year of 1979, had turned away from the family business to take up the struggle—jihad—against the godless Soviet invaders who had crossed into Afghanistan that winter. Through the course of dinner, with the help of Osama's periodic translation, I learned that Hekmatar was also schooled in engineering, and we discussed whether the three of us all being engineers was meaningful or simply coincidental.

"Engineers are trained to be problem solvers; we are simply solving a problem."

"Conflict is technical; it takes a technician to wage war and always has; look at the Roman war machines, the long bow, Viet Cong tiger pits; these are all forms of technology."

"Until the 18th century, there was only one type of engineer: the military engineer. The 18th century saw the arrival of a second branch: civil engineering. The joke now is that civil engineers build the targets that military engineers destroy."

"Engineers are by definition calculating; there is no room for emotion or empathy in engineering; there are only facts."

"We are trained to solve difficult problems, make fact-based decisions, execute effective actions, measure our performance, then improve the system."

"Yes, and we yearn for complex challenges, while at the same time appreciating and seeking the elegance of simple solutions."

"Engineers see things in black and white; there are no nuanced shades of gray for us. Quantitatively there is always a right answer and a wrong answer. Just like there is good and evil, just and unjust."

"Our jihad is simply another set of problems to solve."

"Yes, and American technology offers a highly effective solution to our current problem with the filthy Hinds."

And so on. We three engineers, Afghani, Saudi, and American had all analyzed our respective systems, defined the problem, formulated a solution, just like good engineers do, and were now executing it. Clearly the engineering design process had brought us together this night; that and of course the will of Allah.

Over dessert of pomegranate, honey, and jasmine tea Osama explained the nature of Islamic patriotism through which he viewed all of life.

"In Saudi Arabia, at the time of your American Revolution, there lived a preacher named Mohammed ibn Abdul Wahhab. Wahhab understood that change and modernization brought with it great evil, and he preached a simple message that spoke to the fundamental values of the old days. Wahab held himself as an example, rejected modern comforts, and lived a life of simplicity in the desert, much like the Amish people in your country, Christopher. In many ways he was like our allies in jihad, your conservative Republicans, turning away from the decadence of a liberal future and holding on to the surety of the past. We, his followers, practice this same conservative philosophy, Wahabism. We look towards the day that Saudi Arabia, America, and the world is taken back to those days of purity."

I couldn't believe what I was hearing. Here I was, thousands of miles from home and listening to a Saudi Berg!

"Yes, we have a kind of Wahabism in America, too, now. Some people believe that liberal change has destroyed much of what made our country great. President Reagan is cleaning up from the Carter years, getting rid of solar energy programs, and taking a tougher stance with the Soviets. Come to think of it, President Reagan's campaign slogan was pretty Wahabi: "Let's make America great again." Without President Reagan, we wouldn't all be sitting here today."

Osama nodded. "Exactly, Allah created man from the

clay of the earth, just as we have created this house in which we sit —the requirements of man are fundamental and were established when time began, all else is modern frivolity."

Hekmatyar yawned and brusquely excused himself from the conversation that appeared to be expanding beyond his vocabulary and interest. While Osama and I would sleep on the straw mattresses where we were, Hekmatyar slept elsewhere, and said he would see us kids in the morning. Osama stretched out his long frame on his straw mattresses and gave me a smile.

"Christopher my friend, for us alcohol is explicitly haram, forbidden. But for thousands of years, we have smoked hashish as a tradition, especially the Sufis, and if it is used judiciously to feel a closer connection to Allah, it is not considered haram. It is especially helpful for those of us who fight in the cold harsh mountains making it a staple medicinal. Have you heard of hashish?"

"Yes, many people in America smoke marijuana, and sometimes hashish if it is available."

"Excellent, so you are familiar with it! Would you like to get stoned?"

Before I could answer, Osama had pulled a finger-sized bar of black hashish from one of the top pockets of his field jacket. He held the bottom of the bar with his right index finger and thumb and deftly heated the top of the bar with the flame from a stainless steel lighter he held in his left hand, the sweet aroma quickly reaching across the table to where I sat. He let the edge cool slightly, then crumbled the loosened grains into a cigarette paper filled with tobacco, rolled it, lit it and passed it to me.

"This is some really good product from Mazar-i-sharif, so be careful, it can sneak up on you."

The golden light of burning kerosene and candles danced across the clay walls that now enclosed the sweet smell of hashish and jasmine. I am not sure how much we smoked, but it was enough so that I got a bit unstuck. I am unsure where I went, but I am confident I went somewhere. I am unsure what I saw there, but I know it was profound. Coming back was a bit rough, but when my autonomic system slowly returned, I was able to concentrate on more than just breathing and could relax. I looked over at Osama, who had his eyes closed and was humming softly to himself. How long had I been gone? An hour? A minute? I glanced at my Rolex. It was almost midnight. I had no idea when we had fired up that joint. I looked back again at Osama, relaxed, smiling to himself, and enjoying his own internal music. I closed my eyes, shrugged my shoulders up and down to relax and passed out.

"*Sabah al khayr sadiqi*, the good morning for you, Christopher my friend."

I opened my eyes. A pale light streamed through the window, softly illuminating Osama's smiling face, his breath steaming in the cold air.

"*Sabah al noor sadiqi*, the morning light for you Osama my friend."

"Come, let us walk."

I quickly laced my boots and grabbed the black cotton turban I had bought in Karachi, wrapping it several times around my neck. I then ducked through the low doorway, following Osama out into the early morning mist. We walked out the back of the camp, pausing to splash icy water on our faces from the basin, gasping and grinning at each other in silence. A narrow trail led up the escarpment, and I followed the backs of Osama's sandals as they navigated the small rocky steps and crevices. After an hour of dancing along the trail, we came to a ridge and Osama paused. I finally looked up from the ground and drew a breath.

"My God!"

"Yes—*bismillah*!"

The not-yet-arrived sun illuminated the backs of the Hindu Kush Mountains, etching their massive dark gray faces into a rosy sky.

"Sit, this is a good place to await al shams the sun and make salat al-fajr, our morning prayer. We mujahideen consider a splash of water or even a handful of dust to suffice for wudu, our ablutions, and our daily prayers are often communicated internally, given our informal circumstances and constraints."

We found a small piece of flat ground, leaned against some rocks, and stretched out, feet pointing towards the rising sun. The air was still and sweet, with the smell of fresh mountain herbs that had been crushed by our passing. It was cold, and we jammed hands into trouser pockets, shrugged necks into jacket collars, and tried to minimize any uncovered surface area from which heat could be lost. And then the sun appeared above the peaks, and with it the arrival of the wind, providing radiant warmth and a subtle chill, and rising from somewhere within me the strains of the Largo from Dvořák's Symphony No. 9 in E minor. I am not a religious person, but at that very specific instant I had a moment of something. For lack of a better description, it felt as if a spiritual entity had passed through my body, touching me to my core, and then departed as quickly as it had arrived, and I began to weep. I was clearly having some sort of significant epiphany, at least for me, but I was also self-conscious and clumsily attempted to hide my tears from Osama. He turned his head slowly towards me and smiled.

"Yes, Christopher, my brother—*Allahu akbar*—God is indeed the greatest."

I spent a week with Osama and his guys, unpacking the Stingers and teaching them how to use them. For obvious reasons, they were quite attentive and as a result learned quickly. The missiles had both infrared and ultraviolet detectors that gave them an uncanny ability to navigate through incidental background noise and deliberate enemy countermeasures in order to reach their targets. In theory, the Stinger was actually pretty easy to operate. The hard part was staying cool while staring down a fast-approaching Hind or MIG and waiting for just the right moment to fire the thing.

During this time, I also learned a bit about my role in the program. Hekmatyar and Osama had agreed to receive the Stingers contingent on their delivery by *albari'*, an innocent. Neither would deal directly with the CIA, and both had found the Pakistani ISI just barely acceptable in past dealings. They had cautioned the Americans and the ISI that there were many dangers a trained professional with ties to either agency might encounter in the mountains, and told them to diligently seek a competent *albari'* technician—or suffer the consequences. When I asked how the Americans had done, he chuckled.

"Christopher, professionally Hekmatyar and I are happy we did it this way. Actually, Hekmatyar is never really happy about anything, but I am especially glad, as I have enjoyed your company. And you should be happy, too, as you are still alive!"

We trained multiple groups of fighters that week. I would deliver the canned lecture, a fighter holding the Stinger, and Osama would translate. One day, I thought I spotted the two ISI guys from our truck wearing local clothing and pakol caps, but I couldn't be sure. The days quickly became routine, and I always looked forward to the evenings when Osama and I could kick back, get high and talk.

"Osama. That's an interesting name. What does it mean?"

"It means the one who is like a lion."

"Well, that's pretty fitting."

Osama chuckled. "Christopher. That is an interesting name too, what does it mean?"

"I was told it means the one who carries Christ in his heart."

"That is excellent. Then all Muslims are Christophers."

"How do you figure that?"

"Well Christopher, as it is written in the Family of Imran in the most Holy Koran, the Messiah Jesus was born to the Virgin Mary and made by Allah to be a messenger to the children of Israel.[1]"

"I did not know that."

"Yes of course my friend. Jesus, whom we call Isa, gave life to a clay bird, restored sight to the blind, healed lepers, and raised men from the dead. He was a great prophet.[2]"

"I learned about these miracles, too, as a kid. And somehow, I feel like I had heard that Jesus was mentioned in the Koran, but I didn't realize it was in such specific context and detail."

Osama dug in his battered olive drab canvas rucksack and pulled out a worn leather-bound Koran. "Listen to this Christopher, and Allah please forgive me for my paraphrasing and Arabic to English translation:

And remember when Allah said: Oh Jesus! Lo! I am gathering you and causing you to ascend unto Me, and I am cleansing you of those who disbelieve and am setting those who follow you above those who disbelieve until the Day of Resurrection. Then unto Me you will all return, and I shall judge between you as to that wherein you used to differ.[3]

As for those who believe and do good works, He will pay them their wages in full. Allah does not love wrongdoers.[4]"

Osama sat back, closed his eyes and took a deep breath. "We mujahideen carry the Holy Koran in our rucksacks and in our hearts. We are compelled to wage jihad both against the evil and injustice of others as well as evil inclinations within ourselves. When we carry the Holy Koran within our hearts, how can we not carry Isa as well?"

One night, a mujahid arrived after dinner. He had a small stature, a large aquiline nose, a face pinched and leathery from the weather, and a dark camel brown pakol cap set at a jaunty angle upon his head. His name was Abdallah, and he was fresh from fighting. Osama and Abdallah exchanged greetings, then went outside by the fire and sat and spoke in Arabic. I stepped out with them and stood to one side, not understanding the conversation, and only learning afterwards what had transpired. It went something like this.

"Abdallah, I am told of your battles in Nangrahar, they have been difficult."

"Yes, last month we lost many men in a single operation. We had taken a position close to the top of a mountain overlooking a valley, and were shooting down at the Soviets with BM-12 rockets and mortars. Our operational *markaz* was not too far from our position. Then, all of a sudden, a VDV company of about 90 men appeared and attacked us from behind. These infidels had climbed straight up the face of the mountain like spiders during the night. They captured our first post and came to within a hundred meters of our BM-12 launchers and rockets and ammunition before we stopped them. We fought for two days there, and many were killed. These were really tough guys. The Russians have also been killing us very efficiently from the sky with their helicopters. They have been capturing young women and girls and defiling them as well."

"Yes, Abdallah, I know, that is why the American is here. We are planning to stop this slaughter from the sky soon. But tell me about the prisoners."

A smile crept across Abdallah's lips. "Ah, you have heard.

Yes, the prisoners. We captured several of the Russian VDV infidel *kuffar* and dispatched them slowly to their hell."

"Yes, that is what I was told. But you were given orders to protect the VDV prisoners and return them to camp so they could be interrogated, no?"

"Yes Sidi Osama, but my jihad called for me to kill these filthy non-believers, and it was more convenient to travel without them. Besides, killing them slowly after seeing so many of our brothers killed by them was very enjoyable."

"Ah, your jihad Abdallah, of course, your jihad, I understand."

What happened next occurred so quickly that I didn't see it all unfold and had to assemble the pieces over the next days. Osama reached under his robe with his left hand, or maybe his hand was already under there. He pulled out a Soviet Makarov pistol, turned to his left, shoved it under Abdallah's chin, and blew the top and back of his head off into his pakol. All of this landed upon the ground in a contained mess a meter away from Abdallah's crumbled body that looked very small now. I jumped and took several steps back from the fire as Osama holstered the pistol

"What just happened? Why did you do that?"

"Christopher, my friend, we are all of us like prisms, and our jihad is as a beam of light. Our ability to accurately absorb, organize, and transmit this light determines how true of a representation of the struggle we live and communicate to others. Because we are flawed humans, we inadvertently bend this light, preferentially peel off specific wavelengths, and project the results for others to see. The degree to which we alter this light and are cognizant of it is, as with a prism, dependent upon our internal properties and our orientation. Often the changes we make are subtle, but sometimes that beam of light we began with becomes a confusing breccia of multicolored mirages that dance from wall to wall, now on the ceiling, now on the floor. Sometimes we must shatter the prism in order to stop this twisted projection from happening."

"But he wasn't just an inanimate prism, he was your friend, wasn't he?"

"Yes, I have known Abdallah since before we came to Afghanistan. He was a great soldier and a true patriot. I loved him as one can love a brother, and that is why I killed him so quickly and kindly preserved his face. But Abdallah had bent the message beyond recognition and as a result he was fighting his jihad not our jihad—his patriotic cause, not ours —and there is a critical distinction between the two. It is true the Russians rape the Afghan women and kill the children for sport, but it is the regular and support forces that mostly commit these crimes during their *prochiyoska* or so-called combing operations. The VDV, *vozdushno-desantnye voyska* airborne special forces, and the *razvedchiki* reconnaissance troops are highly trained and disciplined, and they are singu-larly dedicated to killing us *basmachi*, which is what they have called resistance fighters for over fifty years now. The regular forces are poorly educated conscripts and criminals that have received very little military training. They are igno-rant human filth. Sadly, this is nothing new in warfare and not unique to these godless Russians. Your Christian crusaders did the same to us one thousand years ago and your ignorant criminal American GIs did the same to the Germans, Koreans, and Vietnamese. They raped the women and killed the children because that is how the world has always worked, or not worked.[5] In each of those conflicts it was individual ignorant American filth fighting their own personal jihad, instead of the collective jihad waged by fighters of character, who committed those atrocities. I saw that Abdallah's personal jihad had twisted him. It was too attractive, too powerful to change, and because of this I had to stop him before he was allowed to define and defile our jihad with his actions. He was a good friend, and I will miss him dearly, but jihad is the business of Allah. We may be compelled to kill in our jihad, and sometimes that involves taking the lives of innocent people, but we are also compelled to take no pleasure in that killing. Now come, let's go inside and warm up."

I have thought back often to the events of that night and tried to consider them from multiple perspectives. A metaphor I return to involves setting out with a group of travelers on a journey along a high road, call this road your collective jihad or ethos, the true path to your intended destination. The road to hell is paved with good intentions and incremental bad ones as well, and as you travel, opportunities arise to veer off course, to take a path off the high clear ridge road and down into the tangled and dusty wadi. Some seek to divert the group down off the ridge, down into those blasted lands below, claiming, and in fact believing, that down below resides the true path, not along the high road. Their actions endanger the group arriving at its intended destination. Their actions endanger your life and that of the other travelers. What is your moral obligation to yourself? What is your moral obligation to the group?

Now what of those who might seek to take a country off the high road and down into their dark vision of the true national path in the name of patriotism? Consider one hundred people boarding an airliner bound for Alabama and one of them, who calls himself a true patriot, hijacking the jet to Arkansas. There is swift clarity to the analysis of this simple scenario, where the will of the many is forcefully subverted by the few, and the violent resolution of this specific phenomenon is regularly practiced and clearly justified. I think back to college, where Berg saw hippies, liberals and democrats as the few trying to hijack the many down off

the high road, and certainly by 1981 he had a strong mathematical support for this argument, given Ronald Reagan's
four hundred and eighty nine electoral votes. I wonder how
far Berg would go in defense of his ethos in order to save the
nation? Defending a morally superior and broadly embraced
ideal kind of sounds like true patriotism.

But what about a more nuanced scenario wherein one
person wishes to take leave of the group and carve his own
path that, while somewhat parallel, is different? What should
be done with that individual? Ronald Reagan said something
like, the government should protect us from those who
would take us off the high road but should not prevent or
protect those idiots who want to leave of their own accord. I
think he used motorcycles and helmets in the metaphor:
require safe bikes so others are not hurt by faulty vehicles,
but don't require riders to wear helmets, even though riding
without one is stupid. Protect the masses from the few but
allow the few to self-destruct if they so choose.

Although Reagan's argument seems sound and intellectually defensible, history suggests many might not agree. At the
birth of Christianity, Roman Christians killed individual
Arian Christians because the Arians believed in one god
instead of the trinity. They killed Priscillian Christians
because they worshiped at home and outdoors instead of in
dusty converted pagan temples. Both groups diverged from
the narrow doctrine specified by the Emperor's approved
operating manual for Christians and for that they needed to
be corrected. Heck, even in the twentieth century we
witnessed white Evangelical Christians in the American
South killing black Christians, Catholic Christians, and
Mormon Christians because of differences in their Christian
faith paths, naturally with some bigotry sprinkled in as well.[6]
Those same Christians used conspiracy theories to keep individual Catholic Christians from reaching the presidency until

1960, when the Catholic JFK remarkably defeated the Protestant Nixon. Stunningly, Nixon claimed that JFK was elected not despite being Catholic but because he was Catholic and that Nixon himself was the victim of religious bigotry by the electorate whom he claimed was anti-Protestant. Now, in the twenty-first century, Muslims join Jews in bearing the brunt of white Evangelical Christian violence while those same Evangelical Christians complain, just as Nixon did, that they are in fact the real victims of religious discrimination. Objective intellectual and moral arguments seem to fall apart these days when religion is involved, or perhaps to be fair to other religions, they seem to fall apart when Christianity, especially white evangelical Christianity, is involved.

It seems clear that just because you call a path "true" does not make it so. That claim requires legitimacy. Truth must be revealed through examination and analysis, just as a litmus test reveals an acid or a base, and within such a framework right and wrong can be objectively defined. By this, I am not endorsing a simple Manichean conceptual model of black and white. I am merely saying that there can be an objective evaluation of a path or ethos. And if that legitimate path and those upon it are threatened by the few, then doesn't that support a correction, a significant act by which to eliminate that threat? Bentham said, do that which results in the greatest good for the greatest number of people. He didn't say specifically, however, exactly what to do if someone got in your way, but his math seems simple.

I think I was accepting of the conceptual model I heard Osama propose that night because his moral high ground stood in such sharp contrast with Abdallah's low ground. But what about a situation where the topography lacks such clarity and subjectivity is the only altimeter? Who decides then what is high and what is low, what is right and what is wrong, what is patriotism and what is sedition? The analysis of path purity requires purity from those who analyze the path. And if politics becomes even more like religion, then objectivity is thrown completely out the window and history becomes our guide to the madness that will likely ensue.

Although I continue to be somewhat conflicted on this topic, I have arrived at a stasis. Allow stupid people do stupid things as long as they don't hurt anyone else. But, if push comes to shove, sacrificing the life of one individual to save the lives of five is worth considering. I think Berg would agree, at least with the second point. He never was very tolerant of stupidity, so I am not so sure about the first one.

And then it was time to go. Waqas was anxious to get back to Karachi. But I was not. Whether it was the altitude, the hash, or the hand of Allah, I felt closer to the cosmos here and closer to Osama than I had ever felt towards anyone before. Although we were peers in years, his wisdom and vision set him apart, and simply being in his company inspired within me a feeling of heightened spirituality and a deeper sense of self. I felt sure he would survive, especially armed with Stingers now, and his life after this conflict would be one of remarkable significance.

Waqas and I saddled up in the truck compartment that he had been cleaning for several days and I reached my hand out the window and took Osama's hand in mine. "I love you, *sadiqi.*"

Osama paused and looked deep into my eyes and he smiled sadly. "Christopher, it is difficult for me to feel much these days given the violence I must engage in and the suffering I see. But I can tell you this, you have made me feel a kinship I have not felt in a long time and for that I am grateful. *Alhamdulillah.* Listen, I tell you simply that you and I will always be brothers, and this moment will always be ours, and that is a great gift from Allah. Let us never forget this. *Baraka allahufik sadiqi.* May Allah bless you, my friend."

Waqas and I retraced our route, and along the way we spoke carefully about our experiences that week in the mountains. While I expressed surprise by the friendship, I felt I had built with Osama, Waqas was not.

"Christopher, we Muslims believe all of mankind has arisen from Adam and Eve and one person has no superiority over another because of skin color and things like that. We define superiority based upon piety and good actions. Your piety is clear to others, as are your good deeds. This is why Osama opened his heart to you."

We said our goodbyes outside my hotel in Karachi, the evening sky clouded with wood smoke, and the call to prayer echoing through filthy twisting alleys and off the weathered facades of buildings. And then he was gone in a cloud of diesel. Although we never spoke of it, I am fairly confident that simple Waqas was probably quite a bit more complex than he appeared on the surface, and his first stop that night was to see his superior at ISI and only after that his family. I had been in my hotel room for less than two minutes when there was a knock. I opened the door to two Pakistani goons in black suits, yellowed white shirts and black ties who brought me down to an ISI office for a debriefing; thankfully CIA from the embassy was also present. I thought it went well. I stuck to the logistics of the material transfer, the technical details surrounding the QC of the Stingers, and an overall view of the instructions I had provided for their use and the aptitude of the fighters. They wanted to know more about people, but I told them I didn't mingle much with the natives. Both the ISI and CIA seemed satisfied with my report, and after asking a few more questions, they stood up and let me go back home to America.[7]

TEN

DARWIN

My time in Pakistan is hot, filthy, and magical—the first visit and every subsequent one I make there in beyond-space time. Upon returning back to this bench in Zilker Park, I lose the magical and am left with just the filth and heat. It's a bit like people in pandemic Manhattan; divorced from the magic of the city—restaurants, cafes, and theater—what are they left with? Back in college, Laurie regaled us with stories of New Jersey summers and how people there would escape from hot, filthy cities and suburbs to the crowded Jersey Shore, where they would wallow in an ocean filled with used condoms, cigarette butts, dead fish, and thousands of other sweaty people. She said her family wouldn't be caught dead at the Jersey Shore. Instead, they rented a house for a month each summer at Ogunquit in Maine, relaxing on the cool beach and periodically dipping in to refresh themselves in the frigid gin-clear waters. Sometimes I slip back to Laurie's childhood and see both the horror and privilege she experienced. More often, I watch as she progresses through her career. I close my eyes and she begins to appear through a smoky haze as I slip toward her.

Laurie pushed and squeezed her way through the crowd. There was debris on the floor, the air was thick with cigarette smoke, and the final psychedelic bars of the Talking Heads' "Burning Down the House" resonated off the walls. The multi-level, multi-bar Bayou Club made her feel like she was back in college. The club was located on K Street in an old two-story white brick building under the Whitehurst Freeway in Georgetown, and it was one of the hottest venues in the DC area. Hard liquor cascaded through a myriad of pipes from a second-floor reservoir to the standing-room-only crowd of ground floor patrons, who consumed as much as the system could deliver. As Laurie continued her struggle towards the bar, two leering preppies, faces plump with baby fat, approached, and one with a bow tie reached behind as he passed and gave her ass a lecherous squeeze. Laurie swiftly bent her knees, cocking her upper body and hips slightly right then pivoting hard left to deliver a surgical blow with her right fist to the preppy's left kidney, then rebounded without significantly altering her original trajectory. The preppy inhaled sharply then exhaled a terrible sigh, his knees buckling from the pain.

His friend stopped and turned to him. "What's wrong, Tucky? You OK?"

Tucky, upright again with a hand on his friend's shoulder, turned to see who was responsible, but Laurie had already disappeared into the dense crowd. Steel-eyed, she continued her serpentine travel, spotted a gap at the bar, and flagged the bartender, smiled sweetly at him, and ordered three double vodka tonics and a club soda with a slice of lime. It was Sunday, February 2, 1986. The temperature almost hit seventy degrees that day in Washington, and Laurie had leveraged this peculiar weather phenomenon by wriggling into a black leather mini skirt for the evening. She was out with three Senate staffers from prominent petrochemical producing states, and was preparing them for tomorrow's meeting. She was getting them shitfaced and horny. The doubles were doing their part and her dirty dancing was taking care of the rest. John Cougar's "Small Town" started playing on the stereo. Who the fuck dances to this shit? she thought. Laurie looked over at the bartender dispensing vodka into the drinks from the upstairs reservoir, and her mind began to wander down the maddening engineering path it often took when she was out drinking.

Density, gravity, height: rho, g, z. Let's see, vodka, density about one gram per cubic centimeter. The acceleration of gravity is nine point eight meters per second squared, so call it ten. Height is about five meters to the bottom of the upstairs reservoir. That's fifty thousand Newtons per square meter or fifty kilopascals, close to ten pounds per square inch, about one fifth of my shower head...

Mercifully, the bartender returned with the drinks before the wrestling match with the solution to vodka velocity out of the gun began. She wished she didn't have to babysit these children tonight and could have herself a real drink, but business is business, and this was actually kind of fun. Laurie tossed a fifty on the bar, grabbed her drinks and headed back to the boys. They were huddled in a back corner and had been sneaking sniffs of bad cocaine from a bullet vial every time she left them alone. They thought she had not noticed, but Laurie didn't miss anything. She set the drinks down as Night Ranger's Sister Christian started playing. As the first staffer reached for his drink, she grabbed his hand. "Come on Texas, it's time for a slow dance!"

Although the building was four years old, the smell of paint, construction adhesives, and new carpeting was still potent. The Hart building had been completed in 1982 to ease the strain on the United States Senate's existing facilities, and at $137 million it was the most expensive public building in existence. Its nine-story façade was decidedly anti-neoclassical in design, favoring the vertical elongation of windows, yet fabricated of timeless white marble. The building was named for Senator Philip Hart, a Michigan Democrat described in the inscription above its entrance as a man of incorruptible integrity and personal courage, strengthened by inner grace and outer gentleness. Laurie sneered at the inscription, walked briskly through the sun-filled nine-story atrium, and caught an elevator to the fifth floor, where her meeting was scheduled. As she entered the conference room, she saw it was already filled with familiar but worn-out faces. The male staffers were all her age, but they looked much older that morning, with gray skin, sagging jowls and bloodshot eyes. The partying the night before in Georgetown had taken its toll, just as Laurie had planned, and they were now prepared for her show.

"Hi boys! It sure is a beautiful morning in America! Y'all ready to hear about the latest and greatest?"

Billy, the staffer from Texas, called the meeting to order with a short speech framing the importance of the petro-chemical industry—not just for Texas but for America—trying his best to smile at Laurie seated across the table from him, but managing only a grotesque grimace. Laurie smiled back sweetly. This was theater, which was part of winning, and winning was everything, and everything was the promise of power and compensation beyond the wildest dreams of most Americans, which meant being superior to most Americans, which made Laurie happy.

So began Laurie's first formal infiltration of the United States Congress. It was the Ninety-ninth Congress of the United States of America in February 1986, and she was on Capitol Hill lobbying for Upland about a new, cost-effective technique for treating hazardous waste called land farming. For many years, landfills—or leaky holes in the ground—had been the cheapest, and therefore the most popular destination, for hazardous industrial wastes. But landfills were receiving significant bad press these days as those chemicals had been leaking out of the landfills and into people's drinking water, so Laurie was getting out in front of the inevitable end of the landfill party. The Chemical Manufacturers Association, the CMA, whose argument for decades had been that landfilling of hazardous waste was not a problem, were harbingers of this end, and they had recently acknowledged publicly that landfills should be destinations of last resort for American industry. Coming from the CMA, this was the kiss of death. Laurie had many previous off-the-record interactions in anticipation of this event, plowing the field and sowing the seeds so to speak. She was poised to make her first major fortune—if things went as she had planned.

Unlike Berg, Laurie had moved very quickly through the ranks at Upland, assuming leadership roles, managing projects, and producing significant financial results. She had been noticed. As a dedicated warrior for free enterprise, she was also a dependable go-to girl. She was good looking, well-spoken, and knowledgeable about the legal and technical dimensions of toxic waste. She could be put in front of regulators and sweet talk them into deals beyond the reach of a mere male. Congress was a bunch of pussies compared to the EPA regulators. They were much more corrupt and perverted and much easier to manipulate. Their staffers were even sleazier and easier, and that's where Laurie had started her campaign. This morning she wore a low-cut blouse, a slit skirt, and almond-toe pumps, topped off with her trademark librarian frames with non-prescription lenses—she looked ready to get busy.

"Boys, I am here today to talk to you about the future of the treatment of industrial byproducts in America."

Laurie never used the words "hazardous" or "toxic" or "waste". These were materials that had arisen from America's industries, and were proof of the Nation's ability to create.

"The byproducts of American chemical industry are natural organic compounds, and as such can be composted— just as some of your parents do with their eggshells and grass clippings in the backyard."

Many of the staffers nodded their heads while some simply stared down Laurie's blouse. She had them either way.

"Most of the byproducts we are talking about are easily digested by bacteria—or 'bugs' as we call them. In fact, these materials are like pizza and cheeseburgers to these bugs and, given the availability of the appropriate beverages, they simply can't get enough of them."

A low ripple of laughter ran though the room. She knew she had them now. They were laughing through their hangovers.

"Often what limits the ability for these bugs to consume all that pizza is their ability to get oxygen to breathe, that's all. Boys, at Upland we have done extensive testing with industrial byproduct application to soil along with active tilling using conventional plows to get air to those bugs. Our data show that, given a structured approach, 99% of the byproducts of American industry can be converted to carbon dioxide—which by the way is an excellent plant food—and rich organic mulch in which to grow crops. All we, Upland and the American chemical industry, need is your approval to move forward with this remarkable technology, and we can begin a new era of industrial chemical farming here in America."

Of course, it was all bullshit, but to Laurie so were the draconian laws that kept interfering with industry's ability to make money. The data Laurie had alluded to were fudged. Land farming might work with human shit, but given the recalcitrant chemical wastes that Upland and other petrochemical manufacturers generated, land farming was about as useful as a bicycle is to a fish. Those shit-eating bugs would chip their teeth on Uplands chlorinated byproducts, but these liberal arts assholes in Congress didn't know that. Upland's goal was simple—get permission to land farm its byproducts, which they would do in a conveniently remote location. There, they would allow the most volatile toxic chemicals to evaporate during the tilling operations. The Mexican tractor drivers plowing the toxic fields and the low-income folks living down wind of the farm would suck up those volatile chemicals in their lungs. What do you expect if you are an illegal alien or don't get an education, fresh air? Those folks were getting what they had earned. And Upland could deal with the chemicals that could not be consumed by bugs when regulators found out what had accumulated in these fields—maybe fifty years from now, and long after Laurie was retired. Until then, Upland could put the money they had saved on proper treatment and disposal toward making more money. Just like J.R. Upland always said: business, unlike biology, is in fact Darwinian.

ELEVEN

CONNECTIONS

B erg always used to say, if you can't stand the heat, then crank up the AC. It is impossible to keep Berg out of my mind for long, especially under this punishing Texas summer sun that has turned the asphalt path sticky and shiny. It has always been this way. His spirit seems to live in a cerebral cavity somewhere up there, coming out like a charming Dracula or a jitterbugging werewolf at the full moon to shake me out of my doldrums. I slip off my bench into beyond-space-time and he appears, howling at me.

For Berg, forgetting about the constant roar of the generators was easy, but the pneumatic hammer pounding the legs of the oil production platform jacket into the ocean bottom took some getting used to. Offshore oilfield work was noisy and hot if you were outside. It was noisy and cold and smelly if you were inside where the air conditioning was cranked up and recycled to keep the crew quarters and TV rooms like a diesel tainted meat locker. Over the mechanical cacophony on the derrick barge, Berg listened intently to Junior as they sipped their hot chicory-laced coffee in the ice-cold mess.

"Listen Berg, it's all yoojenix, you got it? Y-O-O-J-E-N-I-X."

"No, not really. What the hell is yoojenix Junior?"

"Yoojenix explains the differences between the blacks and the whites, between Christians and Jews. It's evolutionary man, just like the way the flu changes every year. Us white evangelical Christian people been on an evolutionary super-highway; them others took the fucking low road. We is biologically different and evolutionarily superior, and that's a scientific fucking fact, period. Listen, the dude what discovered yoojenix was a friend of Einstein, man. They fucking worked together on it, and that's the truth!"

"Funny, I never learned about it in college."

"That's the deal man, them liberal professors won't never teach 'bout yoojenix because of the im-plo-cashins. Why the fuck would some Jewboy at a college want to explain how he's sub-human and inferior to you? Huh? Tell me? See—yoojenix won't never be taught in them non-Christian colleges 'til all those left-wing Jews get chased out—it's that simple."

"Well Junior, that actually makes sense to me. You know, most of the classes I took were math and science, but in the few liberal arts classes they forced me to take, I had some pretty lefty professors."

"Why the fuck you think they call 'em *Liberal* Arts, Boy, huh?"

"Ah, good one, Junior!"

Later that same day, Berg got a letter from me—one I wrote after getting back home from Pakistan. I had addressed the letter to his company because I didn't know where he lived. Back then, before I began slipping, I never knew he received it because he never answered it. Receiving this letter was auspicious because (a) Berg had never received a letter offshore in all his years of work, (b) Berg had never received a letter from me, onshore or offshore, ever, and (c) although he did not know it at the time, the contents of my letter would help alter his life trajectory. Perhaps this is part of why I return to this specific beyond-space-time so often. Berg did not so much read the letter as he did consume it, barely breathing, and rereading sentences and paragraphs. What he read brought blood to his cheeks, goose bumps to his neck, and chills. It also pissed him off that I was knee-deep in seemingly fighting the Soviets single-handed in Afghanistan. Berg finished the letter, sat back, and stared at the fly strip hanging from the ceiling of the mess room. What was he doing to serve his country? His eyes followed a fly as it slowly circled the sticky yellow strip, its trajectory of concentric circles growing smaller and smaller.

Berg had been shooting a dirty little shallow water sparker job for three weeks in the Ship Shoal block. He met Captain Jack on the crew boat ride home when his hitch was up, dodging squalls across the Gulf then up the Atchafalaya to Morgan City, the Gomorrah of Louisiana. The sea had started picking up, and the sparker boat had left Berg on a nearby derrick barge. When the crew boat arrived, he had climbed on the personnel basket, a large foam donut that you stand on with a netting interior in which all your gear goes, and the crane operator lifted him into the darkening dusk sky and hovered over the crew boat waiting below. The Gulf was running a six-to-eight-foot sea by now, and the crew boat jockeyed back and forth, trying to position the small cleared-off portion of the rear deck under the basket as a landing zone. It wasn't working. Berg hovered over the boat as it drifted back and forth, wallowing from side to side in the troughs, then suddenly as he drifted over the large bin in which the garbage from the barge was stored, the crane operator got a signal from the crew boat below and dropped Berg unceremoniously the last ten feet. He landed in the deep cushion of garbage bags and empty cardboard boxes. He quickly kicked his gear out of the basket and into the garbage, shoved the basket away from his head as the crane retrieved it minus its contents back to the derrick barge above. Berg gathered his gear and climbed out of the bin. What the fuck? He headed up to the bridge to see who had arranged this inelegant landing. Captain Jack was at the helm, and he was fixing to hook it up and bring the boat up to speed. The Captain stood six feet, four inches tall, with hands like well-used baseball mitts. He had pale skin from living in the air-conditioned wheelhouse, spiky blond hair with darker roots that hinted at bleach, and drove his crew boat like he drove his Corvette: with significant expertise and significant speed. They were on the road home.

People who think New Orleans is decadent haven't been to Morgan City. After exchanging a few words about the offload and working things out, Captain Jack and Berg had proceeded to rock out in the air-conditioned bridge to Van Halen at distortion volume as the captain worked the throttles and danced the boat through the swell and closer to the mouth of the Atchafalaya River. The Atchafalaya was flat calm, and once they got in the river, he wound the boat gracefully up the S-shaped meanders and they made record time. Despite the bumpy start, the two of them clicked on the ride home, Berg learning that Captain Jack lived across the Lake from him in Texas over on Clear Lake Shores. They fully bonded later that night as they sprinkled their hard-earned oilfield cash on every perky bare breast in the scores of topless bars down the strip, from the highly structured silicone implants at Mr. Lucky's to the free agents shaking it at the Holiday Inn. By the next day, Captain Jack and Berg were brothers.

Back in Clear Lake they'd go fishing when fate gave them time off together. Sometimes they'd take Berg's Mako down to the Texas City power plant outfall and catch pigmy sea trout and two-headed catfish. The Captain said that once you'd eaten a two-headed catfish, you'd never go back to regular farm-raised—and he was right. The Captain knew his fish, spending most of his time offshore, either fishing or jerking off to Hustler, waiting to pick up someone or something from the thousands of production platforms and drill rigs that peppered the Gulf. The two of them always stocked up well for their fishing expeditions, regardless of the destination: filling one of the two bait wells with ice, a couple dozen cans of coke, and a couple of bottles of rum. The Captain only drank 151 Bacardi. He said the first drink with 151 mixed strong was like doing a hit of crack. There was no talking him out of it and Berg walked the plank with Captain Jack and hit the Bacardi crack pipe as well.

Every once in a while, Captain Jack would disappear on his sailboat during his off time; nobody knew where he went, but when he appeared again, he always had an open cockpit tan and cocaine—good coke, and lots of it. People would try to pry out of him where he had been, but it was no use. For Captain Jack, lying was a sport that he was well practiced in, and he regularly stretched the truth about the most trivial things—like the length of his sailboat or the year of his car. If somebody confronted him regarding an untruth, he would simply shrug it off, saying he was just having some fun and engaging in a little "truthful hyperbole." Tom Brewer, an overweight perpetually rumpled and sweaty attorney from down in the Rio Grande Valley, who was probably in his early forties but looked like he was in his early sixties, claimed behind Captain Jack's back that he knew some details about how the Captain was hooked up with an outfit running coke up from down south. Captain Jack was clear with Berg about his distrust of Brewer. He would often bark about it from between grinding teeth when he was loaded up on his own coke.

"That motherfucker isn't a real fucking attorney. All he does is public defender work and that don't pay shit. He's a CI—confidential informant—mark my fucking words. I highly recommend you keep your distance from him, amigo."

But when it came down to it, nobody in Clear Lake really knew much about anybody. People came and went down there, and it was no coincidence that when the band played Jimmy Buffet's Banana Republic at the Turtle Club everyone sang along loudly when they got to that part about running tons of ganja and running from the IRS. Clear Lake was an end-of-the-road kind of place, and what someone was or did wasn't as important as what they were when they were wasted: entertaining or an asshole. And despite his warnings to Berg, Brewer was the first person the Captain called when he ran out of coke in between episodes and needed a stash. It was complicated. Brewer always seemed to have either awesome coke or none at all, much like the Captain. Both of them were binary, either one or zero. When Brewer was on, he would produce the most remarkable rocks Berg had ever seen, much like Captain Jack's: shiny white with pinkish-yellow hues, sparkling and cleaving like sheets of mica. The first time Berg saw one of Brewer's rocks, he had gasped and commented on its plumage. The "lawyer" was nonchalant.

"Son, the problem is that you have been snorting reconstituted bullshit all your life and you just don't know any better. Some sorry motherfucker with a GED takes good blow like this, hits it with a bunch of bullshit inositol, some manitol, and maybe lidocaine if he's really special, grinds the mess up, pisses on it, compresses the shit out of it, then dries it out for you to snort. Bullshit. That's the final product that you have been consuming: GED, moronic, bullshit. It's time for you to grow up, son."

One night, Berg walked into the Turtle Club as Brewer was walking out. Well, Brewer was not so much walking as rolling like a gigantic tumbleweed in an unsteady wind. He was very fucked up.

"Berg Berg Berg Berg Berg—perfect perfect perfect perfect! Let's go man, let's GO NOW, we have a date with destiny."

"Where are we going?"

"Destiny man, to your destiny, trust me, you won't regret it."

Berg looked in through the window at the usual cast of characters gathered around the bar, nursing their drinks, staring at the TV, and looked back at Brewer with his filthy suit, loosened tie, un-tucked and soiled white shirt, and bloodshot eyes. Then he thought about me, his old friend Christopher, and how I had seemingly stumbled into my destiny in Pakistan, and he found it strangely fortuitous that instead of his ten-speed, he had instead driven his Jeep that night, planning to have only one or two cocktails and then call it an early evening.

"OK, why not? Let's go, you crazy fuck."

The drive to Galveston was convulsive, with Brewer oscillating between states of catatonia and eruptions of saliva-punctuated diatribe, continuing to rail against bad cocaine and preaching the virtues of flake. As they approached the Galveston Causeway on the Gulf Freeway, Brewer became more consistently agitated and began barking directions to Berg, both geographic and behavioral.

"When we get across the causeway, we're gonna bang a right at the Post Office down 53rd Street, when we get there, you're gonna listen and keep your mouth shut unless spoken to—god gave you two ears and only *one* mouth, motherfucker, and that is not a coincidence. These guys are Vietnam vets and you do *not* want to fuck around with them. OK, take a left on Avenue R."

Berg swung the Jeep left.

"No goddamit, I said Avenue R ½, not Avenue R, OK hang a right, then another right. Shit, can't you get anything straight, boy! OK, OK slow down, slow down. There, now cut your engine, shut off your lights, and stop in front of that house."

The house Brewer had indicated looked derelict. It was a 1940s vintage bungalow with rotting wooden siding and sagging gutters. A slight yellow glow emanated from the two small dirty glass panes at the top of the front door. But for that, the place appeared abandoned.

Brewer opened the door and rolled out of the Jeep onto the neutral ground. "Goddamit, did I just fall in dogshit? Dammit Berg, you need to be more careful."

Brewer waddled crookedly up the degraded concrete walkway to the house, Berg following at a safe distance to stay out of his corona of saliva. At the door, Brewer paused, gave a poisonous backward glance towards Berg, then knocked softly, three taps, one tap, two taps, then stood back. The front door eased open enough for a bearded face holding bloodshot eyes to squint out at them.

"What the fuck?"

"Snook, it's me Brewer, let me the fuck in."

The door swung open, and Brewer and Berg slipped inside. The vestibule was almost pitch black, curtains dividing it from the living room. Stepping through the heavy curtains into the bright light of the living room left Berg squinting.

Snook examined him like an insect. "Brewer, who in the fuck is this?"

Snook was tall and hunched over a bit, as if the ceiling

was too low. He had long, greasy brown hair streaked with gray and sported orange balloon surfer pants from which two skinny white ankles protruded. He wore a tie-dyed T-shirt that contained two equally skinny white arms, and a plaid bathrobe hung loosely from his narrow shoulders. He twitched and moved continuously and looked like he had not slept in a few days.

"Don't worry Snook, this is Berg, he's good people, ease up."

The room had a peculiar smell. There was a strong foundation of old books combined with tropical wood, and overtones of mold spores born from a century of hurricanes mingled with the scent of powerful cigars, both combusted and not. The place was filled to the ceiling with old furniture, tapestries, statues, and artifacts. A toilet flushed somewhere in the interior of the house, and soon after a giant of a man rounded the corner into the living room. Snook glanced at the monster, then at Brewer and Berg, then the monster grimaced, drew a Colt 1911 from beneath his tent-like shirt, racked the slide, pointed it at Berg's face and the two of them locked eyes.

"Who fucking sent you here?"

Berg, maintaining eye contact, slowly reached up and took hold of the Colt's barrel. He steadily withdrew the pistol from the monster's paw and, with a swipe of his hand to the side, cleared the stubby stovepiped 45 caliber round that nobody but he had noticed had jammed the pistol. He ejected the magazine, loaded the round, returned the magazine, spun the pistol around, and holding the barrel, he returned the Colt to the giant, grips first.

"Nobody sent me. This crazy fat motherfucker kidnapped me, and I guess I am here to party."

The giant's eyes were wide, his face looking first at Berg then at the pistol, incredulous. Snook regained his composure and quickly stepped into the gap. "Brewer, Berg, this is Lucky. Lucky, these are some compadres from up Clear Lake way. They're cool, as you can see. Lucky is an old high school friend from Wisconsin just down visiting from Arkansas, isn't that right, Lucky?"

Lucky looked the three of them over, stone-faced, eyes squinting; then a wide grin spread slowly across his face. "Yeah, I'm not from Texas, boys, but I got here as fast as I could."

Brewer and Berg both laughed, perhaps a bit too loudly, and Lucky holstered the Colt. Snook looked around at the seating possibilities, then swiped some newspapers off a couple of chairs. "Listen, everybody sit the fuck down, y'all are making me nervous."

They all settled into various modes of recline in an assortment of seating that was high on stains and low on springs. Brewer was still sweating profusely and twitching in his chair. "Hey, I just know y'all are up for getting tweaked, and my friend Berg here is in the market for some quantity, so how about breaking out some product and letting us take it for a spin around the block."

Berg shot a sideways glance at Brewer; this was the first he had heard about being interested in quantity.

"This can be arranged; this can definitely be arranged. Lucky got here a little while ago and we were just about to open a case of whiskey."

Lucky stuck out his jungle boot and shoved a cardboard Old Smuggler Whiskey box across the floor to Snook, who opened it and extracted a football-shaped object wrapped in duct tape. A four-inch switchblade appeared out of Snook's bathrobe pocket and in an instant he clicked it open, cut a neat right-angled U in the football, opened the door he had created, licked his index finger and poked it deep into the hole. His finger emerged covered in white shiny flakes and he quickly thrust it into his mouth, closed his eyes, tilted his head back, and hummed. "Mmmmmmmm…dat's da shit."

Lucky chuckled, reached over and grabbed the kilo of cocaine and the knife. He stabbed the blade into the hole and sniffed the small pile that emerged on its tip in one quick inhale.

That was how it started. Lucky was an ex-Marine who was moving cocaine up from Central America for the CIA to fund the Contras while Congress jerked off and discussed whether aid to these patriots was appropriate. The Sandinistas had successfully sued the United States in the International Court of Justice, prevailing in their contention that the US had supported insidious acts, including psychological operations to prepare fighters to kill civilians in support of their cause. In 1985, Congress decided that, given their continued murder of women and children, aiding the anti-communist rebels was in poor taste and they severed the lifeline supplying the Contra Freedom Fighters with the third Boland Amendment, which effectively said:

No funds available to the Central Intelligence Agency, the Department of Defense, or any other agency or entity of the United States involved in intelligence activities may be spent in supporting directly or indirectly military or para-military operations in Nicaragua by any nation, organization, group, movement, or individual.

The CIA said fuck Congress, fuck Boland, and simply took things into their own hands. Just as they had funded covert operations in Southeast Asia during the conflict in Vietnam by running heroin in Air America aircraft, they now went into the business of moving coke to support their friends in Central America. It was no coincidence that America was flooded with heroin in the 1960s and 1970s until the Vietnam War ended and the heroin supply dried up as well.[1] Now coke was appearing on American streets, high purity coke, and lots of it. People called him Lucky because his real name meant rabbit's foot in some foreign language.

"Listen man, this is patriotic coke. White folks know how to handle their coke, but they are only a small market. Those spooks in the ghetto are genetically programmed not to handle it, which makes them really great customers. And it's not even them who are really paying the bills for this shit anyways, after all most of the spooks that buy this shit are on welfare. It's the fucking Congress who gives the spooks the money—the spooks give us the money Congress gave 'em—and we turn that money into guns for the Contras. Congress should be buying the goddamn guns in the first place, but they are a bunch of paralytic pussies that couldn't make a decision if it promised them a blowjob in exchange. So it's actually pretty fucking poetic that the spooks get fucked up, we get our money, the boys in the jungle get their guns, and Congress gets stuck with the bill at the end of the evening."

Lucky was working with an operation transshipping coke through an Arkansas airfield. The word was the operation had the secret approval of the hip young democrat Governor. This whiskey box contained just a few keys that had fallen off the back of the airplane, a little something to help fund Lucky's retirement. The mother load of dope was already heading to inner cities across America to get converted into cash, and then guns, for the quick trip back down south.

The more coke Berg did, the more fucked up he got—which is what is supposed to happen—and the more impressed he became with the quality of the product, and of the provenance. This was coke from the source. This was the real deal—agency snoot. This blow was saving the lives of real patriots fighting the soviets in the jungles of Nicaragua. And then it happened, like a modern-day Ezekiel experiencing the burning wheel in a wheel or Tesla seeing the sky above him filled with tongues of living flame and AC current circuit diagrams: Berg, in that moment of spectacular drug-induced clarity, saw his once-in-a-lifetime vision. He too would do something meaningful, like I was doing with the mujahideen, something that would help America kick those fucking Commies' asses, something that could make him shitloads of money. He needed to sell himself to these guys. He needed to go to work with Lucky and make his vision a reality.

TWELVE

PANAMA

H eart surgery has been a double-edged sword for me. On the one hand, I have been reduced to a tottering old man, with just enough stamina to stagger from my condominium to the park each day, where I collapse on this bench and am pummeled by the relentless heat. That sucks. On the other hand, I am lucky to be alive and able to visit now with those close to me: my human Aspen tree relatives, in beyond-space-time. These visits have opened my eyes to layers of life I had not heretofore been aware of and, in some cases, given me a greater appreciation of the effect my presence on this earth has had on others. It also serves to connect me to the contemporaneously unshared lives of those close to me from whom I had drifted. I feel this especially with Berg, who had effectively disappeared from my space-time after college. It is magical to be on the bridge of a crew boat listening to him howling along to Van Halen's "Panama" with all his might. I sometimes wonder if this was a premonition for Berg of things yet to come in his space-time.

1989 was bittersweet. The year began with two Navy F-

14 Tomcats knocking down two Libyan MIG-23s over the Gulf of Sidra. Two weeks later, Patrick Edward Purdy, a mildly retarded white supremacist, killed five elementary school children and wounded thirty-two others with a Chinese AK-47, a record for non-university school massacres. Two days after that shooting, we watched as President Reagan left office after eight years that had seen America achieve world domination. Bush, who many hoped would carry on Reagan's legacy, spoke at his inauguration about the promise of freshening democratic winds of change across the world, and of the pathogenic scourge of cocaine that had arrived on our shores.

In February, the last Soviet tanks rolled out of Afghanistan, marking the end of the victorious struggle of god-fearing Arabs and their American brothers over the godless communists. President Bush signed a treaty with Canada to mitigate acid rain, an atmospheric phenomenon that some said was the greatest hoax to be perpetrated against the American people, and a socialist plot designed to destroy American industry.

In March, a massive geomagnetic cosmic storm knocked out the entire Hydro-Québec power grid, darkening large areas of New England. President Bush signed a bill banning the import of foreign assault weapons in order to keep them out of the hands of drug dealers—and perhaps mildly retarded white supremacists as well.

In April, the Bush government took over the Lincoln Savings and Loan Association, which had collapsed. The government, which means the American taxpayer, would eventually be on the hook for $200 million as a result of this take-over. Those on the left said Lincoln's collapse was the result of Reagan's deregulation and that only re-regulation could fix it. Chinese patriots begin demonstrations for democracy in Tiananmen Square. One protester faced down a tank holding nothing but shopping bags. The communist Chinese government would kill ten thousand of these protesters before it's all over.

In May, the Russians broke ground for their first McDonalds, and began issuing Visa credit cards. The Hungarians took down their razor wire Iron Curtain fences. President Bush sent two thousand American soldiers to Panama to arrest our former friend Manuel Noriega for allegedly running drugs. In June, the Ayatollah Khomeini retired from life and in July, President Botha of South Africa agreed to meet with the former communist terrorist Nelson Mandela, and Nintendo made its debut.

In August, the presidents of five Central American nations informed the United States that the patriotic Contras who had been selflessly sacrificing in their struggle against the Communist Sandinistas in Nicaragua should now stop fighting and get real jobs. The Cartels in Colombia declared war against the government, and coincidentally America watched President Bush hold up a bag with several ounces of crack cocaine his guys had scored across the street from the White House, saying that we need to do something about drugs in America. Doc McGhee, a music promoter, got the Scorpions, Skid Row, Mötley Crüe, Ozzy Osbourne, and a bunch of other bands together through his Make a Difference Foundation to perform at the Moscow Music Peace Festival to promote international cooperation in fighting the drug war in Russia. Klaus Meine of the Scorpions would go on to write about his experience in Moscow in the Cold War ballad "Winds of Change", although some argued that in actuality the CIA were the authors, and the Scorpions merely the delivery boys.

In September, East Germans began flooding into Hungary and beyond. American financial support of our friend Pol Pot finally paid off, and Vietnam withdrew from

Cambodia. In October Nathan's opened a hot dog stand in Moscow, and an earthquake shut down the World Series in California.

In November, the house of communist cards collapsed, along with its most hideous manifestation, the Berlin Wall. On Thursday December 7th, Steven Michael Kalish testified in a Lafayette, Louisiana courtroom that he had given the Panamanian Manuel Noriega millions of dollars to facilitate his cocaine smuggling and money laundering operations in Panama and that Doc McGhee, recently returned from his anti-drug concert in Moscow, was his link to the Colombian drug supplier. On Christmas day, Romanian dictator Ceausescu and his wife were executed, and by the last day of 1989, the Soviet Empire was pretty much finished. America had won.

In 1990, the covert investments the US had made into Central America paid off and Nicaragua, a country the size of Alabama, became a constitutional democracy with a female president, President Violeta Barrios de Chamorro of the UNO party, the amalgam of the Nicaraguan Contras, at the helm. The economic and social reforms of the Sandinistas seemed to be a thing of the past; however, to the consternation of the UNO party, President Chamorro chose to work with the Sandinistas to gradually transition the police and armed forces to a new world order. She had chosen to give credence to claims of torture, terrorism, and the assassination of civilians by the Contras.

World structures had been slowly changing through the 1980s while Berg was offshore, and many of those structures finally collapsed at the end of the decade. But this inconvenient peace didn't put his newfound enterprise with Lucky and the boys out of business. He had missed much of the first wave, running tons of dope, making tons of money, and supporting the freedom fighters in the Nicaraguan jungles.

The second wave simply eliminated the last step where the drug profits were recycled into weapons for the Contras. The first steps of the process were left more than intact: run the dope and make even more money.

In the 1980s, while the murderous Pablo Escobar was flying small loads from the Bahamas into Miami-Opa Locka airport using Cessna 210s, the CIA was elegantly moving significant freight into major metropolitan airports.[1] A friendly cartel would move the coke from Colombia to Costa Rica. The product was packaged in kilogram quantities, wrapped in plastic, and tied with twine, wrapped again in several pages of Bogota's *El Tiempo* newspaper, then wrapped tightly again in duct tape so that the kilograms resembled gray footballs. The CIA loaded their giant Boeing 707s in Costa Rica with thousands of footballs and flew them straight into the US. Once landed, a long-established network efficiently moved the coke throughout the homeland. Some simply loaded rental cars right at the airport with two 50 kilo duffel bags in the trunk, parked them in several garages, then gave a car key to the distributor, along with the parking space number and a bill for $1 million. The distributor would pick up the product and leave the car key and cash behind in the trunk of the locked vehicle. The product would be quickly dispersed without anybody even seeing anybody else. Those domestic network distributors were usually movers who had gotten caught and given a choice: move tons of product and make tons of cash, or do tons of time. For most, the positive and negative motivations were both significant and the choice clear. When the money came in, it was used at first to fund black ops and later to purchase the bread-and-butter weapons and munitions that the Contras needed and Congress had made illegal through the Boland Amendment.[2]

In 1990, when hostilities ended in Nicaragua and the

Contras no longer needed weapons, the CIA no longer needed the covert flights. However, they kept going for a while, with planes returning south empty now instead of laden with guns. The profits were shared amongst the participants instead of being diverted to the gun merchants. It didn't take long to make so many millions in cash that they had to weigh the bundles in duffel bags instead of counting it. But they didn't have long to play this game, because as they all knew, "pigs get fat and hogs eventually get slaughtered," So after a few months of major movements, they burned the 707s in Costa Rica, kept the cartel and the distributors and moved to water deliveries from Panama in coordination with friendly US Customs agents in Florida. Customs would regularly schedule controlled deliveries of cocaine into the US in order to set up and gain physical evidence on a South American supplier or a domestic buyer.[3] Berg's group planned to simply add a hidden layer beneath the controlled load, and after Customs took their stash to do whatever with, the bottom layer would be quietly collected and fed to the usual distributors and the game continued. They called it a semi-controlled delivery.

Given his gift for persuasion, Berg had talked his way into the cabal and out of his offshore job during that very long coke fueled night and day and night in Galveston. Lucky and the guys were happy to have someone willing, capable, and dumb enough to take significant risks. And the risks were real. Several months after the Galveston meeting, Lucky's airplane was shot down over Nicaragua carrying a load of weapons to the Contras, and although he survived, he could never come back to the group.

Berg was relegated to purely domestic operations for several years, where he did well, capitalizing on his technical academic training in mathematics and management, especially with respect to delivery and logistics. In his senior year at UNH, he recalled gazing listlessly out the windows of Kingsbury Hall at the fall New Hampshire colors while the Professor droned on about project planning and project management and the iron triangle, blah blah blah blah. Toward the end of class, he stopped talking, put down the chalk, rubbed his dusty white hands on his pant legs then turned and spoke directly to the class—which in itself was memorable—about the next course module, Integrated Inventory Management, or I2M. I2M was a structured approach to managing the flow of stocks, especially with respect to the streamlining and optimization of supply chains to better satisfy customers and gain a competitive edge on the marketplace. Berg could not recall hearing about customers or marketplace or business in his four years of engineering education, and this recognition of a world outside academia was refreshing enough for him to stop looking out the window. There was also growing interest in research on the topic in 1979 and one of Berg's classmates in civil engineering later went on to do his graduate thesis on the topic that is now called Supply Chain Management. Berg hadn't directly applied much of his university education in the oilfields, and thought it was cool that this pragmatic topic that had caught his interest would now be so useful to him in managing the movement of drugs, guns, and money.

The conflict and air transport of weapons quickly wound down in 1989, and Berg stepped up, leveraging his gift for persuasion and offshore experience, and got himself assigned as the group's representative on their first semi-controlled offshore delivery experiment. They would move a test load of one hundred keys from Panama to Florida. The United States had recently cleaned house in Panama, invading the country and arresting the dictator, Manuel Noriega. Noriega had an acne-scarred face that earned him the name Pineapple, active beady eyes, and a propensity to take bold corrupt acts in broad daylight. He had started as a paid CIA collaborator in the 1950s and then worked his way up to become the leader of the hemisphere's first narcokleptocracy. The American government was fine with this while he kept quiet, behaved reasonably, and helped their covert operations in Central America. But Noriega became a bit too flamboyant by Washington standards, hanging out with guys like Fidel Castro and Muammar Gaddafi and kicking out Barletta—Panama's democratically elected president—and as a result, he had to go.

There were already thirteen thousand American troops in Panama before the American invasion began, including the 193rd Infantry Brigade, a battalion from the 7th Infantry Division, a mechanized battalion from the 5th Infantry Division, two companies of Marines and a basket full of military police, Air Force, and Navy personnel. The initial invasion force of seven thousand airlifted troops arrived in the early morning hours of December 20th 1989, and was comprised of a brigade of all-stars from the 82nd Airborne, the 75th Infantry Rangers and a mélange of five or six battalions filled with other tactically useful assets like Green Berets, SEALs and psychological operations specialists. It is said that Noriega's drunken sex that night with a prostitute at a recreation center right next to Tocumen airfield was interrupted when an American gunship began priming the drop zone with 105 mm cannon fire as Airborne Rangers drifted down out of the early morning sky.

One priority target of the invasion was Noriega's house at Fort Amador and what was inside: if not Noriega himself, then evidence of his involvement in the drug business. Noriega wasn't there. After the two-story house was secured, First Lieutenant Donnie Warner—a West Point graduate from the Midwest—entered with Private First Class Louis D'Angelo from Brooklyn, New York at his side. As they walked through the modestly appointed home, instead of finding file cabinets and hard drives filled with hard and electronic records, they found a very different type of strategic evidence. On the living room table was a cow's tongue with a nail driven through it. In the bedroom, three mummified iguanas were wrapped in a banana leaf. Elsewhere in the house they found dozens of burned prayer candles fixed to surfaces in pools of melted wax, feathers, rotten chicken eggs with peculiar writing on them and photographs of people ranging from Ronald Reagan to Adolf Hitler. This was Noriega's Santería laboratory.

D'Angelo quickly crossed himself, pulled a large gold crucifix embossed with a bas-relief Jesus held around his neck by a heavy gold chain from beneath his service uniform, and kissed it to ward off the effects of this dark primitive mélange. "Jeez Lieutenant, how can people still believe in all these freaky old religious rituals?"

Warner looked at D'Angelo clutching his crucifix, raised his eyebrows wearily, nodded, then looked away and continued his sweep through the house.

According to Colin Powell, the Chairman of the Joint Chiefs of Staff at the time, the invasion was named Operation Just Cause so that anybody who had a problem with it would have to say the words "Just Cause" within their criticism, like the United Nations General Assembly which passed a resolution stating the operation was a flagrant violation of international law. The invasion added to the poverty and homelessness of the Noriega years, with tens of thousands of people internally displaced as a result of the urban warfare that destroyed their homes. It also left things in an untidy state, which was good for the group. You don't eliminate a narcokleptocracy easily, and you certainly don't do it by destroying civilian homes and arresting one man. The narco-machinery was still in place, and despite the bump in the road, the show pretty much just went on.[4]

In late November of 1991, after hurricane season ended, Berg was given a one-way ticket from Houston to Colón, Panama, with the flight scheduled to arrive in the late afternoon. Colón was still an unsettled mess almost two years after the invasion, and he was instructed to meet the delivery captain at the bar in the American Trade Hotel at seven that evening. Berg strolled into the hotel wearing a linen short-sleeved shirt with his sea bag slung over his left shoulder, matching linen slacks, and Sperry boat shoes with no socks. There were a dozen people seated at the bar but only one wearing dark blue yachting cargo shorts, Sperry boat shoes with no socks, a white polo shirt, and a red Mount Gay Rum Antigua Race Week ball cap with Oakley sunglasses fixed around the brim. He had his back to Berg and an empty drink in front of him. Berg sat down two seats away and slowly turned to make eye contact.

His neighbor did the same. "Jesus fucking Christ, you, Berg, you? Please don't tell me you're the fucking hall monitor for those shitbirds on this fiasco?"

The captain was no other than his old friend from Texas. For many years, Captain Jack had been making controlled deliveries for Customs in *Dreamweaver*, his beefy Morgan 51-foot Out Island Ketch, filled down below with spare parts of anything that might go bad offshore, and with plenty of room for additional cargo. That's where the periodic cocaine had come from, a little spillover from the delivery. Captain Jack had painted a new name on the transom for this trip, *Blowback*, but other than that it was the same boat Berg had partied on in Texas. It's a small world sometimes, especially in the drug business. Captain Jack's hair was now a dark shade of sienna brown, and he had a mustache.

"Let me get us drinks, Captain. 151 and Coke?"

"Fuck this place, Berg. Let's get down the road to a more appropriate venue where we have ten times the buying power." Captain Jack threw $5 on the bar.

"Where's that?"

"Only my very favorite place in Colón. Trust me, you'll love it. It's a shit-ton classier than anyplace we partied at in Morgan City. And we can walk there. Come on."

They headed out of the hotel, reminiscing about the madness they had gotten into in Texas and chuckling about fate throwing them together now. The captain navigated effortlessly through the filthy narrow streets, while Berg with his eyes to the ground leapt from island to island of moist pavement surrounded by what seemed a sea of feces, offal and garbage, trying desperately to keep his boat shoes from getting soiled. "Jeez, these streets are a real mess, were they like this before the invasion?"

"Berg, Colón is a Central American shithole. There's nothing an invasion can do to fuck it up any more than it already was."

"And what is that nasty sour fucking smell?"

Captain Jack paused and kicked at several of the thousands of feral cats that filled the city like slinking furry slime, lifted the lid of a trash can and tilted it toward Berg. "Fucking cats! Is this what you smell?"

Berg gagged. "Yes, ughhhh, what the fuck is that shit in there?"

"Rotten chicken feathers, my friend, that's what you've been smelling. These Panamanians love their chickens fresh, and they kill and pluck 'em at home, even here in the city."

"What's up with these cats too?"

"Yeah, no shit. I was in Cuba just the other day. Come to think of it, Colón looks a little like Havana, and you know what?"

"What? Wait, you were in Cuba? What the hell were you doing there?"

"Never mind why I was there; the important thing is I didn't see a single fucking cat in Havana. So, I ask the dude I'm with, I say, hey amigo, where did all your cats go to? And he looks at me real seriously and says, 'we have eaten them all.'"

"They ate them?"

"Yeah, life's been pretty fucked up since the Soviet Union imploded. The Cubans lost their welfare money, so they have to work now. The cats are part of the price they have to pay for emancipation. So anyways, I ask this dude, so how come if there are no cats because you ate them, there are still so many goddamn dogs running around? Right? I mean there's lots more meat on a dog than on a cat. I would have thought the dogs would have been the first to go, then the cats. Well, this dude puffs out his chest, looks at me like I just called his sister a whore and says, 'amigo, we are Cubans, we would never eat our dogs!' Hey, all this talk of eating has got me hungry. Good thing that Chicas Locas, which has the finest Latin ass in town, also has outstanding fried chicken. We're almost there."

The streets got narrower, and the smell grew worse, until they finally rounded a corner to the buzzing neon violet marquis for Chicas Locas, where they went inside. The bar was already loud and busy, and required a subtle elbow here and there to navigate through the maze of ripening Panamanian men who surrounded the stage, clutching large bottles of Balboa beer and shouting periodically and incoherently at the ceiling while watching a hard-bodied indigenous girl with tiny breasts slither up and down the brass pole. The captain moved quickly through the crowd and found a relatively quiet table in the back corner of the bar where they could watch the show and talk.

They sat down, and the Captain quickly and efficiently slid his hand up the skirt of a passing waitress, tweaking an unseen part of her anatomy. "Yo por favor, amiga, dos 151 and Coca Colas for me and for my amigo."

"OK, dos 151 and cola."

"No no no no no. Dos for mío and dos for himo, comprende?"

"Aha, sí, sí sí, cuatro Jack151 y cola en total."

"That's right, now you've got it, sweetie!"

Despite his many trips down south, the captain had not mastered any real Spanish, not even enough to clearly order his favorite beverage. When the drinks arrived, they each slammed one, coughed, then settled back to sip the second in a more civilized fashion.

"So Cappy, you gotta tell me, how did you get started in this business? You must have gotten busted and had to make a deal, huh?"

"No way man, I'm a patriot. President Bush personally gave me the ensign I'm flying on my boat right now. I am a patriotic warrior in the war on drugs and I always have been. And Bush, shit, he's a smuggler at heart, man. His family ran booze into Walkers Point up in Maine during prohibition and the motherfucker has one of the early cigarette boats built by his good friend David Aronow, may he rest in peace. I heard Bush's favorite thing to do is to hook that fucker up and lose the Secret Service in the mudflats between Cape Porpoise and Stage Harbor while he listens to Jan Hammer on a loop in the cassette deck at distortion volume. Bush is cool, Berg, very cool. He's total Miami Vice."

"That shit about Bush is pretty crazy. But how do you figure that patriotic stuff? The drugs come in and then get distributed. I know that people get busted as a result, but the blow is still out there on the streets of America. Not that I'm complaining or anything."

"That's not my end of the deal, amigo. Somebody else has got all that figured out. I'm just the delivery boy. I move the shit where they tell me."

"And the stuff you skim off the top that we've been doing in Texas? War on drugs? We've been partying in Clear Lake with drug war drugs!"

"Berg, you ask too many fucking questions. Listen, bottom line, we had some great times in Texas and Louisiana, but this run's gonna be different—you understand that, don't you?"

"You bet, Cappy, this is your world, your boat and your show. I am along for the ride to help out as best as I can."

"I like that, I like the way you put that just now—along for the ride—help out. All right, enough shop talk, let's check out the local pussy, shall we? Holy shit, now that's some real talent over there!"

Berg and Captain Jack had a long night together, got drunk on rum, bought a large bag of shitty coke and did it on the back of the toilet at Chicas Locas, had table dances and a hand job each, and in their own way worked out most of the potential rough spots they thought might arise working together. They staggered onto *Blowback* as the sun came up, waking the first mate Couvillon in the process.

"Couvillon, this is Berg, he is our human cargo, and he and I go way back. He understands that he is to stay out of our fucking way unless we say otherwise. He gets it. OK?"

"OK, Cap. Push off at sunset?"

"Sounds like a plan. Night night boys."

The Captain crawled back into his stateroom, drew the curtains, and despite the residual coke in his bloodstream, passed out. They pushed off that night and sailed east, around the corner about one hundred miles to the San Blas Islands, arriving and anchoring at dusk the next day. They called it an early night, to complete the recovery from the episode in Colón. The Captain woke up the next morning and was extremely pissed off. "Goddamn it, those little fuckers stole our fucking sugar!"

The San Blas Indian kids were brown skinned with twinkling Asian eyes. They wore nothing but bathing suits for clothes and lived their lives on and in the sea. Every time Captain Jack would pull in, the kids would wait until night then paddle their cayucos out to the boat, reach in the open portholes and grab whatever was conveniently within their reach. Last night it had been sugar from the galley.

"That's it. I have had it with these little san blastards."

Captain Jack went back and began rummaging through the head. Berg looked on, keeping a safe distance. The Captain was pleasant enough with a rum and coke in his hand and a half naked girl swinging around on a brass pole, but his mood had been foul since they had left Colón. He made it clear at regular intervals that he was the captain and there were rules that were going to be followed. Rule number one was nobody used his real name. Captain Jack was Ahab and Berg understood why. The first mate Couvillon was Little Bear, also for obvious reasons. Captain Jack gave Berg his name: Sea Squirt, or just Squirt for short. The Captain said it's because Sea Squirts are all mouth and asshole and grow up to be hermaphrodites like Jamie Lee Curtis. He was still a little pissed about this deal being linked in a way to Brewer, and also just wanted to be extra sure Berg understood who was boss. Captain Jack came back in the galley with a satisfied smile and set a large bottle on the sill. "That will fix them."

"What's that?"

"This, my little Sea Squirt, is first fucking rate American Ex Lax chewing gum that, once they have stolen it and commenced to chewing as much as their little san blastard mouths can handle, will keep those kids shitting in the bushes until long after we have bugged out of here."

The time to pick up the load was approaching. The new moon offered an entire night of darkness, which sometimes was necessary if something got messed up. As twilight faded to dark, they switched on the masthead light and fastened large rubber fenders to the port side of the boat. Almost instantly a voice crackled calmly over the radio. "Sky to Night, Sky to Night, over."

"Night to Sky. Come on in."

The 40-foot wooden fishing boat slowly took form as it approached out of the darkness and came along side. Not a word was spoken between the two captains and the delivery crew got to work under the bright deck lights heaving duffel bags up and across to the crew on *Blowback*. Each duffel bag had a spray-painted dot, either red or green. The red bags were loaded first deep within the bowels of the boat. The green bags were loaded last and stacked under berths and in the main salon. They loaded 500 green dot kilos for Customs and 100 red dot kilos for the organization that night. The delivery boat departed without a wave and Ahab, Little Bear and the Squirt went down below. The Captain unzipped a duffel bag pulled out a gray football with a green dot and set it on the table in the main salon. "Boys, they say never get high on your own supply. I say that's a bunch of bullshit. Never say never!"

The Captain cut a 3-sided door in the football, drove his rigging knife into the aperture lifting out an eighth of an ounce in one scoop, dumped it on a Sail magazine, crushed the shiny, flaky rocks with the butt end of the knife handle and looked around. Berg had seen this before.

"Goddamn it, Little Bear, go get us a fucking straw, would you?"

Little Bear did as he was told and they snorted the pile,

weighed anchor, and began grinding their teeth and heading north. The trip home was magical. They played with dolphins and caught kingfish by day, and watched shooting stars at night. Theoretically they were supposed to run roughly on six-hour shifts, Squirt and Little Bear on for six, then Captain Ahab on for six. But the Captain preferred sailing alone, and after the sun had set. In practice, they rarely saw him during the day, and they stayed out of his way at night, unaware of his presence except for when they heard him singing along in his loud monotone to whatever cassette was playing through the cockpit speakers, be it The Allman Brothers or Seals and Crofts, two of his favorites. The Captain had a significant soft side to him that he revealed through this singing, only after dark and in private, however much he managed to mangle the lyrics.

Breakfasts, they seem to come and go, oh yeah
There's tipsy flies upon my toast
Blowing cookies, making chum
Be home tomorrow, we'll have some fun
Back on home he's gonna run
To sweet Patricia

The trip was uneventful, which it should have been, given the Coast Guard had been warned off of them by Customs. They were also updated on the position and vectors of other major traffic, so watches were more about fixing food and drinks and changing the music than responding to a changing environment. After that first blow out night when they left the San Blas Islands, the Captain had banned coke for the rest of the trip. Instead, he ran all night long on a potent mixture of Swiss Miss and instant coffee that he called Swiss Bitch. They ate well, sailed more than they motored, and the days passed in a pleasant rhythm, unpunctuated by mechanical failure or foul weather.

The crew of *Blowback* arrived in Tampa Bay before dawn, tied up in a prearranged slip at the Vinoy Hotel Marina, closed the hatches, cranked up the air conditioning and crashed. They were woken an hour later by the barrel of an AR15 attached to a bushy bearded head hollering down from the companionway. "All right motherfuckers, freeze! Keep your hands where I can see them!"

Couvillon and Berg were paralyzed and played dead. Captain Jack appeared from his rear stateroom, scratching his balls. "Fuck you Pedro, I just got to sleep, goddammit. Get down here and make yourself useful, you little prick. I need me some Swiss Bitch."

Pedro, the group's friendly Customs guy, laughed as he slung the rifle over his left shoulder and backed down the companionway into the main salon. The Captain and Pedro arranged for the controlled unload to happen that day and then for our special cargo to go out later that night. It all went so smoothly that when Berg reported back to the others on the delivery, not only were they confident in the business model, they were all a bit jealous of his experience.

When Berg went south, everybody seemed to lose track of him. I hadn't actually heard directly from him over the years—as you know, he never answered my letters—but he had kept in touch with Laurie, and she and I spoke on the phone from time to time. When his communications with her simply stopped, we wondered if maybe he had been killed in a dope deal gone bad. Or maybe he had just gotten a job selling insurance and was ashamed to admit it. Truth was, we were all getting older and had already grown significantly apart, and Berg's silence was further dampened by the background noise of the changing world.

The Texas air has taken on a crystalline texture today, and I am able to push it around with my hand and watch the resulting fluid lines flow like smoke in a wind tunnel. The flow lines drift off the tips of my fingers like five biplanes in formation at an airshow, the trails beginning in such remarkable alignment, descending rapidly with distance into a delightful chaos of colors that remind me of fall in New England. The bench pushes uncomfortably into my tailbone, and I shift my bulk, ease the pressure, close my eyes, and relax once again.

It is a stiflingly hot late spring in 2007, and I breathe easier as I enter the dimly lit crisply air-conditioned Papasitos Mexican restaurant on I-35 in Austin. I am met by the familiar oily smell of warm paper-thin corn tortillas and the sounds of mariachi and sizzling fajitas, all of which have become intoxicants for me since moving to Texas. I come here often, perhaps too often, and the restaurant has become a comfortable extension of my home. But tonight is different: tonight I am here for a date, and I am uncomfortable. Our office manager Mary arranged the date, despite my protestations, with a friend from her condominium complex named Darla. Mary said I needed to get a life, and Darla was supposedly a real "hoot," whatever that means, so I agreed, and now here I am. I arrived early because that is my normal practice, and tonight I needed a bit more time to think and prepare. I take a seat at the bar, order a sweet tea, and think about topics of conversation I might employ. What do you talk to a woman about? Current events? History? It's Texas, so maybe guns? Everyone travels, so that would probably work. My job keeps me on the road a lot, so I don't really travel much for pleasure. When I get time off I normally either don't take it or just stay home and shoot and read. An exception was a trip I took a couple of years earlier, up north to Virginia in February 2005, of which I still have vivid memories. Yes, that could be a good conversation starter.

The fifty-degree temperature at eleven in the morning in Lexington City reminded me of New England in the fall, and I walked the Washington and Lee University footpaths with familiarity, despite it being my first visit—that familiarity born from the basic physical commonality of many old post-secondary schools and the ever-present cluster of my fellow conference attendees. I had taken a long weekend away from Texas to attend a conference at the Virginia Military Institute on "Leadership with Integrity" that included workshops, parades, and receptions. What had caught my eye about the conference was the keynote speaker, former NATO Ambassador David Abshire, who I had heard about as a kid, as he was my father's platoon leader in Korea for whom he had expressed great admiration and respect. My real interest, though, was in Abshire's role in the Reagan White House after the Iran Contra affair, when a cabal of Reagan's senior administration sold missiles to an embargoed Iran as a secret payment to help free American hostages. Once the hostages were freed, the proceeds from the continued missile sales to the Iranians were used to supply weapons to the Contras in Nicaragua, which was banned by the Boland Amendment.[1] I thought about how similar—but at the same time very different—this black operation was from mine that had happened concurrently in Pakistan. I wondered, how does anyone clean up a mess like that without acquiring a stink?

I walked the brick path across the grassy expanse that is the approach to the ivy-covered brick façade of the Lee Chapel, stepped through the simple white doors, and quickly found a third-row seat beneath the substantial dark wood lectern and gazed up at the low arched white ceiling as others got settled. A hush descended upon the room, and I looked up to see Abshire take the stage from the left and approach the lectern. He was tall, with a shiny pate and graying brown hair at the sides, wearing wire rimmed glasses that framed smiling eyes. Abshire conjured my childhood memories of Art Linkletter, gazing front to back and side to side, seeking to make eye contact with every person in attendance—even for a millisecond. He arranged his notes on the lectern, looked down, and took a quick sip from a glass of water, then raised his eyes and began to speak.[2]

"Many historians would argue that FDR and Churchill were the two greatest men of the twentieth century. Together they saved Europe and the world from Hitler's tyranny and Japan's imperialism. Why then, would these two giants choose George C. Marshall as the greatest man they ever knew? After all, Roosevelt was a charismatic speaker and political personality who took America through the Great Depression and the Second World War. Churchill was an extraordinary writer, classical orator, and accomplished historian. He combined these abilities to mobilize a defeatist nation during World War II. Why then, with all their talents, did each not choose the other, but rather Marshall, as the greatest?"

Abshire had swiftly captured my attention on a topic I had heretofore not given a nanosecond of consideration. I only knew Marshall vaguely in the post World War II context as a preface to the word "Plan." After a pause, allowing the question to settle in, he continued.

"As I researched this perplexing issue for my speech and essay, I found the answer to be stunning. It cuts to the heart of what is the most sacred part of truly great character-based leadership. It makes us think that maybe we live in an age of diminished expectations. Under close examination, the most stunning characteristic about Marshall is that he was not a leader of blind ambition who sought power and self-aggrandizement but, to the contrary, he was an unparalleled servant-leader. When he was willing to sacrifice himself and his career in speaking out to Pershing and to Roosevelt, Marshall moved beyond servant leadership and practiced sacrificial leadership. Although these virtues of character can be traced back to a time even before Plato, they are conspicuously uncommon in public life today. As I study and work with the Presidency, I know how easily a President becomes isolated and often intentionally cut off from dissenting views. If only a member of Nixon or Clinton's staff had spoken up and said early on, 'Get it all out,' these Presidencies may have come through untainted. When President Reagan called me back from NATO on December 26, 1986 to take charge of the Iran-Contra investigation, I had an easier job than most. When Reagan first phoned me, he already knew his Presidency was in deep trouble. Over the next three months, I met with the President alone in the White House a dozen times. My job was set up so that I reported to him alone to "tell it like it is" and for me to be utterly frank with him. Previously, he had been so misled by subordinates; he did not want to be misled by me. Reagan told me that there would be no executive privilege, and one of my roles was "to get everything out" to ensure no cover-ups and to restore trust in the White House."

I was impressed with what Abshire was saying: his assessment of Marshall and his description of his role in the wake of Reagan's Iran Contra. I wanted to ask him about George H.W. Bush, Gerald Ford's Director of the CIA, and Reagan's Vice President, and what he thought H.W.'s role in Iran Contra really was. For example, just last month a business associate with substantial intelligence connections had shown me a secret document from June 25, 1984 that he thought I would find of interest. Considering it was January, and the document had already been marked for declassification at the end of December 2005, neither of us considered it a terrible breach of security for us to share in this 11-month premature preview. Anyway, the document contained minutes from a meeting where Bush had an interesting conversation with Reagan that indicated he was open to creative Contra problem solving.[3]

Bush: How can anyone object to the US encouraging third parties to provide help to the anti-Sandinistas under the finding? The only problem that might come up is if the United States were to promise to give these third parties something in return so that some people could interpret this as some kind of exchange.

Mr. McFarlane: I propose that there be no authority for anyone to seek third party support for the anti-Sandinistas until we have the information we need, and I certainly hope none of this discussion will be made public in any way.

President Reagan: If such a story gets out, we'll all be hanging by our thumbs in front of the White House until we find out who did it.

My phone chimed in my pocket, and I pulled it out and looked at the screen: "hi darlin i am running a bit late lol be there any minute"

It is interesting how communication modes and vehicles change with time. It seems I transmit and receive more text messages now than I do telephone calls. I set the phone on the bar and watched as bowls of queso, chips, and guacamole, and plates of multicolored enchiladas and tacos ringed by sweating bottles of Dos Equis, swept by me on an exceptionally large tray carried by a particularly small Hispanic girl.

Bush subsequently arranged that third party deal with Honduran President Roberto Suazo Córdova in March of 1985, trading covert aid to the Honduran military in return for their support of the Contra war effort. Regarding his involvement with the Iranians, Amiram Nir, an adviser to Yitzhak Shamir on counterterrorism, reportedly briefed H.W. in Israel on the hostage situation. This fact could have significantly countered Bush's assertions to the contrary if Nir had gone public with the information, as he told Bob Woodward he would because of Oliver North's attempts to throw Nir under the bus for the whole mess. Fortunately for Bush, Nir—traveling under the assumed name Pat Weber—died fortuitously in a plane crash in Mexico before he had that opportunity. H.W. later claimed no knowledge of the Iran-Contra affair, despite his diary entry on November 5, 1986:

On the news at this time is the question of the hostages. There is some discussion of Bud McFarlane having been held prisoner in Iran for 4 days. I'm one of the few people that know fully the details, and there is a lot of flack and misinformation out there. It is not a subject we can talk about.[4]

And finally, on his way out of the White House on Christmas Eve 1992, Bush granted executive clemency to Caspar Weinberger, former Secretary of Defense, Elliott Abrams, former assistant secretary of state for Central America, Duane Clarridge, Alan Fiers, Clair George, all former CIA officials, and Robert McFarlane, former National Security Adviser, for their criminal conduct related to the Iran-Contra affair. All of them except Weinberger and Clarridge had already pleaded or been found guilty of various criminal activities associated with Iran Contra. He wrote at the time about his primary clemency criterion: First, the common denominator of their motivation—whether their actions were right or wrong—was patriotism.[5]

Depending upon the optics of your prism, this clemency demonstrated either that powerful people with powerful allies can commit serious crimes in high office and deliberately abuse the public trust without consequence, or that in the mid 1980's, the outcome of the struggle against the Soviet Union was far from clear and, while some may have hesitated to act, the best and most dedicated patriots stepped forward and took chances for the good of the country. There are always loose ends and unknowns in complex systems and, in the end as so often happens, we hit a metaphorical brick wall and are simply left with a basket filled with few facts and many speculations, and we must decide what to do with them. The facts are that H.W. Bush was an intelligent, informed, thoughtful man. He raised a family and served his country. He helped defeat the Soviet Union, yet was careful not to gloat on this success or declare victory. He built a broad and substantial international coalition and drove Saddam Hussein out of Kuwait and back into Iraq—and then, like George Washington, like a patriotic servant leader, he dissolved the coalition and went home. He led a life of honor, decency, and fairness. Through my prism, the rest becomes subjectively optical and anecdotal.

I felt a tap on my shoulder and turned to see a zaftig, large-busted woman with an unusually tall frame in a form fitted blouse and tight blue jeans capped by a thin gold belt, with a hefty mane of symmetrically streaked blond hair set atop a slightly cocked theatrically-attractive, makeup-enhanced head, holding an unnaturally broad smile. She looked me right in the eyes and extended a limp right hand. "Christopher, I presume?"

"Yes, Darla?"

"In the flesh, Honey! What's that you're drinking?"

"Iced tea."

"Yay—great idea!" Darla looked at the bartender with smoky eyes and purred. "Two Long Island Iced Teas and make 'em good ones, baby!"

We made some small talk while the bartender mixed our drinks, then followed the hostess to a dimly lit booth in the back of the restaurant where the two of us settled in. In addition to being as tall as me at about six feet, Darla had a deep contralto voice that had me struggling to get rid of the Kinks song rolling through my head and the urge to call her Lola.

"So, Mary tells me y'all sell weapons—so that's pretty cool!"

"Yes, we're making a real killing these days—get it?"

"Why, yes I do—and that's very funny, Christopher!"

"Yes, well, I tell my customers that I only deal in significant weapon systems. So if you want 'small arms,' I'll have to introduce you to my friend T. Rex in Berlin—get it?"

"Mmmmmm...not sure I got that one, but that's OK. Excuse me señorita, dos más Long Island iced teas, por favor. Gracias! Now Christopher, where did you get that fabulous accent?"

"Well, I am originally from Massachusetts, right outside of Boston."

"Oh, I just love Boston!"

"Ah, so you've been there!"

"No, I've never actually visited Boston, but I love to travel and hope to visit some day. How about you, do you travel much outside work?"

I was delighted. What a great lead into my Abshire story!

"Yes, as a matter of fact I was just recalling a visit I made to Virginia…"

"Let me guess, Williamsburg, right?"

"No, I was at a conference in…"

"Richmond!"

"No, Lexington City."

"Never heard of it. Let me guess, golf vacation, right?"

"No, I went up for a conference."

The waitress arrived with our drinks and took our orders. I decided to eat healthy and ordered the shrimp brochette. Darla did the same with a side of fries, no salt. We ordered some queso with fresh jalapeños to get us started.

"Well Christopher, that is so interesting. I like to travel too, and in fact I just got back from Kentucky."

"What were you doing up there?"

"Well, I was on a museum visit."

"Visiting a museum, what an intellectual holiday. That's really great."

"Yes, I know!"

"What museum did you visit?"

"The Creation Museum in Petersburg, and let me tell you what a remarkably blessed place it is."

"The Creation Museum? I have never heard of it. Is it an innovation or manufacturing museum or something like that?"

"Well, in a way. It's about the manufacture of our planet and of us."

"I'm not sure I follow you."

"Well, this museum provides the proof that God made the earth and everything on it six thousand years ago, and he made it in six days. God loves science![6]"

My head began to spin, and I thought I had better slow down on the drinks—they were quite powerful, and the conversation had taken a strange turn. "Ah, well, tell me a bit about this museum."

"Well, you walk into the museum and move through a series of rooms with displays, each room filled with facts and evidence. The first room proves how the dinosaurs were all killed by Noah's flood four thousand years ago."

"Dinosaurs were killed four thousand years ago?"

"Why yes, and this is supported by all the stories we have about monsters and dragons and whatnot. Those stories are talking about the struggles between men and dinosaurs!"

"So, I was taught something quite different, that the earth is 4.5 billion years old and that dinosaurs lived tens of millions of years before man, and the physical evidence for this is in the fossil record."

"Yes, they had a room about that too! You see Christopher, the trouble started when Adam and Eve ate the fruit of the tree of knowledge, and they became corrupted. That's what knowledge does, you know, it corrupts. Anyway, the world after the flood, the one we live in now, is one in which many people rely solely on things like reasoning and science and stuff like that, and that is what leads to all the confusion."

"But what about the evidence, the fossils, the radiometric dating, and all of that?"

"Oh, I don't quite know what you are talking about, but I can tell you that evil is real and the devil places things everywhere to deceive us, so why not radioactive fossils or whatever in rocks too, right? Ah, here comes our food! Yay!"

I wasn't sure what to make of this conversation. Initially I thought Darla was joking with me, but she was not. I was also a bit disappointed that she had taken the conversation down this intellectual alleyway and that I did not have the opportunity to use my Abshire story on her. Oh well. The food arrived and Darla picked up the saltshaker and, shaking it like a maraca, quickly dispensed several grams on her fries.

"I thought you wanted fries with no salt."

"Mmm hmmm, that's what I ordered honey."

"Yes, but you just salted them prodigiously."

"Yes, that's right, I love salty fries and so does everyone else and because of that there are piles of old salted fries lying around back there in the kitchen right now. By ordering them without salt, I force the kitchen to make me a brand new batch of fresh fries. Then I just add the salt on those delicious piping hot babies myself."

"That's genius."

"Yes, I think so. Well, bone apateet Christopher!"

We enjoyed our food with requisite oohs and ahs and smiles, and as we were finishing Darla snapped her fingers at our waitress who was hurrying by, quickly got our check and handed it to me. She leaned over, put her arm around the back of my neck and purred in my ear. "Christopher, I am having so much fun with you! Let's go to your place for a nightcap. I'll leave my car here."

The rest of the evening is a bit of a blur. I read an article in a men's magazine once about what every successful man should keep in his home bar and had acquired the requisite products. I had not touched very much of anything, as I had not received any visitors, so there was a lot for Darla to choose from. The Belvedere vodka was still in the freezer, and she squealed when she spotted it. We consumed most of the bottle, which was a somewhat unusual departure for me from my moderate alcohol consumption, and then we had sex, which was a radical departure from my normally monastic lifestyle. I felt the sex was quite adequate, although I did not ejaculate. I think Darla enjoyed it as well. She had mounted me with hands firmly planted on either side of my head, her head tucked down like a rugby player in a scrum, her stiff blond hair tickling my face. She moved her robust hips, thrusting back and forth like a mechanical bull rider at Gilley's, faster and faster until she gasped, squealed, threw back her head, arched her back and urinated on me. When she was done, and it was a considerable volume, she gave a low basso profundo grunt, looked down at me and made eye contact for the first time. "Ummmgh. Shit yeah y'all."

Then she quickly dismounted, stood up, went to the bathroom, showered, dressed, kissed me hard on the lips and walked out the door to catch the cab she had already called. She was very efficient. I was a bit startled by Darla's urination, but not being extremely sexually practiced, I thought perhaps this was the norm—until I did some research and found that orgasmic urinary incontinence is in fact somewhat rare. I purchased a new mattress for several thousand dollars and, although our date had been very interesting, I did not respond to Darla's follow up texts seeking another date, as the cost-benefit ratio of new mattress to sex was too great for my budget.

Although I never saw Darla again, her embrace of creationism and wholesale rejection of elementary science really stuck with me. Her approach to physical evidence, rational thought, and expert consensus reminded me of the so-called global warming controversy, something that had me questioning my political affinity. Since college, I had voted Republican, because of Berg and Laurie and because the platform seemed to make sense, especially a strong defense. But as the years progressed, I had found it increasingly difficult to reconcile my political allegiance with the anti-science dogma of many Republican politicians and the failure of others to denounce that nonsense. I had listened as global warming denial shifted from "the earth is not warming and the climate is not changing" to "of course the climate is changing, just like it's changed since the earth was first created by God six thousand years ago." Eventually, given the current atmospheric trend, this position will probably evolve to its final state, and the same people will tell us how great it is that carbon dioxide emissions are warming the planet and feeding plants at the same time, a position espoused back in 1896 by the Nobel Laureate Svante Arrhenius, who quantified the effect of increasing carbon dioxide on the temperature of the ground. Arrhenius, who grew up in Sweden during the period climatologists call the Little Ice Age, looked forward to a coal combustion-induced global warming where future Swedes would live under a warmer sky, in a milder environment.[7]

In one of my monthly calls to my parents, I brought up the topic with my father, leaving out the intimate details about my night with Darla of course, and asked him his thoughts.

"Christopher, the demonization of science has been going on for hundreds, perhaps even thousands of years, so that is nothing new. Look at Galileo. He reviews the work of Copernicus, checks the math, and then dares to agree out loud that the earth orbits the sun and not vice versa. For this heresy, one of the greatest scientists of all time finds himself sitting uncomfortably in a dark musty room, on a hard wooden bench, at the table of the Inquisition, while at the other end an ignorant Roman inquisitor informs him that he is an absurd fool and asks if he would like to be burned at the stake. He says no thank you, and promises to be good, and is rewarded with house arrest for the rest of his life.[8]"

I am sitting in my warmly lit, book-filled living room, on my jade green velvet couch with my feet up on an antique ochre Berber print ottoman, and I have my father on speakerphone. I can see him in my mind's eye in his study, settled in his burgundy wingback chair by the window looking out at the woods, thick Bokhara rug beneath his leather-slippered feet, and a glass of sherry on the reading table beside him. I nod to myself in agreement with what he has said, but press him further. "Yes, the event is clear. But the reasoning behind it is what eludes me: how do people who are clearly unqualified to render an opinion on a scientific topic arrive in a position where they can do so? And once there, why do they elect to risk doing such significant damage with their unqualified opinions?"

"Aha, root cause analysis, excellent choice. Let's start with the elites and non-elites. When Galileo was alive, the Catholic elites had invested in a geocentric universe and, like insecure parents, did not want to be shown to be fallible in any way, shape, or form by their children. Let's turn to today for an interesting look at the non-elites. There's this fellow, Robert Sungenis, a Ph.D. who recently published a thousand-plus page treatise on how Galileo was wrong and the church was right, and in fact the earth does not rotate and we do not live in a heliocentric system.[9]"

"Oh, come on dad that's ridiculous. Number one, how is someone with a Ph.D. not an elite of some sort, and number two, he sounds like he has a psychological problem not a mathematical one."

"Valid argument son—I use him strategically to make my points. Number one, his Ph.D. is in religious studies from Calamus International University. Calamus is an unaccredited sham school, the campus is an answering service in the Turks and Caicos Islands, and the administrative offices reside within a post office box in London.[10] So he is a non-elite masquerading as an elite because he recognizes his lack of credentials and expertise. That is a plus for him as it makes him a con man and not a narcissist, and that is the first distinction I think we must make in categorizing these creatures: whether they are strategic con men or simply mentally ill."

"Okay, strategic versus sick, I am with you so far, but can we take a look at global warming?"

"Of course, let's start with strategic versus sick, as you put it. You pick your favorite contrarian and I'll pick mine."

"That's easy, I pick Senator James Inhofe from Oklahoma."

"Good, Inhofe is a politician. I choose the scientist Fred Singer, one of Inhofe's crowd. Sound good to you?"

"I have certainly heard of him, and his science fits right in with Inhofe, so let's go."

"OK, what do we know about Inhofe?"

"Inhofe has been a Senator since 1994 and now, after thirteen years, we find him currently chairing the Committee on Environment and Public Works. When it comes to elite versus non-elite, I guess, in a way, he might be a bit like Sungenis. Inhofe lied for years, saying he had earned a B.A. in economics (not exactly a powerhouse degree) from the University of Tulsa (not exactly a powerhouse university) back in 1959. In fact, he finished the degree in 1973, well after getting involved in politics, and only after getting called out on the flaw in his resume. His business experience includes the mismanagement and collapse of his company, Quaker Life Insurance, and management of the subsequent lawsuits. He gave a painfully long speech in 2003, where he said global warming is the greatest hoax ever perpetrated on the American people and it has been cooked up by a massive conspiracy involving far left environmental extremists. He even referenced your guy Fred Singer in that speech."

"Okay, so is this non-elite politician strategic or is he sick?"

"Well, Oklahoma is a poor state with an unbalanced economy that depends in large part upon petroleum. That influence must play a role in his actions."

"And Inhofe represents Oklahomans, not Americans or

Africans or Peruvians or people in Micronesia or the Maldive Islands, correct? In order to protect your mother and me today, would you lie about something that might be a problem for some unknown people somewhere far away at some unknown time in the future and call it a hoax? I think you would. I say Inhofe is a micro-patriot who is lying in order to save his collective Oklahoma family at the expense of other people's families. What do you think?"

"Jeez, I'm not sure I can move him that quickly from unqualified liar to patriot. But let's set him aside and move to Singer, I want to hear your approach to him."

"Excellent. I now present to you, Siegfried Fred Singer. He holds a Ph.D. in physics—a significant degree and area of study—from Princeton, which is a real and excellent school."

"All right, I think we can place him in the elite box. So, is he strategic or sick?"

"Throughout a multi-decadal career in which he accomplished significant scientific feats within his area of expertise, physics, he has also been consistently wrong about scientific issues outside his bailiwick. According to Singer, secondhand tobacco smoke was not a problem, acid rain was not a problem, CFCs were not destroying ozone, and ultraviolet radiation from the sun does not cause skin cancer. He has consistently argued that all environmental issues are political issues, and all environmental advocates are communists."

"He is clearly an elite, but he sounds kind of crazy. Sick?"

"Well, in 1938, the Jewish 14-year-old Siegfried Singer left his parents behind and escaped Nazi Austria on a *kindertransport* to England, eventually making his way across the Atlantic to the United States. Might this early horrific part of his life have affected him emotionally? Might his subsequent experiences in America have given him a heightened sense of patriotism for his adopted country? He earned his Ph.D. in 1948, the year the United States began screening federal employees' backgrounds for communist and other totalitarian affiliations. Might living through the McCarthy era have reawakened in him a fear of totalitarianism, this time from the communists instead of the Nazis, the greens instead of the browns?[11]"

"Yes, I see your point. So, we label him sick, but with an excuse?"

"Christopher, I am not sure. It seems to me that there are people in this world who call themselves patriots because they love their family, tribe, state, or country to the exception of all else. Their love is very real to them, but it is a distinctly personal affection that is not necessarily shared by others and in fact may be terribly detrimental to others. Because of this, we can have a dozen of these folks in a room, all calling themselves patriots and calling each other traitor, communist, Nazi, and so on. This type of patriotism, while perhaps well intentioned, can be quite destructive."

I close my eyes and I am back in the mountains, the crisp air and smell of wood smoke mingling with roasting curried lamb. I see the kind eyes of my friend Osama and recall his words about jihad, and how Abdallah had bent the message beyond recognition and was fighting his own personal jihad, perhaps just like Inhofe and Singer are today.

"Christopher, are you there?"

"Yes, I was just thinking about what you said. It makes good sense, and I am able to set it firmly within my experiential context. This was an excellent conversation, but I know it's late, and I don't want to keep you. Tell mom I said hello."

FOURTEEN

THE WITCH IS DEAD

(ZILKER PARK, AUGUST 11, 2020, 10:43 CST)

Karachi. Donkey shit and diesel and that suffocating heat. Karachi? No. I'm still in Texas with these Day-Glo gelatin rivers and the bongos and the hissing of the hot pavement. I find myself struggling to breathe, and consciously focus on engaging my diaphragm. As I decouple from my sympathetic nervous system and allow the parasympathetic to guide my internal elephant, my heart rate decreases as does the panic and I close my eyes with a sigh of relief.

I didn't see my friend Osama again until he declared war on America in August of 1997. There he was on CNN, being interviewed by Peter Bergen.[1] It was the same Osama: that infectious smile, trim and fit, just a bit gray in the beard.

"The US today has set a double standard, calling whoever goes against its injustice, a terrorist. It wants to occupy our countries, steal our resources, impose agents on us to rule us, and then wants us to agree to all this. If we refuse to do so, it says we are terrorists."

When I heard him say that I thought, hey, he's telling the truth. This is what we do. This is what everyone does. Yesterday's freedom fighters are today's terrorists, and today's villains are tomorrow's heroes. But isn't that traditionally the way things go? A good day for the lion is a bad day for the zebra, and all that? The men who set out to kill twenty five thousand innocent civilians at Dresden, sixty six thousand at Hiroshima, and thirty nine thousand at Nagasaki were sentient human beings who were loved by their families and friends. They killed over one hundred thousand innocent civilians in particularly terrible ways and we don't call them animals or monsters; we call them heroes. The prize belongs to the victor to refract reality and write history.

I had been an unquestioning, perhaps even childlike, patriot until the Bergen interview. After that, my relationship with patriotism changed. I think I grew up a bit and saw my country in the same light I saw my parents when I left childhood behind. Like my country, my parents had flaws, they had setbacks, and they made mistakes. But they were my parents. Loving my parents unconditionally while recognizing these realities were not mutually exclusive. Loving my country unconditionally while recognizing the realities Osama had pointed out and appreciating his position were also not mutually exclusive. America's support for Israel and by default its complicity in the killing of women and children in Palestine, Lebanon, Syria, and so on and so forth, was born out of our unconditional love for Israel. As a mature nation, we should admit and be willing to accept the repercussions for sanctioning this killing by our beloved friend. If we are not willing to accept the possible consequences, then we should say "we love you Israel, but you're on your own."

Well, four years later, Osama made good on his promise to take his jihad to America, and the towers came down killing almost three thousand of our innocent civilians. I was not surprised to learn that the masterminds of the hijackings that terrible day—Mohamed Atta and Khalid Sheikh Mohamed—were both engineers, just like Hekmatyar, Osama, and me, and more than half of the twenty-five suicidal conspirators that day were engineers too.[2] We were all problem solvers who had used our technical and reasoning skills in support of our jihad. I mourned the loss of life that day with my fellow Americans. But details slowly leaked out in the aftermath that President Bush knew there was activity in our country consistent with preparations for hijackings or other types of attacks, including recent surveillance of federal buildings in New York. In fact, he had been unambiguously informed in a Presidential Daily Briefing on August 6, 2001 "Bin Laden determined to attack inside the U.S.."[3] This made me want to scream at my country.

"You approved of and supported the killing of innocent women and children in the Middle East. You knew the possible consequences of these actions before you took them. Osama told you he would punish you for these acts. You then learned that he was preparing to punish you and the vehicle for that punishment and you either did not listen or you did not care."

This is a shameful onion to peel, and presents a logical disconnection if we as Americans attempt to absolve ourselves of any culpability. Either we support killing and are very prepared to prevent or deal with the knock-on effects and consequences, or we shouldn't support killing. Even small children understand that you cannot have your cake and eat it too.

I was in State College on business at Penn State's Applied Research Lab, ARL, in spring of 2011. The Arbor Day Foundation recognizes State College as a "Tree City" and because of the prolific flowering in spring the town is a histamine hell for those with allergies—thankfully, not me. On the surface, the town has all the appearances of a tranquil bucolic village, with classic Sears homes and tidy neighborhoods. I was staying downtown at the Days Inn on Pugh Street. They have an indoor swimming pool and a good Mexican restaurant, Mad Mex. My multi-leg flights from Austin to the tiny State College airport had been successively delayed, and I had arrived late Sunday night on the first day of May for my meetings the next morning at ARL. The student population has always tended towards dull misogynistic boys who eat lots of red meat, drink too much cheap booze, and can't handle their alcohol, and the girls who enjoy being with boys like this. Not surprisingly, during the 1960s Penn State saw significantly fewer Vietnam War protests than other universities of similar size in America. While students at Harvard and other schools forced their administrations to remove the military training Reserve Officer Training Corps (ROTC) from campuses, the anemic student activism at Penn State resulted in the administration simply changing the name of the Ordinance Research Laboratory, ORL, where torpedo and other weapons research was conducted, to the Applied Research Laboratory, or ARL, where torpedo and other weapons research continued to be conducted.

It was unseasonably warm that day, and I was finishing a late dinner of fajitas around eleven, outdoors under a patio heater at Mad Mex, when suddenly I heard an awful sound. It was as if all the buildings around me groaned, moaned and wailed simultaneously. It sounded like a giant wounded animal. I set my napkin down, and looked around, wide-eyed. The sound quickly transitioned to the slamming of doors and cries of "to the Canyon." Thankfully, my waitress had just approached my table to see how I was doing. She had dreadlocks and was unusually tall, with tattoo vines creeping up her forearms and a pierced nose with a single red ruby stud. While I was nonplussed, she was unruffled and serene.

What was that? What is going on?"

"Something must have happened on TV, and now all the idiots are going to Beaver Canyon to riot."

"Riot?"

"Yeah, they do it all the time. If a basketball team wins, they riot. If a basketball team loses, they riot. It's the same with football. Riot at the Arts Fest too. They're morons."

"Beaver Canyon?"

"Yeah, the gap between the high-rise apartments right down the street."

"What happened?"

"Who knows? I personally don't watch TV, and don't date guys who do. It rots your brain and makes you fat and stupid. No offence. You should go check out the scene in the Canyon for yourself. It's just a couple of blocks right down the street, and it's guaranteed to be a freak show. Just don't get too deep into the crowd, or you might get puked on. Those children are all cretins."

I thanked her, paid my check, and walked down the hill to Beaver Avenue. To my right was a dense corridor of high-rise apartments, and the road between them was already filled with several thousand students. Some were just milling about while others jumped on parked cars and climbed streetlights like psychotic chimps and attempted to rock them loose from their footings.

As I got closer, I saw that some kids were draped in American flags and others were wearing T-shirts imprinted with a variety of nationalistic and obscene symbols. "God Bless the USA" was blasting out of gigantic speakers from a fifth-floor apartment, confetti quickly put together with ripped-up school notebooks and colored balloons drifted down from balconies, with people either singing along or howling maniacally. As I approached the edge of the crowd the music ended, and a deafening chant began.

USA! USA! USA! USA!
FUCK BIN LADEN! FUCK BIN LADEN! FUCK
BIN LADEN!
USA! USA! USA! USA!

A skyrocket suddenly sailed whistling over my head, and I ducked. It hit the apartment building behind me, fell to the ground and exploded. A student next to me laughed. "Don't worry dude, it's just a bottle rocket."

"What's going on here?"

"Haven't you heard? They killed Bin Laden!"

I had walked into the heart of several thousand young Americans celebrating the death of Osama. The cheering was deafening, and there was dancing and laughter. I can understand feeling relief when someone you love that is in terrible pain passes away. I can understand a feeling of closure and maybe even satisfaction when someone who has caused you great personal harm passes away. But I cannot understand how human beings can take pleasure in the killing of another human being in general, and express their feelings in gleeful celebration. While the munchkins celebrated the death of the wicked witch of the east in the Wizard of Oz, Dorothy—the one human present—stood aghast and apologetic that her house had been the instrument of that death. To me, celebrating death like this is not human, not even in Oz, and it exceeds mere schadenfreude. It is social sadism. Only the sickest of the Nazis worked in concentration camps and only the sickest of those took pleasure in killing. The American prison system, which is not especially known for the sensitivity of its workers, would not tolerate an executioner who laughed and cheered as he administered a lethal injection. Families, who attend the execution of murderers responsible for the death of a loved one, usually do so in solemnity. Yet celebrations took place all across America that night, just like in rural State College, with hundreds of thousands of social sadists laughing and chanting as they got drunk, cheering like they had won a football game. Ding, dong, Osama is dead.[4]

The initial collective cheer from my fellow Americans that night had sounded to me like a wounded animal, and perhaps that was a foreshadowing of how I felt that night about the death of my friend. Wounded. When I considered the event later, my thoughts were more dispassionate. Osama believed he was acting in support of the downtrodden, he believed his actions were just, he knew the possible consequences of his actions when he took them, and he knew it was inevitable that he would eventually be found and killed. I am sure he was prepared to die the night the American SEALs came knocking. I see him smiling, closing his eyes, and humming to himself as they burst into his room.

FIFTEEN

ENGINEERING DEATH
(ZILKER PARK, AUGUST 11, 2020, 10:51 CST)

L ike a skin diver coming up for air in a lake surrounded by a forest fire, the radiant heat sears my wet face, and the air chokes me and burns my lungs. You would think I would be used to the heat by now. Some say it is the combination of heat and humidity that is so brutal. Over thirty years in Texas and I am affected like this, just sitting in the park on a bench. How is that possible? And what is that hissing? It is like a lone cicada rattling high in a far-off tree not stopping to take a breath: subtle, indistinct, and incessant. This acquired weakness doesn't make sense. Where is that resilience I had in Pakistan? Morocco? Dubai? How does one's thermal capacity decrease? Dubai is one of the hottest and also the most humid places on the planet in the summer. The sun and sea obey Clausius and Clapeyron, and the Gulf boils under the punishing rays to create something reminiscent of the steam room at the Gellért Hotel in Budapest. But back in the day—when I was still intact, still myself—I alone walked its streets, only slightly uncomfortable and not at all discomfited, while luxury cars whistled by, their climate-controlled occupants—

wrapped head to toe in robes—gaping at me with incomprehension.

The flight from Austin to Dubai in 2010 could typically take as much as twenty-four hours with connections. Some people dislike long flights, but I enjoy them. In first class, the high frequency hiss of the air conditioning and the low frequency rumble of the turbines combine in a synergy that I find calming. There is a churchlike solitude to air travel as well. The restricted space facilitates a meditative focus on one's immediate environment, whether that is working, reading a novel, or watching a movie. Many people grumble about airline food, but I enjoy the nuts and appetizers followed by a multiple small portion meal. It reminds me a bit of tapas in a Sevilla bar, absent the jamón ibérico pig haunch and the rustic atmosphere.

I exit the plane, move through the jetway, and enter the airport, where I pick up my pace, avoiding the jetlagged meander of other passengers, and navigate through Terminal 3 towards immigration. I am looking forward to seeing my associate and friend Mohamed Salem, with whom I had been doing business for several years. Mohamed was my age and had relocated from Syria to Dubai with his family in 1980 at the start of the Iran-Iraq war. Mohamed's family was Sunni Muslim and had been uncomfortable with the appearance of a theocratic alliance between Baathist Syria and Shia Iran. Mohamed's father was a trader and the family had significant diplomatic and business connections in the region. Mohamed followed in his father's footsteps, arranging arms purchases and whatnot with clients throughout the Middle East, and North and East Africa. These transactions usually involved wealthy Gulf State families, but bulk sales often paralleled unrest and the clients for those sales remained unknown to me. I typically supplied Mohamed with small arms, but sales of shoulder-fired Rocket Propelled Grenades (RPGs) and small refurbished BGM-71 Tube-launched

Optically tracked Wire-guided missiles (TOWs), both of them effective on heavily armored passenger vehicles, were becoming increasingly popular for the private security details of royal relatives and other mystery clients that were not my business to know. Similarly, although Mohamed was aware of much of my experience in the region, I had kept my first weapons delivery to Pakistan to myself—while Mohamed would surely have found the story delightful, it was simply not necessary.

Mohamed lived with his younger brother Ibrahim in a classic villa built in the 1960s in Jumeirah, a neighborhood on the coast. A ten-foot-tall wall ringed the property and enclosed the main house and two small outbuildings, all whitewashed and, while reminiscent of Frank Lloyd Wright, tastefully punctuated with classic Moorish arches. Inside, numbered lithographs by Picasso and Chagall mingled with larger works in oil by other less well-known artists hung on the alabaster plaster walls. The central living area was laid out like a salon Marocain, dominated by an expanse of low, heavily pillowed couches and hardwood tables daintily edged in Berber silver. The dining room hosted a massive antique Italian Baroque table with Spode Blue Italian table settings and Lalique crystal glassware. An occasional thick silk Persian rug and tall banana plants in large faux Ming fishbowls broke the continuity of the broad expanse of large black and white floor tiles. The air was cool and dry, and contained a complex mix of ancient scents. Earthy oud oil, extracted from resin produced by infected Asian agarwood trees, familiar to mystics for millennia, was cold-diffused from unseen places, while mounds of copal resin from Amazonian burseracea trees, considered by Incans and Mayans to be food of the gods, were burned prominently in antique Chinese bronze censers.

Outside, bougainvillea, date palms, and mature olive trees punctuated the xeriscaped grounds where Ibrahim collected and cured the dates and olives when they matured. The compound was a block off the beach and, not that anyone else walked in Dubai, an easy walk for me from the Burj Al Arab, my hotel of choice in the city ever since it opened in December 1999. Mohamed had secured a ninety-nine-year lease in this desirable nonfreehold zone, and he enjoyed hosting dinners at his home. As Ibrahim was a fixture at these dinners, over the years I got to know him a bit. He was an unemployed Islamic scholar and martial arts expert. I divined this when we first met, from the *salah* prayer callous on his forehead and his propensity to crack his equally calloused knuckles and thick neck. In subsequent conversations and tours of the house, I learned just how dedicated he was to both pursuits: his workout room accommodating mats and a one-hundred-pound heavy bag, along with a small silk rug where he respected the five Muslim prayers of *Fajr* at dawn, *Zuhr* at midday, *Asr* in the afternoon, *Maghrib* in the dim light of dusk after the sun set, and *Isha* in the true darkness of night.

From time to time, Mohamed would host a large dinner party, but more often than not, it was just the three of us dining together. Mohamed and I never talked business at dinner, instead using the time to explore diverse topics where we had experiential or intellectual overlap. We especially enjoyed unpackaging historical accounts of past events that were perhaps never present, including widely accepted contemporary western myths as well as more archaic visions. A white skinned god visits pre-Inca South Americans living a hunter-gatherer existence, instructs them in the arts of civilization, shows them plants with which they can both cure sickness and alter consciousness, and introduces them to pottery and instructs them in its manufacture.[1] The earliest archaeological remains of ancient pottery we have found support an intrusive event of this nature, as they are not crude and plain, but intricate and geometrically adorned—with reflections of the potter's hallucinations. Mainland Neolithic Greeks living in crude circular rock huts with goatskin roofs suddenly abandon their simple matriarchal worship of female idols with remarkably large breasts and vulvae for that of a complex polytheistic pantheon.[2] Was this rejection and the subsequent cultural and intellectual Mycenaean enlightenment the result of intrusion by charismatic Proto-Indo-Europeans?[3] What then caused the subsequent collapse of Mycenaean Greece and the Dark Age dominated by Big Man leadership that preceded the enlightened Hellenic period—and what led to that enlightenment? Is Homer's Odysseus a fantasy character like Washington Irving's Christopher Columbus, or does he provide us with a deeper insight into the people and period? Given the English were driven out of France after one hundred years of war, was the English longbow really a mechanically effective weapon, or was it simply the first psychological divorce between the killer and the killed?[4] Was the North African pirate kingdom of Salé perhaps the first and best example of true democratic capitalism?[5] And so on.

Ibrahim would also lead us to discuss the decaying morality of the Emirate of Dubai as evidenced by its embrace of western culture—including dress, music, and movies. Because alcohol consumption often leads to other offences, the Prophet Muhammad, may peace be upon him, deemed drinking alcoholic beverages to be the mother of all other vices, *ummal-Khaba'ith*, his proscription recorded in the Hadith with eighty lashes required as punishment for their consumption. From a numerical standpoint, an argument can be made that Dubai is not really a Muslim city at all. Most of the population is comprised of migrant workers from Hindu India and the Catholic Philippines. And because one person's *haram* is another's freedom or pleasure, there are multiple venues for alcohol and prostitutes in Dubai, ranging from elegant brothels serving slip and slides for expats, to back alleys where migrant workers are minimally and swiftly serviced and then dispatched.

There are many legal frameworks around the world that differ, yet are not necessarily mutually exclusive. Dubai, while embracing elements of Sharia law, subjugates it to an extent within western civil and criminal structures. This seems to work, as the crime rate is quite low. While I recognize the broad legitimacy of Sharia law in the Middle East, just as I do that of Mosaic law in the West, and see its constructive place within this greater context, I still have questions about specific elements that trouble me. During a discussion on the topic one evening over dinner, I shared an experience I had in Asia several years prior to stimulate discussion on the topic. "Ibrahim, I must admit that although my experience with Sharia law and *hudud* is not extensive, it left an impression upon me. I was in Brunei on business several years ago and took a side trip to see mainland Malaysia while I was in the neighborhood. I contracted a Malay driver in Kuala Lumpur—Ahmad—for five days, and told him that I wanted to see the country top to bottom, but I didn't want to visit any of the usual tourist sights. Early one morning, we were in Kelantan province and heading off the beaten track a bit towards Orang Asli country when we approached a small village. A roadblock had been set up at the village edge and a young man in ill-fitting dark blue police attire and beret carrying a 9 mm Czech Scorpion EVO 3 submachine gun waved us to a stop. The EVO 3 is a decent weapon, firing 1150 rounds per minute with very little muzzle rise.

Although there are multiple Picatinny rails for tactical attachments, this officer's weapon was bare bones with iron sights. Anyway, my driver Ahmad got out of the car, smiling broadly with his hands up in the air, and walked towards the young man. They exchanged greetings and I watched as the young man relaxed a bit and began smiling along with Ahmad, speaking in earnest, and pointing up the road to the village. Ahmad patted the young man on the shoulder and returned to the car.

"He turned to me and said, 'Mr. Christopher, we have arrived in this village at a very sensitive time. A villager returned home to find a man in the house stealing his valuables and, in the resulting confrontation, the homeowner was killed. The thief was caught, and he is to be punished today.'

"'Why is there a roadblock here?' I asked.

"He replied, 'Well, the thief was tried under a new proposed Syariah law that has not quite been approved yet by the national government, so they are being a bit cautious.'

"Ibrahim, they call Sharia "Syariah" in Malaysia. Personally, I prefer Sharia as Syariah sounds a bit like an intestinal disorder.

"I asked Ahmad, 'What is the punishment for theft and murder under Syariah?'

"'It is *salib*, Mr. Christopher, crucifixion.'

"'Crucifixion?' I responded, wondering if I had heard him correctly.

"'Yes, Mr. Christopher,' he said.

"'Ahmad, have you ever been to a crucifixion?' I asked a bit hesitantly.

"'No, Mr. Christopher, never, but I would very much like to attend this one,' he replied.

"Ibrahim, the Quran says that life, which God has made sacred, should not be taken except by way of justice and due process of law, and I respect that. But I felt that in the

Syariah proposed in Kelantan there were clear inequities. For example, a married woman who is raped is considered to have had unlawful carnal intercourse, *zina*, and is stoned to death, while at the same time, a man who has intercourse with an animal or a human corpse is only imprisoned for up to five years.[6] That does not seem fair to me. But setting these aside, I simply could not sanction crucifixion as a form of justice that day. Perhaps that is because of the stigma inherent in this form of execution that has been cultivated by Christians over the last two millennia. After all, killing another human by electric chair, firing squad, the gas chamber or hanging all result in the same end point and each is brutal in its own way.

"A prisoner is strapped into the electric chair and receives a stream of electrons pressurized to one thousand volts that quickly causes him to defecate, urinate, vomit blood, and then begins cooking his body. Like a pig on a spit, his flesh swells and begins to crackle and smoke and his eyeballs are ejected from their sockets and onto his cheeks.

"A firing squad lines up, each shooter armed with a 30-caliber carbine, one carbine loaded with a blank as consideration for the shooters' feelings. The shooters aim for the heart and if successful, the prisoner bleeds out over a couple of minutes. If they miss the heart, then the process of bleeding out takes a bit longer.

"The condemned is strapped to a perforated seat beneath which sits a pail of sulfuric acid. At the appropriate time, sodium cyanide crystals are released into the pail. The crystals react with the acid to form hydrogen cyanide gas. Prisoners often hold their breath for as long as possible as the gas hisses and begins rising up from beneath them, which makes sense, but they eventually gasp for air and inhale a large dose of the poison. Once dissolved in the lung tissue, cyanide enters the bloodstream, pollutes the mitochondrial enzyme, cytochrome oxidase, and prevents oxygen uptake at this most fundamental level. Thus begins the simultaneous suffocation of every cell in the body. The prisoner's skin flushes red, then begins to turn blue. As the central nervous system is particularly dependent upon oxygen, the first significant effects are seen here, pain registering on the face, turning to horror as cellular strangulation progresses, the prisoner's eyes bulging, and drool flowing from the slack mouth. Seizures are frequently precursors to respiratory failure, followed by heart failure and death.

"When a prisoner is hung, one of several things can happen. If the rope is too short, it can take as long as an hour for death to occur by slow strangulation. Inside the prisoner's hood his face swells, his eyes bulge, and his tongue extends. Outside the hood, there is violent thrashing of the limbs, defecation, and urination. If the rope is too long, as was the case for the former chief of Saddam Hussein's secret police, Barzan Ibrahim al-Tikriti, decapitation occurs. Ideally, the rope should be carefully prepared so that the neck is quickly snapped, but hanging is an archaic and imperfect art.

"Alexander the Great brought crucifixion back west with him from Mesopotamia and employed it across North Africa and the Middle East. In its simplest form, the prisoner is hung vertically by his arms from a cross-member the Romans called the *patibulum*. Although several researchers in the last one hundred years have conducted physical crucifixion experiments on graduate students, these experiments were of course terminated prior to death. Although we cannot know, pathologists, physicians and surgeons generally agree that death by crucifixion absent intervention is a multi-day process with death arriving rapidly either by cardiac rupture or heart failure, or more gradually through hypovolemic shock, acidosis, pulmonary embolism, or simply by the voluntary surrender of life.[7]

"Each process is revolting. Historically, the crucifixion process was looked at as the most degrading form of execution. Today, in context with other methods, it is probably the religious symbolism that makes it so troubling, not necessarily the pathway or outcome.

"From my perspective, while the fundamental framework of Syriah, or Sharia, or God's will for mankind seems as solid as any other religious framework, all of these codified punishments appear to be in need of some updating. But perhaps of greater importance to me that day was a feeling that, even in my respectful attendance, I would be invading something deeply private. Birth and death are the most sacred and important events of our lives. Although others may be present to offer assistance—either in our arrival or exit—we are significantly alone in these events, perhaps by design, and that should be respected."

Ibrahim, at first leaning forward, his eyes fixed like those of a cat upon a mouse, had gradually relaxed in his seat, his eyes softening and a look of disappointment growing. "So, Christopher, in the end you made the decision not to attend this crucifixion?"

"No, despite my moral analysis, something deeper within me drew me toward this event. I thought my attendance would be different and I would be a respectful spectator."

"Perhaps you possess a strong inner sense of justice?"

"No, truthfully, I believe it was simple juvenile fascination dressed up in adult clothes. I wish it were something different. It was neither the absence of something moral within me nor the presence of something evil. Just primal fascination supported by justification."

Ibrahim licked his lips and leaned forward again, eyes focusing. "Could you please continue the story now?"

"Yes, of course. Well, I looked at my driver Ahmad, his eyes betraying the same primal emotion that I was feeling.

'Yes, Ahmad, why not, after all, we're here. Let's attend this crucifixion.'

"Ahmad smiled and turned quickly before I could change my mind, waved out the window at the Policeman, started the car, and we drove slowly into the village.

"The village was unremarkable for Malaysia. Large warehouses and industry buildings with blue roofs and poorer inhabitants at the village outskirts near the agricultural fields in small homes with gray corrugated steel roofs. Within the heart of the town, low single- and two-story homes with red clay tiled roofs and small gardens. In the town center stood a municipal building and a small circular park with manicured trees. In front of the municipal building a large stage had been set up and people were gathering in front of it.

"Ahmad parked the car on a side street, and we walked toward the square. All the feeder streets had been blocked to traffic, and it appeared that most of the village men were gathering for this event. I only saw a few women. Ahmad and I found a spot near the stage that was under a tree in the park and out of the way. My experience as a foreigner in Malaysia was different from any other place I had visited, in that nobody really gave me a second glance—much less approached and spoke to me. At times I felt like a ghost, and that was a nice feeling. At nine o'clock, the bell in the municipal building rang and the front doors of the building were opened, and the low murmuring of the crowd hushed. A man dressed in a long zinc gray robe wearing a black skullcap walked out followed by two black-robed men escorting a prisoner. He was short and stocky, draped within a white robe with a black hood covering his head. They had bound his hands behind his back and his feet loosely together with light ropes such that he walked with a shuffle, his shoulders arched, guided by his two escorts. They ascended to the center of the stage where the prisoner was made to kneel by his escorts who then released their hold on him and stepped to the side. The man in gray turned and addressed the crowd in Malay, and Ahmad leaned toward me and whispered in my ear. 'Mr. Christopher, the judicial official is announcing this man's crimes now: murder, during the commission of a theft. He is pronouncing the sentence.'

"I had turned to listen to Ahmad, and in the time I took my eyes from the stage, the official finished speaking. I turned back to the stage just as the escort on the right swiftly and fluidly withdrew a large, curved sword from beneath his robe, swung it in a graceful arc and brought it down on the neck of the kneeling prisoner. The head was cleanly severed and rolled away from us. My gasp broke the silence of the crowd. The prisoner's headless body remained kneeling and, before it could fall over, was quickly supported by the escort on the left while his partner cleaned his blade and sheathed his sword. Then, the two of them dragged the body across the stage, flipped it roughly on its back and after some manipulations that we could not see from our vantage point, hoisted a crucifix upon which the headless prisoner was strapped by his arms. His bound legs, still tied together, hung free of the crucifix, swaying slowly back and forth. That was it. It was over. I felt confused. I felt ill. I felt relieved."

Ibrahim furrowed his brows. "I don't understand. What did you find confusing?"

"I thought that the prisoner would be crucified alive and not beheaded, so I was not prepared to watch his death but was spared the beginning of his suffering."

"You thought Sharia would require this man be crucified alive?"

"Yes, I did."

"What kind of monsters would crucify a man alive? The Romans stopped this primitive abomination almost two thousand years ago. Japanese and Nazi soldiers crucified prisoners in the Second World War, but this ranked low on the list of other atrocities those animals committed. We Muslims are neither primitive nor are we animals. Sharia seeks justice, but only within the framework of mercy. Beheading is clinically the most merciful way to deliberately end a life. The subsequent crucifixion serves as a warning to others, not as torture." Ibrahim then rose quickly, excused himself from the table and left the villa for the evening.

I looked over at Mohamed who had been sitting quietly at the head of the table. "Mohamed, I think I unintentionally offended your brother Ibrahim and I hope I have not offended you as well."

"Christopher, I have not taken any offence and in fact found this conversation to be fascinating and quite informative."

"Well, that is a relief. But what about Ibrahim? He left in a hurry."

Mohamed got up from his chair and motioned for me to follow him to the patio for an after-dinner cigar. "Trust me, I know my brother, he would have informed you directly if he were offended. I think he found your story inspiring. He goes out every night around this time, ostensibly for exercise. I think he is actually out hunting Russian prostitutes, but I cannot be sure."

"Hunting prostitutes?"

Mohamed chuckled. "Yes, these Russian and Ukrainian whores have been turning up dead, knocked unconscious with a strong blow to the back of the neck followed by an icepick through the ear and into the brain. It is very quick and very humane and something I can easily imagine my brother doing. He has adopted this Emirate as his home in a way that I have not. Perhaps because I was a bit older when we came here, I will always see myself as a Syrian. Ibrahim was a very young child when we arrived, and he sees himself as a patriotic defender of his homeland's values. I am happy living as an expatriate. While I find the whores objectionable, I would never kill one, nor do I weep for their demise. I am a bit lukewarm on the subject. But enough of this morbid discussion, let's talk weapons, shall we?"

And so, we spent the remainder of that evening chatting, as we had so many times before, sipping chilled tart pomegranate juice and taking in the sweet smoke from our Cuban Cohibas comingled with the warm velvety sea breeze from the Arabian Gulf.

SIXTEEN

THOSE PEOPLE

(ZILKER PARK, AUGUST 11, 2020, 11:03 CST)

I n 2014, Jimmy McCauley changed my own life by ending the lives of my parents. The profound significance of the event left such scarring on the inclined plane of my beyond-space-time that I find myself returning to this high friction point—to Jimmy and his past—perhaps as often as I do to the lives of Berg and Laurie. I am inextricably linked to his rough, haunting life of ignorance, depravity, nobility, and redemption and as a result have come to know him quite well.

Jimmy's father, Billy, was a five-foot-tall descendent of Irish immigrants. He had an eighth-grade education and poor eyesight that required him to wear coke-bottle-thick, black-framed glasses. Billy also had a short man complex, a predictably short temper, and a significant drinking problem. He learned about Pearl Harbor on Monday, December 8, 1941 at the Granite Works in Athol, Massachusetts where he worked. After his shift, and after drinking at the pub that sat conveniently halfway between the quarry and his rundown house, Billy made his way home, beat and raped his equally short shrinking violet wife Mary, and then passed out. Sadly, the beating was not unusual. Even today, especially in rural America, many men beat their wives after their favorite sports team suffers an upset loss.[1] Fewer rape them afterwards. In this case, the national loss at Pearl Harbor resulted in the conception of Jimmy McCauley and his birth exactly nine months later. Jimmy was conceived in and born into violence, his formative years spent in a house surrounded by ignorance, madness, and filth.

"Mary you get over here and put that goddam apple on your head right now or I'll crack your fucking skull!"

Jimmy, at seven years old, knew what the apple meant, and while that understanding was formed from a familiarity of experience, that familiarity did not lessen the metallic taste of fear. His mother, whimpering and obedient in the face of the inevitable, shuffled to her place at the end of the long dark musty hallway, placed the apple upon her head and closed her eyes as she always did. Jimmy stood in the kitchen doorway, out of the way. The game was about to begin.

"Those fuckers said I couldn't see good enough to go shoot Japs and Nazis, well fuck them, we show them don't we Mary, we show them every time how goddamn good I can see, don't we?"

"Yes Jimmy, we do, we do, please let's just show them so I can get back to fixing dinner, please?"

"Shut the fuck up!" Billy pulled his 22-caliber revolver out from under a couch pillow, opened and checked the cylinder. It was filled with 22 short bullets appropriate for indoor firing.

"Hail Mary, full of grace, the Lord is with thee."

"Shut the fuck up!" He snapped the cylinder closed.

"Blessed are you among women and blessed is the fruit of thy womb…"

"Mary, I said shut the fuck up already!" Billy took a deep breath, held it, aimed the pistol at the apple on his wife's head, squinted his eyes, relaxed, and exhaled as he squeezed the trigger. This demonstration by his father had happened so often that Jimmy was mentally prepared for the sharp crack of the 22 and for the back of the apple to explode, leaving its sticky debris on the pock marked wall. Despite his poor vision and alcohol consumption, his father was in fact a good shot. But this time when the pistol cracked, his mother's head snapped back a bit, and although sticky debris still covered the wall, the apple remained intact. A small red dot, like a Hindu *bindi*, appeared in the middle of Mary's forehead, and after what seemed an eternity she slumped to the floor. Jimmy stared, transfixed. Billy shoved his huge glasses up on his small head with a filthy calloused stub of a finger, sniffed and turned to Jimmy with a confused look.

"Your saw that, she fucking moved, that's what she did, it was her fault, not mine, she fucking moved!"

Jimmy shrunk back, peering warily as his father rose up from the couch.

"Don't you fucking look at me like that you little piece of shit, this was not my fault!" Billy beat Jimmy unconscious, then headed down to the pub, got drunk, walked outside, sat down on the curb, pulled out the pistol and shot himself in the temple.

There was no hospital in Athol at the time, so they brought Jimmy down to Saint Vincent's in Worcester. When he recovered enough from the beating, they moved him from the hospital over to Saint Anne's orphanage, just down the road on Granite Street. The orphanage was founded by French Canadian Catholic nuns with the purchase of the old Ellsworth farm that sat on 160 acres in what is now downtown Worcester and in January 1893 ten sisters and fifty children moved into the renovated and newly constructed complex. In 1949, when seven-year-old Jimmy arrived in a faded black Plymouth, he saw two structures along Granite

Street: a Victorian wood building that housed administration and dining areas, and a large four story brick dormitory. Behind these stood another massive brick dormitory which was connected to the one up front by a breezeway. Out back were several terraced play areas. To the left stood a circular in-ground cement swimming pool. Jimmy's eyes were wide and his mouth agape. To him, Saint Anne's looked just like the mansion of a wealthy family. Father Alfred Berthiaume was the head priest and Sister Dolores the head nun. She and most of the nuns were French Canadian and sprinkled *mon petits* and *très bien* throughout their speech. Traditionally, each little boy that arrived got a big brother as a mentor. Jimmy, while young, was just a bit too old to qualify as little and was on his own. The nuns disciplined with sticks, rulers, locked some kids in closets, and twisted ears. It was traditional Catholic tough love for that time.

The boys slept together in large dormitory rooms with fifty beds. Some kids were terribly lonely and cried at night but not Jimmy. For him, living at Saint Anne's was safe and predictable. These were things he had never experienced before. There were corn flakes for breakfast every morning, a meal he had rarely experienced at home, and lots of delicious garlicky blood sausages made from the pigs the nuns kept across the street. It was also fun. The girls went to events, like one at Holy Cross College where they got to dance on stage with Dick Clark and Connie Francis, Annette and the Mouseketeers. And one day, the boys were outside playing when the Budweiser horses and wagon came riding up.

For many of the kids, Jimmy included, swimming in summer and skating and sledding in winter were things they had never experienced before, and they thrived at Saint Anne's. But Jimmy struggled in his classes. He was bright and understood logic and reason, but he had trouble with the simple mechanics of reading, writing, and arithmetic. He also could not grasp the simple paradigm of the almighty that the sisters proffered. Atypical for his age, Jimmy had a significantly developed and visceral understanding of life and death after watching his mother be killed. This understanding left little room for him to accept the sisters' loving yet omniscient god whose will according to their dogma was perhaps responsible for this murderous act. When quizzed regarding his beliefs, Jimmy sounded a lot like Charles Darwin responding to the frustrated sisters.

"Sister, there's so many bad people and bad things in this here world, and I just can't believe that God designed it to be like this. Why would he deliberately create a cat so that it has fun torturing a mouse before killing it, or humans who enjoy hurting other humans? I can't imagine a loving God wanted my father to kill my mother. But I'm sort of confused because I also can't imagine that the world and all of us in it are just accidents.

"I guess what I'm trying to say is that I believe in something. But right now, I see things running sort of like you teach us in science class, kind of like physics. You know, maybe all of this, the planets, the world, the people are all like wind-up toys that God made and then let loose inside the universe, with rules like gravity and stuff like that to keep us penned in, and then whatever happens just happens. It's kind of like when Father Alfred tells us the school rules every year and then sets us loose.

"But who am I, Sister? I'm just a kid trying to be honest with ya. I'm just not sure I'm ready to sign on to anything yet, you know? Maybe you can just let me keep listening to you and keep thinking and praying really hard about all this stuff and I'll develop some of my own ideas as I grow up?"

Catholic sisters are not usually known for liberal open-mindedness, but knowing Jimmy's sad history and setting his questioning within that context, the sisters of St. Anne's rose above their dogma and arrived at an acceptance of the boy's personal ethos. Given the time and place, this in itself was perhaps a true miracle and proof of a higher power.

The goal of St. Anne's was to place kids with foster families as soon as possible, and most boys were gone before they turned twelve. Jimmy's love of St. Anne's and willingness to help the sisters with the upkeep of the place beyond what was required of him did not go unnoticed. While the other kids came and went, Jimmy settled in, eventually walking down the hill out back each day to attend the Providence Street Junior High School. On September 8, 1959, his seventeenth birthday, Jimmy asked Father Alfred for his signature so that he could enlist in the military, which the Father did with pride. Jimmy had developed into an obedient and reliable young man, and would fit in well in the armed forces. He approached a Marine recruiter, took the tests, and, while a bit skinny and small of stature, was found to be physically, medically, and morally fit and, although lacking a high school diploma, in possession of sufficient aptitude to absorb the rigorous training in store.

The night sky lit up with parachute flares and tracer rounds, and incoming rockets left stomach-punching bass thuds in the warm clear sea. In a little over a year, Jimmy had transitioned from a successful training at Paris Island to his first Marine Corps adventure aboard the amphibious Landing Craft Infantry assault ship, LCI Barbara J. He had boarded the ship in Miami the first week of January 1961 for what was supposed to be an important operation and for which he had eagerly volunteered. Winter in Miami was like summer in New England. The warm breezes were unlike anything Jimmy had experienced during training in South Carolina, and the warmth helped him felt at ease with the world.

The Barbara J. left Miami and headed to Vieques Island

off the east coast of Puerto Rico for invasion training. Jimmy and his comrades still did not know what was in store for them, but it was beginning to look interesting. In late March, Jimmy and the Barbara J., back from training, departed Stock Island, Key West, Florida for Puerto Cabezas, Nicaragua and arrived on April 2, 1961. There, he and his group learned their mission. The Barbara J. was to help invade and liberate Cuba. The ship would land Jimmy and several hundred other fighters comprised of US Marines and Cuban nationals on Red Beach, in a place called Bahía de Cochinos, or the Bay of Pigs, on the southwest side of the island. They were told the Cuban people would welcome them as liberators and join them in the fight, which made sense and gave all the fellows a pretty good feeling about the mission. But what gave Jimmy and the other Marines particular pragmatic comfort was the guarantee of supporting US air strikes on Cuban air bases so Castro's air force couldn't come kill them.

The Barbara J. arrived on station with the other ships of the invasion fleet at 1730 hours on April 16, 1961. The ships circled and formed a column, and then began their run in to the beaches. Five miles from the mouth of Bahía de Cochinos, the Barbara J. left the column and began heading toward her target, Red Beach at Playa Largo, the bitter north end of the Bay. That's about the time the incoming rockets arrived. Even though they all missed, the concussions busted open the riveted seams of the Barbara J. and she began taking on water. Down below, the Marines were already sweating from the heat and the rockets and cascades of warm seawater inspired additional perspiration, curses and prayers.

"Yea though I walk through the valley of the shadow of death I shall fear no evil for thou art with me and thy rod and staff…"

"Fuck rods and staffs Annunziato, pray to your god for some fucking air cover!"

Barbara J.'s run into Red Beach was aborted and she rounded back towards the mouth of the Bay with instructions to head back out to sea about 15 miles and wait. That's when the Cuban Air Force arrived in the form of a Hawker Sea Fury, coming in low and fast from the beach. Thankfully the plane only made one short strafing pass at the Barbara J., missing her with a quiver of rockets but punching several holes in the superstructure with 20 MM cannon rounds. That night, the leaky Barbara J. was ordered to unload Jimmy and the 499 other fighters into a Landing Craft Utility (LCU) for a run into the beach. The troops geared up but were then told to stand down, as calculations showed the LCU wouldn't arrive at Red Beach until after sunrise. Jimmy began to realize that this great adventure was turning into something quite different, and they were all about to get the royal shaft. His Marine Corps training had emphasized repetition, precision, predictability, and dependability. Here they were with conflicting orders, knee-jerk responses, leaking ships, no air cover, and an active Cuban Air Force. At about noon the Barbara J. along with three LCUs, loaded with supplies, started for the beach again with a predicted landing time of 1800 hours and guaranteed air cover. On the way in, the brigade commander on the beach radioed that some of his troops were now fighting in the water and he was out of ammunition and under direct fire from Cuban tanks 500 yards away. In his last transmission he said he was destroying his equipment and heading for the woods. That was when the Barbara J. turned around and Jimmy went home.[2]

The Bay of Pigs marked a watershed for Jimmy. He had enlisted and trained to kill bad guys, save his buddies, protect America, be honorable, and make a difference. Instead, he was lied to about the mission and then sealed inside a piss and vomit filled pressure cooker for several days where the Cubans were allowed to shoot at him without him being able to shoot back. The brave men they landed on the beach to do their jobs were not given the air support they were promised and were then left there to die when things unwound. Once the Cubans had finished off everyone on the beach, the Marines were ordered to turn tail and run. He had a lot to think about.

The remainder of Jimmy's time in the Marines was marked with drinking, absences without leave and time in the brig. But just like the medical student in the back of the classroom who gets poor grades is still called Doctor in the end, despite his poor performance Jimmy received an honorable discharge and left the Marine Corps in 1962. He watched the Cuban missile crisis that year on television in a bar, only glancing away from the screen long enough to spit his dip into an empty Coke bottle. The next year, in a different bar, he bought everyone a celebratory drink when the programming was stopped to announce the assassination of President Kennedy. Jimmy understood what it felt like to be left hanging out to dry by a democrat politician, and he would be dipped in shit and deep-fried before he ever voted for one.

Jimmy had been making $275 each month for his three years in the Marines. He drank up one year of saved pay while enlisted. He drank up another year of savings after his discharge while working odd jobs in New Orleans and Daytona. That still left him with some cash to take him to his next stop in life. One morning, he woke up in his rooming house in Florida. He was hung over like every other morning, but he felt unsettled. Maybe it was the understanding that his pot of gold was running out. Maybe he was just bored and needed something new. Maybe it was a desire to revisit the past and confront old ghosts. Whatever it was, in 1964 Jimmy went back home to New England and to his old hometown of Athol, where as a veteran he quickly found a job with the Massachusetts Department of Transportation, MassDOT District 2.

In addition to the work, the MassDOT offered Jimmy companionship with other fellows similar to him, simple decent guys that had also never finished high school. They were a peculiar group with a worldview shaped by their experiences in Massachusetts north of Route 495. These were guys who only strayed south to Boston maybe once every few years for a Red Sox game. But Jimmy was different. He had travelled, seen the world, and had adventures beyond their imaginations. The fellows gradually learned this and became an enthusiastic audience for Jimmy's war and drinking stories. They listened intently to him as he complained about democrat presidents messing up the country with things like civil rights, his views set firmly within a cracker-based Daytona Beach worldview. And they never tired of Jimmy recounting his Bay of Pigs experience. No matter how many times he told the story of buying everyone a beer when Kennedy was assassinated, they laughed like they were hearing it for the first time, slapping each other on the back and shaking their heads in amazement and admiration. Jimmy was becoming a legend in his old hometown, and that made him feel good. Reliving Cuba in those stories also felt good. That island adventure, regardless of how short an experience and how messed up it turned out to be, was strangely enough the high point of his life.

The work at DOT was straightforward and predictable, and there was plenty of time to goof off. He found a girl, Meghan Krawchuk, who reminded him of the gauzy memories he still had of his mother. She was three years younger than Jimmy, the second child of three, and like most middle children, felt overlooked when she was a kid. The oldest had the longest relationship with her parents and the youngest was the baby everyone paid attention to. Meghan leveraged school in an effort to gain her parents affection. She studied hard and strove to always be the teacher's pet, which she usually attained.

In early September, 1957, the year Meghan started eighth grade in Athol, while she was fretting about her belly fat and pimples, nine black students were trying to attend school at Central High in Little Rock, Arkansas and not get lynched. Despite the physical threats and abuse from American and Confederate flag-carrying Arkansans that America watched on TV, and with the help of the Army's 101st Airborne Division sent personally by President Eisenhower, those kids were finally able to attend school in late September.

Americans, especially rural Americans, searched for and found on their TV sets simple answers to complex questions about the world outside their small towns. Meghan found answers to her questions on race at home. Although there were no black families in Athol, Meghan's parents—like many others—had strong views formed almost exclusively by what they watched on the fuzzy black and white screen in the living room and conversations they had when they got together at things like church events with people informed by their TVs. Their conclusions were simple. Blacks are coddled too much and white people are treated unfairly. Blacks are lazy and white folks are industrious. Blacks are less evolved and can never attain the mental status of a white person. All of these beliefs helped the racially sequestered and poorly educated of Athol make sense of what they felt was the overwhelming complexity of the modern world. It also allowed them to feel consistently superior to an entire race of human beings. This was the wisdom conferred upon Meghan by her parents, intellectual gifts she could in turn pass on to her children.

In social studies class that fall, Mrs. Gibson gave the class a weekend assignment: learn what happened at Central High School in Little Rock and explain why it happened? Meghan worked hard on her answer and listened more closely to her parents talk around the house about what they had watched on TV and discussed at church. She came up with a "three-point" approach that Mrs. Gibson encouraged them to use: "It's easy for most people to remember three things, but it gets harder as you increase that number. So, if you are going to give a speech, try to limit it to three parts."

By Sunday night Meghan had her three points:

1. The kids and teachers at Central High didn't want black kids attending their school. Black kids never attended Central High before so why should they now?

2. Black kids are not as smart as white kids. That isn't their fault, it's just how God made them. Because they are not as smart, they go to different schools so that they can learn slower and don't hold the smarter white kids back.

3. The teachers and students tried to keep the black kids from attending Central High and told them to go back to their own High School, but President Eisenhower said they needed to let those kids attend. Now the white kids won't get as good an education.

On Monday Meghan was the first to raise her hand when Mrs. Gibson asked who would like to present first. She was dressed in tight blue jeans cuffed up to just below her knees, white bobby socks, loafers, a red and white plaid button down shirt and a denim jacket with the word "Princess" across the back that her Aunt Helen had embroidered in flowing yellow script. She walked briskly to the front of the class with a swagger born of so many academic victories and delivered her three-point answer with authority. When she concluded, Mrs. Gibson, who usually showered Meghan with praise, looked uncomfortably at the floor. "All right Meghan, that is certainly one way to look at it. Who would like to comment or share their three points?"

Robin Lakewood quickly raised his hand. Robin's father, Peter, worked at Harvard Forest, just down the road in Petersham. The 4,000-acre forest was used by the Faculty of Arts and Sciences of Harvard University for student research. Peter was a laboratory support technician and kept the electrical and plumbing systems running smoothly. This position exposed him to a broad range of research being conducted by faculty and students from around the world in the new field of ecology. Robin's mother Laura had a greenhouse and sold cut flowers to shops in Boston. Both of his parents were free thinkers and a bit Bohemian for the time and place, and consequently Robin was a bit different from the rest of the kids in Athol. He walked slowly to the front of the classroom. Robin was tall for his age, slender, and dressed in blue jeans cuffed once at the bottom of each leg with a simple white t-shirt tucked into his waist and a pair of fresh white Keds his mother had just bought him for the start of the school year. His three points were:

"One: three years ago, the Supreme Court said it was unfair to prevent kids in America from attending their local school just because of their skin color. Last year, there were no black kids at Central High even though there are more than five hundred black kids who live near Central High. Most of those kids want to attend Central High, but only seventeen were allowed to attend this year, and eight of those kids chickened out before school started.

"Two: the kids chickened out because they knew how

mean the white people could be and how they hated black people just because of their skin color. Turns out they were right. The first day of school one hundred white soldiers from Arkansas and four hundred mean white people didn't allow them to attend school, yelled at them and called them terrible names, knocked one girl down, and threatened to kill them all.

"Three: this mean behavior kept going, so President Eisenhower sent soldiers from up north to make those southern white people stop being mean to those kids. He did that because our Declaration of Independence says that all people are created equal including black people and that God gave us all the same rights which includes being able to go to your neighborhood school."

Mrs. Gibson smiled, brushed her eyes, and gave Robin a hug. The realization of what had just happened first became clear in the pit of Meghan's stomach, followed by her brain, which then triggered a desire within her to run. After that, Meghan lost her passion for Mrs. Gibson's social studies class, and her grades in general slipped for the rest of her school experience. She was a smart girl and self aware enough to realize that Robin had unintentionally taken a piece of her that day. As a result, she felt smaller and inferior, whereas before she had been on top. This clarity of understanding filled her with a very specific hatred for smarty-pants people like Robin—elites—that would deepen and serve to influence her throughout the rest of her life.

Jimmy diligently courted Meghan and married her in 1967, in what they referred to as their "redneck summer of love". Meghan was a looker, a bit heavy through the middle, but definitely above his pay grade, as he used to say. She was also smart, being as she had graduated from high school. For Meghan, Jimmy wasn't necessarily what she had dreamed about as a young girl, the handsome prince who would sweep her away and out of Athol. But he was charming, he was kind of a war hero, he had a job with the state, and he needed looking after. She was also ready to get away from her parents. Meghan quickly took over as the family brain, keeping the household books and paying the bills with Jimmy's paycheck and by working from time to time as a waitress in the always-struggling downtown of Athol.

Jimmy had found an Oedipal mother in Meghan, replacing the one he had lost in Athol so many years ago. In the early years of their marriage, he found her infantilizing to be both sweet and comforting. Together they bought motor-cycles, snowmobiles, and lots of TV sets. Jimmy brought home from work his role of resident philosopher and social funny man and, during the short New England summers, they had cookouts nearly every weekend—with lots of guests, whom he regaled with stories of far-off places.

Over the years they raised two children, Timmy and Shannon, who both arrived during the early 1970s. The kids grew up seeing their father was well respected by his friends because of his worldly experiences and his sense of humor. Although they also saw that he was dependent upon their mother due to her superior intellect, Timmy and Shannon were encouraged by Jimmy and Meghan to recognize both of their parents' god-given "country common sense" that allowed them to figure anything out and made them subject experts on everything. Jimmy let Meghan orchestrate the kids' academic and social lives, given she was the brains of the family. Meghan got Shannon a new satin jacket every year with "Princess" embroidered on the back, and back-channeled her into cheerleading, even though she was a little thick in the middle like her mom and was always the base of the pyramid. From the time Shannon was four years old, Meghan had annual Glamour Shots photos taken of her daughter, which she hung around the house wherever she could find an empty space on the wall that was not covered by inspirational phrases like "Live! Laugh! Love!" She pushed Timmy, who had a small frame like his dad, into wrestling, despite his reluctance. Meghan felt that boys needed to play sports, and that wrestling was where kids who weren't good at any of the other sports could go. She was also convinced this might help his low self-confidence. Jimmy thought wrestling was for homos but kept his mouth shut. Timmy was regularly thrown, choked, pinned, and humiliated, both on and off the mat, but kept at it nonetheless to please his mother.

As teenagers in the late 1980s, the kids informed Jimmy and Meghan that they had figured out their parents were in fact two full of shit dumbass rubes, then both of them shuffled successively out of high school and into their own rundown apartments in downtown Athol. Jimmy and Meghan were very proud. They had successfully parented two young adults and ensured they got a good education and then got out of the house. The kids found minimum wage jobs with no effort and no responsibilities in the 1980s, cocaine in the 1990s, and transitioned to crystal meth in the early 2000s. They dragged Jimmy and Meghan through each addiction replete with illness, money problems, unwanted pregnancies, and unemployment. Each new drug discovery, new grandchild, new crisis, further damaged the post-kids American dream that Jimmy and Meghan had seen themselves living, progressively draining their finances, and invalidating their parenting.

As a coping mechanism during the kids' cocaine period, Meghan was born again and found Jesus in a small white evangelical church filled with other people with problems, whether drugs, pornography, alcohol or whatever. The church was a mixed bag of damaged fruits, and she felt at ease with these people, many of whom were even more messed up than she was. Meghan studied the Bible fastidiously during her honeymoon with Jesus, and quickly added fifty pounds to her already expanding frame. She found the flawed characters of the Old Testament comfortingly familiar. Many could have been cut right out of Athol. There was murder, theft, and fornication—and wonderful supporting justifications for so many of the thoughts she had that people like Robin Lakewood made her feel bad about.

Justification for slavery and racism (Genesis): "Cursed be Canaan; a servant of servants shall he be unto his brethren." Check.

Hatred for homosexuals (Leviticus): "If a man lies with a male as with a woman, both of them have committed an abomination; they shall surely be put to death." Check.

Knocking up someone else's wife (Samuel): "One evening David got up from his bed and walked around on the roof of the palace. From the roof he saw a woman bathing. The woman was very beautiful, and David sent someone to find out about her. The man said, 'She is Bathsheba, the daughter of Eliam and the wife of Uriah the Hittite.' Then David sent messengers to get her. She came to him, and he slept with her. Then she went back home. The woman conceived and sent word to David, saying, 'I am pregnant.'" Check.

Dirty deeds (Samuel): "In the morning David wrote a letter to Joab and sent it with Uriah. In it he wrote, 'Put Uriah out in front where the fighting is fiercest. Then withdraw from him so he will be struck down and die.' So while Joab had the city under siege, he put Uriah at a place where he knew the strongest defenders were. When the men of the city came out and fought against Joab, some of the men in David's army fell; moreover, Uriah the Hittite died." Check.

Kill those who hold different beliefs (Deuteronomy): "Only in the cities of these peoples that the Lord your God is giving you as an inheritance, you shall not leave alive anything that breathes. But you shall utterly destroy them:

the Hittite and the Amorite, the Canaanite and the Perizzite, the Hivite and the Jebusite, as the Lord your God has commanded you, so that they may not teach you to do according to all their detestable things which they have done for their gods, so that you would sin against the Lord your God." Check.

And on and on and on it went. The Old Testament was so rich with what Meghan needed most that she very rarely ventured into the Gospels of the New Testament. Quite frankly, Jesus sounded a lot like Robin Lakewood, kind of aloof and condescending. During this transformation period, Meghan began to hoard. She called it "collecting". It started with broken electronics, dishware, and worn-out shoes, and evolved into old *TV Guides*, magazines, and paper and plastic bags from the supermarket. She quickly covered every flat surface in the house, then shelves overflowed, hallways became choked, and the basement floor a deep sludge of rotting cardboard boxes filled with more debris and filth. Given his ambivalence to religion, notwithstanding the efforts of the sisters at St. Anne's orphanage, Jimmy found Meghan's conversion to be disturbing but understandable. Yet, the hoarding chapped at him. The sisters at St. Anne's and later the Marine Corps had instilled a regimen of cleanliness and order that he had always found comforting. Meghan's born-again clutter and filth were not comforting. But it was the fundamental lack of logic in the whole born-again "collecting" ethos that irritated him the most: hoarding while you're waiting to leave it all behind and bug out of this world with Jesus.

"Meghan, tell me again, when is Jesus coming?"

"I think he's already here Jimmy, yes indeed, my sweet baby Jesus may already be here."

"And what happens now?"

Meghan smiled angelically. "After my Jesus grows up, he

is going to take me up to heaven and then fuck over the entire world, which includes atheists like you, my friend."

Jimmy's lip curled in a grin. "So, given you ain't here for long baby, and you can't take it with you, why do we have all this shit around here? I can't walk down the hallways anymore. Don't you think you should be packing light for your trip with Jesus, you know, maybe just a nightgown, toothbrush, and some slippers?"

"Fuck you Jimmy McCauley, I love you dearly but you're gonna burn in hell."

Jimmy hung in there and retired the day he turned sixty-five. Ten months later he claimed his full social security and, on top of the MassDOT pension, this gave him a comfortable financial cushion upon which to relax and think. So, in 2009, Jimmy retreated to his garage with his tumorous coon dog Stella and his thoughts. He stopped shaving, grew his patchy, stringy gray hair out long, then tied it back in a greasy bun. Then he bought a cowboy hat, boots, and a large silver steer head belt buckle, and wore them every day. Shit, if Meghan could be reborn, then so could he. Jimmy's time at St. Anne's had not imbued in him much religion, and the Marines had failed to instill a respect for authority, but both experiences had trained him to be disciplined, neat, and clean. Hardy Boys novels had taught him the ins and outs of how to build a first-rate clubhouse and he applied this formative knowledge to home improvements. Those centered in the garage gave him the ability to burn gas, oil, coal, or wood to heat the house. There were only three chimney fires as a result. Where Meghan's world inside the house was one of filth and clutter and Jesus, Jimmy's garage was the epitome of juvenile technology, secular order, and cold beer.

When visitors commented on the garage's hygiene, Jimmy always responded the same: "Look, you never know when you might have to do an appendectomy on the floor."

And there were plenty of visitors. His friends from MassDOT appeared almost daily to enjoy Jimmy's refurbished fridge, filled with the cheapest beer he could find that week and a TV tuned alternately to Fox News and the Weather Channel. Jimmy also had an old computer hooked to the internet so he could quickly research things for the guys like: "what animal has the biggest balls?" A search from his garage quickly informed the crew that, holy shit, the balls of Rafinesque's big-eared bats make up more than eight percent of the critter's body mass—apply that calculus to a two-hundred-pound guy in the garage and he'd wind up with sixteen pounds of balls swinging between his legs. Case closed. The slow, methodical, all-day beer drunk soothed the rough edges of their lives, and simple companionship helped them make sense of the complicated, ever-changing world safe within the familiarity of Jimmy's garage. It also allowed Jimmy to keep court, like he used to do at work.

"You know, people ask me, 'Jimmy McCauley' they say, 'your wife is fat, ugly and filthy, so why do you stay married to her?' And I tell 'em, 'cause she's got worms. 'You stay married to her because she's got worms', they say? You bet I do! 'But why', they ask? Because I love to fish!"

Like a bar, closing time at Jimmy's garage was predictable and firm. He would get out an old guitar and sing Lynyrd Skynyrd's "Simple Man", the one song he had taught himself to play. Then Jimmy would turn off the Narragansett beer light and tell everyone to go home.

After two years of steady drinking, Jimmy's initial boredom had evolved into agitation and was on its way to irritation. Then 2012 arrived. There were over seven hundred deaths from opioids in Massachusetts that year and Timmy McCauley was one of them. He had injured his back several years earlier around the time he turned forty, and as a result of managing that pain developed a significant Oxycontin habit like millions of other Americans. In 2012 Timmy's doctor, concerned about his professional liability, felt he should be over the pain and cancelled his prescription. Timmy now had a king-sized addiction, no prescription, and no immediate choice except to get some kind of opioid in his body any way he could. The convenient answer resided within the always-available heroin that had been arriving in increasing quantities in recent years.

The heroin that killed Timmy began its trip towards Athol—and Timmy's central nervous system—in a Mexican poppy field owned by Carlos Jiménez, the head of a small cartel in the border town of Juárez. Carlos smuggled loads across the border through the Sunland Park landfill whose northern boundary is the Southern Pacific railway line and southern boundary a porous chain link fence constituting the border between the United States and the Mexican state of Chihuahua.[3] The landfill operated twenty-four hours a day, seven days a week and, while opposed by residents and citizens groups, was strongly supported by local politicians, many of whom were said to have subsequently retired in style —far away from Sunland Park. The manifests and contents of waste haulers arriving at the gates were all carefully checked before being directed to an active cell for disposal. The empty roll-off trucks would then head quickly out and back towards their original destinations with nothing but a wave from the guard. It was those empty trucks that first started carrying Carlos' marijuana and cocaine up north in 1987, and were now hauling the latest drug in his product line, heroin. Carlos had explained the new business model to his boys in this way.

"Listen amigos, these are patriotic Mexican flowers we grow, and this is patriotic Mexican heroin we make from those flowers. Those dumb white gringos are weak and lazy, and they are all hooked on our shit now. Northern Europeans in general are genetically programmed such that they are easily addicted, which makes them really great customers. But the most important part of this business model is that it's not really them who pay us anyway because most of the white trash that buys our shit are on welfare. It's the American government who gives the white trash the money every month—the white trash in turn gives us that money—we convert that money into guns, girls, and more heroin. The white American trash gets fucked up, we get our money, and the American government, that has very deep pockets, gets stuck with our bill at the end of the evening. What's bad for those pendejos del norte is good for us. What's bad for the American government is good for México. *Que viva México*!"

The boys all answered in unison: "*¡Viva!*"

"OK amigos, *a darle, que es mole de olla!*"

Timmy was cremated and Meghan stashed the plastic bag containing his ashes in the back of a crowded closet where she found a bit of room in a cardboard box filled with old underwear that no longer fit her. Jimmy refused to attend the small service at Meghan's church. He said Timmy had made his own bed, took his own life and that was that: no hand of God, no divine providence, no fate, just death, end of story, period. Shannon, who had been close to her brother, sat silently at the service then went straight home, packed her bags and left town. Some said she had gone to Vegas and was hooking on the strip. Others said she was drying out in an ashram in Arizona. She had simply disappeared herself.

Timmy's death was followed quickly by the Sandy Hook school shooting in December, and the subsequent conspiracy theory that the Muslim President and his socialist government were preparing to confiscate everybody's guns. Jimmy had more than a few guns, and there were plenty of preexisting ersatz intellectual rabbit holes for him to burrow into as the Sandy Hook conspiracy theory evolved.

The San Diego McDonalds shooting in 1984: "Yep fellas, believe you me, a WHOLE bunch of folks got shot up out there in California for sure...BUT...wait for it now...they wasn't shot up by no mentally unstable white survivalist, no siree Bob, they was killed by the Ruskies so as to fool the government into taking our guns away and leave us defenseless for their invasion!"

The San Diego Cleveland Elementary School shooting in 1989: "Yep fellas, believe you me, there was some kids got shot up out there in California for sure...BUT...wait for it now...they wasn't shot up by no white supremacist, no siree Bob, they was killed by hit men hired by the gun-maker Bill Ruger to shut down foreign imports and get rid of his competition!"

The Oklahoma City bombing in 1995: "Yep fellas, believe you me, a WHOLE bunch of folks, mostly little kids, got blowed up down there in Oklahoma for sure...BUT... wait for it now...they wasn't blowed up by no ordinary patriotic white militia boy, no siree Bob, Timmy was part of a black ops Army group back at Fort Bragg smuggling drugs to fund covert activities and this was part of that whole deal, he's just the patsy, just like Oswald."

Jimmy paid special attention to Sandy Hook news on his now perpetual Fox News television and was especially tuned in to the back-story that was metastasizing on the internet. The real facts about the so-called shooting became the prime topic of conversation in the garage.

"You fellas tell me, you think it's a coincidence that there Adam Lanza just woke up one morning and out of the blue decided to shoot up that school and kill those little kids at the exact same time that democrat Hussein Obama was telling the U.N. that he was gonna sign away our gun rights?"

Jimmy kept looking for the answers to Sandy Hook, the

real answers. He knew what shitbirds these democrats were, and the back-story on Sandy Hook smelled like Cuba to him. He found his oracle in Alex Jones. By April 2013 Jones had come out and called bullshit on the shooting: "They staged Sandy Hook. The evidence is just overwhelming. And that's why I'm so desperate and freaked out. This is not fun, you know, getting up here telling you this. Somebody's got to tell you the truth.[4]"

Jimmy's life focus became Sandy Hook and Alex Jones. In March 2014, Jones doubled down on Sandy Hook and Jimmy read his thread after a day of paced deliberate drinking: "I've looked at it and undoubtedly there's a cover-up, there's actors, they're manipulating, they've been caught lying, and they were pre-planning before it and rolled out with it.[5]"

That was it. They had crossed the line. Actors. False flag. Betrayal. Jimmy's beer-soaked brain and Cuba-scarred heart told him he had seen this all once before. Goddammit, this was his country and he had to do something. That night he began planning the mission.

I believe it was at this very instant, at this initial condition, that my parents' future became cross-linked and sensitively dependent upon Jimmy's every thought and move. His battle planning began a butterfly effect, however subtle, that steadily bent his path towards that of my parents. His execution of the plan took their lives at the convergence of those two paths.

Jimmy's idea was to take the battle to the enemy, the democrats, the liberals. He knew where they were. They were encamped in pretty little towns all along Route 495, driving their shiny foreign cars into Boston every day to steal from the poor and put another manufacturer out of business and destroy jobs with their environmental bullshit. His plan, conceived in beer, was to use his 1976 F-150 pickup as a giant middle finger and drive it right into the heart of those Hussein-loving libtards who wanted to take away his second amendment rights with a false flag that any fool could see right through. Jimmy had kept this classic 460 cubic inch carbureted pickup pristine since he bought it used in 1987 and he festooned it with cardboard signs taped to the doors saying "Sandy Hook = False Flag" on the driver side and "when you come for my guns you better bring yours" on the passenger side. These complemented his bumper stickers, one a coiled "Don't Tread on Me" Tea Party snake and another that read, "If Jesus had a gun, he'd still be alive today," which Meghan had found for him. A flagpole with a five-foot by eight-foot quality Chinese-made American flag flapping in the breeze capped the message.

Like a godless prophet with a mission, Jimmy took his message down Route 2 the next morning on Thursday April 10th to confront the liberals in their rush hour, along with a six-pack of Narragansetts in a pail of ice and a fresh tin of Copenhagen dip. Jimmy left around 6:00 so that he could get out east on 495 before 7:30 and focus on the Route 3 and 93 junctions. My retired parents left our home in Stow that morning at 6:30 to head up to New Hampshire for a walk on the beach and some fried clam strips and a cold Stella at Petey's in Rye. I received an unusual message from my mother Elizabeth on my answering machine the day before while I was at the pistol range. The message was unusual not in its primary content, which described the plans for the next day, but in how she ended it. She told me that she would always love me and that she was proud that I was her son. My father James chimed in from the background with a 'me too Christopher.' I never doubted my mother loved me, but this type of message was very out of character for her. The weather was supposed to be unseasonably warm for their beach trip, with the temperature expected to reach into the balmy 60s.

Jimmy had downed two breakfast beers by the time he reached the 495 junctions, and he was really ready for a dip. He smiled as he accelerated into the steady right turning cloverleaf and felt the truck heel over and the comfortable push of the driver door against his left side. He muttered under his breath as he watched the tin of Copenhagen slide off the seat and onto the floor under his feet. While two early morning beers were clearly insufficient to render Jimmy McCauley drunk, they had relaxed him such that as he bent his head down, searching with his right hand to pick up his dip on the straightaway leading to 495, his left foot pressed down harder on the accelerator without him noticing. He was still rummaging around on the floor and accelerating as he merged onto 495 and did not see his truck crossing from the entrance lane to the middle lane, nor did he see my parents in the passing lane on the overpass when he struck their front right quarter panel. The truck's momentum drove their relatively light car into a section of Jersey wall that had been put in place by MassDOT late on a Friday afternoon and was never joined to its neighbors. It collapsed, allowing their Saab to leave the highway, fly through the air, and explode in flames on the train tracks below. Slumped on the side of the road by his barely damaged pickup, Jimmy told the state troopers through tears of shame what had happened, that he had been distracted, that he wasn't drunk, that he tried to save them, that everything was his fault. They listened, saw the empty beer cans in the cab, read him his rights, and took him in.

I didn't see much use in flying up to Massachusetts after my parents' accident as they were gone, and there was nothing that my presence in Stow could do about it. Besides, I had my hands full with sales meetings. I made many of the arrangements for their death certificates, and cremation from Texas, and travelled to Massachusetts a month later to clean out the refrigerator and see about an estate sale for the house and furniture. They kept a tidy New England home, with sparse but excellent Stickley furnishings and thoughtful antiques. The rooms were open, wide-planked pine floor spaces punctuated by a wool or silk oriental, depending upon its placement near or away from a doorway. Walking through the old house, I opened drawers I never had before and removed things I had previously no business touching. Like an archaeologist, I looked for clues about who my parents were in the limited remains they had left behind.

I walked the property out behind the house, enjoying the solitude and quiet of the New England spring, the small buds just opening in trees, and the early birds back from their migration. I stopped and looked down at an old pock-marked, rip-top coke can in the weeds at the edge of the field and picked it up, the soil spilling out of the small round holes in its sides. My parents gave me a BB gun for my ninth birthday. I loved the feel of the wood and metal, the look of the bright brass BBs, and their feel in my hand as I loaded them into the rifle's tubular magazine. I evolved from shooting paper targets to cans, as the cans made a noise and moved when you shot them. Then I graduated to glass jars, as you could destroy the jar with the shooting—providing kinetic, auditory, and structural feedback. The next evolutionary step was a bird, a sparrow that I shot out of a tree at a great distance. I marveled at my marksmanship as the little bird tumbled out of the tree. I was, however, not prepared for the wave of regret I felt as I stood over its beautiful still body, saddened that I had been the agent of its end, and more cognizant of the meaning of death than I had been that morning when I awoke. That was the last creature whose life I took with a gun, and I am happy about that. Not only don't

I shoot animals, I also do not shoot at human forms on paper targets and do not understand those who do. Are they trying to strategically desensitize themselves for the day they have the opportunity to take someone's life? Or is it pure fantasy, cosplay, where these men-children dress up, go to the range, and pretend to kill people? I guess these are unanswerable questions. What I do know is that to this day, when I think back on that sparrow, I still feel sorrow and a bit of shame as well.

I had thought about my parents' death before the accident, but always in highly theoretical terms. They were both born during the Depression, and were in their early eighties when they died. They were quite healthy, and I had assumed they would continue aging into their nineties, with death eventually occurring from the combined failures of naturally aging biological systems. When people at work heard about the accident, some responded by telling me that god works in mysterious ways, or that my parents are happier now that they are dead and with Jesus, or, to paraphrase from a letter written two thousand years ago by a guy who enjoyed persecuting Christians before he became a Christian, "don't worry, the Lord will kick Jimmy McCauley's ass for killing your folks". I am pretty sure that god didn't kill my parents on their way to Petey's that day, and who knows if they are with Jesus now or not. Some people seem to be pretty sure that god is a psychopathic killer and that Jesus runs a death-care center where everyone gets to hang out with him for eternity, eating fish and bread and drinking wine. Although I am unsure of what my parents' conception of the afterlife was, I am pretty sure that even though they enjoyed fish baguettes and wine, they would not appreciate eternity at the feet of anyone, even Jesus, as a reward for a life well lived.

In the end, we are all like aircraft in the sky: destined to end our flights at some point in time. If we don't have a premature equipment failure or a mid-air collision, then we have a long flight and the choice whether to end it in a controlled landing or ignore the low fuel warning and crash. I looked at my responsibility as that of an air traffic controller to eventually bring my parents in for a controlled landing if possible. I had also considered them outliving me, the air controller, given their robust New England constitutions and my bloated Texas corpus, albeit non Christi. The accident beat me and my premature death to the punch and left me feeling not so much alone without them as simply less tethered. Lacking any siblings or close relatives, my parents seemed to function like secondary anchors, not explicitly responsible for my security, but contributory and comforting nonetheless. The world also felt a bit colder and quieter.

I learned much about Jimmy and the accident at the time from an article in the Boston Globe. The writer had done a deep dive on the event and the contrast between the two families. In the time between the wreck and my visit, things got strange. Meghan, always Jimmy's caretaker, took it upon herself to defend her husband from what she said was a liberal conspiracy to railroad him into jail, despite Jimmy having admitted his culpability and having stuck with it. Meghan had seen an Obama/Biden bumper sticker in the Globe photograph of the back of my parents burned out car and, based upon this, claimed that in fact it was my parents who were not simply at fault but were the criminals. According to Meghan's conceptual model, my parents had seen and had deliberately run into Jimmy's truck because of his patriotic signs and flag and now the 495 liberals were trying to pin the blame on her man. She called it a witch-hunt and invoked the forty impoverished people considered outsiders by the Puritan Christians who were jailed for witchcraft in Middlesex County in 1692 as historic proof of her concept.

Jimmy served a year in the Middlesex Jail and House of Correction for the vehicular manslaughter of my parents. Every day Jimmy spent in jail, Meghan protested in front of the Worcester County Superior Court, despite Jimmy's crime occurring in Middlesex County. She had a boombox that played "Simple Man" on a loop and a small forest of cardboard signs. These informed passing readers about the Sandy Hook hoax, guns, the left-wing conspiracy that had imprisoned her husband, and that when Jesus arrived, the liberals would get more than just a boot in their ass. On cold days, she sneeringly informed anyone who would listen about the global warming hoax. Meghan was joined at times by what appeared to be clones carrying model replica AK47s, either bearded faces with fat bellies protruding from beneath too-small t-shirts, or pimply-faced skin and bones swimming in too-large blue jeans, all of them looking uncomfortable in their own skins, each clutching his Chinese toy weapon like a frightened child with a teddy bear.

During that year, I reached out to Jimmy through his attorney. I wanted to talk to him. I wanted to look him in the eye. I wanted to forgive him, but be confident he deserved my forgiveness. I wanted to be sure I was not a patsy. He and I were like loose frayed ends of a torn fabric. I thought if we were brought thoughtfully together, perhaps we could, with a few well-placed metaphysical basting stiches, mend the rip in the universe that the accident had opened up and go on with our lives, not untouched but perhaps more functional. Against his attorney's wishes, and despite Meghan's choleric threats, Jimmy agreed, and I flew from Austin to Boston in September to see him and also to see the leaves begin to turn color. In Texas the summer ends as an abrupt death in January when the leaves change quickly from green to brown and the sky from blue to slate gray. Autumn in New England is like an evening beach party huddled around a fire, a slow wildly colored celebration of summer's passing and does not hint at death. I flew Southwest to Logan, rented a compact car at Budget, and drove to the Best Western in Chelmsford just east of Stow. Several Dunkin Donuts restaurants were conveniently located between my hotel and the jail on Treble Cove Road in Billerica. The next morning, I picked up a large black coffee and a box of ten honey glazed Munchkins, and slowly and deliberately finished them one by one as I headed down Route 3 for the fifteen-minute drive.

The Middlesex Jail and House of Correction sits on a hill surrounded by razor wire across the street from the Vietnam Veterans Park. Entering the Jail is similar to passing through TSA security at the airport, except in addition to weapons, cellphones are also not allowed. Jimmy was housed with a nineteen-year-old kid from Lowell who got busted selling a small quantity of drugs, and they would typically spend eighteen hours each day together in their eighty square foot cell. Jimmy had four hours of visits allotted to him each month and he had agreed to give me one of those hours. When I walked into the common meeting room, I recognized his face right away but was taken aback by how small he stood, and how meek and sad he looked. I held his strong, sinewy hand, and we looked in each other's eyes. As we stood there holding each other, I thought I could feel something escape our bodies—like fog blown from the beach by a freshening breeze, leaving us a clearer space within which to speak. We sat down, and it was then that Jimmy shared with me the more intimate details of his life, the loss of his parents, growing up in an orphanage, the Bay of Pigs debacle, the life he had before Meghan and then with Meghan, his dreams for his children, and the sadness of reality. I would experience this visit again and gain additional appreciation of these and other events in my beyond-space-time recollections after my heart surgery. But much like a movie viewed multiple times, the first viewing is often the most profound.

"Christopher, I lost both my parents in one day, and that messed up my whole life. I'm the last person that would wish that kind of loss on anyone, and now I have gone and done it to you. And for what? Since I been in here, I been doing a lot of reading and Meghan, bless her heart, has been sending me Bible quotes. She sent me one from Leviticus that says because of my sins and because of the sins of my father, I am going to rot away just like he did. And what's awful is that it actually makes sense. I killed your mother and father because I am an ignorant, insecure, alcoholic just like my father who killed my mother. I am a pathetic piece of shit.

"I've also been in group therapy, and my therapist opened my eyes, and those of a couple other fellas to how we got screwed. That Alex Jones guy is a crazy motherfucker, and I am the dumbass who listened to him and charged down the road and did all that damage. I don't blame Jones. He's just a psycho piece of shit. I hold only myself responsible and I'm going to live with the regret I feel until the day I die."

I told Jimmy that I was a gun owner too, and shared the feelings I had in 1994 with the ban on federal assault weapons—especially the part that limited magazine capacity. Despite Presidents Ford, Carter, and Reagan and most of the American people supporting the ban, at the time I had a peculiar feeling that it was the first small step to boiling the frog and limiting our right to bear arms. But I also told him that I didn't understand the current anxiety that many had. Since 2004 I had been able to purchase any firearm I wanted and load it with any brand-new high capacity magazine I liked down in Texas. Jimmy's fight was with the state of Massachusetts, which continued to restrict magazines manufactured after 1994 to ten rounds, and not with President

Obama and the federal government. That was something he said he had not really heard about, much less considered.

"Listen Christopher, there is a big difference between the two of us, and I'm not talking education and money. You sound like you spent your life trying to understand facts and looking for the truth, and you don't need education and money to do that. Before all this happened, I thought I was just like you, maybe even cleverer than you, researching things, cyphering, plotting out all the connections. But really, we're mental opposites. I just retired from a meaningless job that allowed me to think as little as necessary and fuck off as much as possible. I got one kid who's dead from heroin and another that's who knows where doing who knows what and I got a crazy wife who prays every day for the Jews to chase the Muslims out of Jerusalem so that the Rapture can start and the world can finally come to an end. I deliberately went looking for that Alex Jones shit to escape my crappy reality. It wasn't no accident, and he didn't hoodwink me neither—I went out there and hoodwinked myself. His message was simple and consistent, just like fast food, and I didn't give a shit if it was good for me or not. Alex Jones is an asshole, no doubt, but I got nobody to blame but myself for letting him take a shit inside my head."

Jimmy and I spoke at length about many things, much of which had to do with our respective childhoods, and the hour went by very quickly. When it was time for me to leave, the visiting room was still filled with the same battered gray metal folding tables and filthy gray plastic chairs and unpleasant disinfectant smell. But somehow, like mineral rich water filling a cavity in muck can become a crystal-filled geode, the space inside that ugly world within which Jimmy and I coexisted for that time had changed for the better.

I think back often to this unusual and significant meta-morphic transformation that occurred during my visit with

Jimmy. After that visit, he made a point of calling me each year on the fourth of July to catch up on life. I don't really have much to share, so I generally steer him towards Cuba and those days at the Bay of Pigs, as I never tire of hearing about it, and Jimmy never tires of telling the tale. It may sound strange, but over time, I grew to genuinely like Jimmy McCauley. I think he liked me, too, and gradually forgave himself. And that is really good, because I have read that hatred and prejudice are neither worthwhile occupations nor travelling companions on the road of life for decent people.

For Meghan, the accident led her to another indecent rebirth, shifting her struggle greasily away from defending Jimmy to broadly railing against people she thought were like my parents, in order to fill the hole in her life. Meghan's rebirth organically guided her to Donald Trump in 2015. When he announced his candidacy, she heard, for the very first time, someone speak out loud the thoughts that people, like Robin Lakewood, had made her feel too ashamed to say. Meghan joined Trump's Massachusetts campaign, not to flip the eternally blue state to red, but to extend her middle finger to all the liberal smarty-pants that lived down state. Meghan leveraged her ignorance, arrogance, and intelligence within the Trump campaign and rose quickly to the top.

I tried to ignore the news of Meghan that would creep down from Massachusetts to Texas during this time, but it was impossible to completely mute her amplified voice, and her vociferous devotion to Trump even caught the ear of John Oliver. I find Mr. Oliver to be informed and thoughtful, and the content of his show—Last Week Tonight—disturbing. I appreciate him making me feel—even if he makes me feel bad. But he also makes me laugh from time to time, which I am not normally prone to do. One night, he did a brief segment on Meghan and the activism of the Massachusetts Trumpeters, followed by a much longer segment on the rock star Paul Pewson and his activism. Although the segments were not intended to dovetail, I could not help but draw parallels. Both Paul and Meghan were activists, of a retired person's vintage like me, and each was in love with his and her visions of America, which were as similar as Southern Sweet Tea and Long Island Iced Tea. They both thought modern songs had become girly, and used music from the past as a vehicle to express their rage. Unlike John Oliver, who earned a degree from the University of Cambridge, neither Meghan nor Paul possessed much formal education. Meghan had earned her high school diploma, and Paul was a high school dropout. Yet, leveraging this limited education, both Meghan and Paul had formed and held particularly strong beliefs regarding topics they lacked the fundamental knowledge to fully understand. Yet, they both gained voices with which to shout these amplified beliefs at anyone who would listen or was within earshot, as if they were of unique and significant value. Lacking any education or understanding of the subject and, despite watching the number of New England summer heating days increase each year, Meghan became a climate change denier. The equally lacking Paul howled about the impending climate apocalypse, while flying about in his own private jumbo jet. Guiding both of them to these divergent hubristic destinations was a recalcitrant faith in their respective experts, each scientist informing them about that which they did not understand. Paul's experts just fortuitously happened to be real scientists, and correct.

I believe what aided Meghan and Paul in their respective leaps of faith was their blind devotion to Christianity and its attendant dogma that defines truth from falsehood, truth from heresy, and truth from wishful thinking for them. Christian truth deeply permeated both of their lives, allowing each one to lay claim to god and demonize the other. On occasion, Paul confided to interviewers that he might perhaps be the messiah—while Meghan called him out and labeled him a pawn of Satan.

I am confident many of Mr. Oliver's viewers were astute enough to write off Meghan as a disturbed ignorant woman; however, I wonder how many were clear sighted enough to assess Mr. Pewson—who goes by the stage name of Bobo because it is funny—in a similar fashion? I suspect the internal properties of Mr. Oliver's viewers refract Bobo into a much more attractive light spectrum and maybe he is in fact quite different, but I don't think so. Both Meghan and Bobo formed their seminal understanding of reality as infants through experimentation. Ignorant, domineering fathers then informed them exactly how the real crude world works: it's a dog-eat-dog world, kid. Add to this the paradigm of structured mystical theater imposed by the church, and you have a brief, three-component definition of reality common to many on this planet: experimentation, yielding valuable yet infantile information, smothered by jaded paternal opinion born of ignorance, topped with dogmatic religious drama developed thousands of years ago by people with nefarious political motives. Absent lifelong experimentation and learning, Meghan and Bobo, and many others, are left with nothing but this crude kaleidoscope with which to view and interpret the world around them. They are preprogrammed—and in fact prefer—to be inculcated instead of inquiring, and de-formed instead of informed.

Regardless of this implicit bias, I still remain a fan of Mr. Oliver, and his show is really the perfect venue for these types of characters, as his genre of journalism is primarily engineered to make you feel. Print provides information and is the yin to the yang of an idiot with a megaphone, metaphorical or actual, screaming his or her interpretation, misinterpretation, or manipulation of that print at you. But Mr.

Oliver seems to straddle the line between information and indecency, between rational thought and rage, between hubris and self-deprecating humor, and while I continue to reject normal cable news, I have embraced this alternative vehicle he has created, despite remaining unsure of exactly what it is.

In late spring this year, I received a package in the mail. Inside was a letter from Jimmy's attorney telling me that Jimmy had contracted SARS-CoV-2, refused to go to the hospital and had died at home of COVID-19. In his final days, Jimmy left specific instructions that I should receive this package, and the attorney was fulfilling this final responsibility. I unwrapped the plain brown butcher paper package and lifted out a United States Marine Corps Mark 2 Ka-Bar combat knife, strapped within a well oiled and well-worn leather sheath, its compressed leather hilt nicked and darkened over many years by the oils from Jimmy's hand. As I held the knife, I considered what an appropriate object this was in which to inter Jimmy's DNA. I pulled the seven-inch blade from its sheath and ran my thumb across its edge, knowing what I would find. It was razor sharp and well honed.

SEVENTEEN

A CHANGING TIDE

The book of Ecclesiastes says there is a season for everything. This is the season for sweat in Texas. As I return back to my bench from beyond-space-time, the physical reality of my shirt's soaked armpits and the progressive dampening of my crotch remind me of this fact. Yes indeed, there is a season for everything. And when the time came for Berg, Laurie, and me to break down and refrain from embracing, we did. I had understood time and distance would broaden the divergences of our lives, but I hadn't considered the potential extent. Although I had reached out to him once by mail, I had not seen or spoken to Berg since 1980. Laurie and I had been a bit better at keeping in touch, but not much. It was shortly after the 2016 election when I saw a brief story on CNN about her. She had been appointed Director of the Office of Continuous Improvement (OCI) in the Office of the Administrator of the United States Environmental Protection Agency. The OCI's mission was to track all Agency actions of importance and respond swiftly to any perceived threats, whatever that means. I got her email address from the Agency website and sent her a brief note with my contact information. Several weeks later I got a late-night call from her. We hadn't spoken in almost 20 years. I could hear in her voice that she had consumed a bit of wine.

"Christopher, Christopher, Christopher it was soooooo great to get your email! How are Youuuuu?"

"I'm OK I guess, how are things in New York—or is it DC?"

Laurie still had an apartment in Manhattan on the Upper East Side that she had bought for a song in the mid-1980s. At the time she had furnished it with a king mattress on the floor, some folding chairs in the living room, no food in the refrigerator, and a plan to decorate properly one day. Almost thirty years later, the apartment was now worth several million dollars, and the furnishings had not increased or changed. Since her appointment at OCI she had rented a place in DC that came furnished.

"Oh, I'm not in New York or DC right now. I bought a condo in Jackson Hole and I'm out here getting some work done and skiing."

"A condo in Wyoming and skiing with friends, that sounds amazing!"

"Well I'm skiing, but not with friends. The men around here are all predatory idiotic assholes who think they are god's gift to the world and the women are dumb fucking cunts. But, hey, enough about me, what's up with you?"

I began to tell her of my growing health concerns, my seemingly pointless job selling products I hoped would never actually be used for their intended purpose, and my lack of friends, but she cut me off.

"That's great, that's great, that's great! Yeah, I don't have any friends in New York either, but who cares about that stuff? I'm in DC now and this new administration has been ordained by God and is the portal to the land of our dreams!"

"What dreams are those?"

"Come on, Christopher, our dreams in college of strong authoritative government, fiscal unrestraint, and giving the finger to the rest of the world. Deregulating industry so they can do what they need to do. Shutting down the tree huggers so we don't have to listen to their whining. Freedom to say whatever you want to whomever you want, whether they happen to be rich or poor, a professional athlete or a handicapped journalist. Call a loser a loser and treat him appropriately, instead of throwing money at him. Make America great again. Those dreams!"

Did I really have those dreams back then? I think I might have felt myself slip a bit that night, reaching back for understanding, but I'm not sure. I do remember that I fought the feeling. I also recall really trying to understand and relate to the emotion I felt gushing out of the phone.

"I'm not sure, Laurie. I'm a bit confused these days. I think a lot about you and Berg and our lives together back then, but I have read that memories are deformable and reborn in a slightly different form each time they are recalled.[1] I think this is correct, as many of my memories seem incongruous with what I see and hear in the world these days. I remember quite clearly that we had great aspirations, but I am less clear now on the precise specifics."

"Well, Berg, that rat bastard, he really struck gold."

"Gold?"

"Yeah, gold, I am speaking figuratively, of course. Remember, the last time you and I spoke, he had gone silent on me for a while, and we were both a bit concerned? Well, about five years ago I got a call from him, out of the blue. Not only was he alive, he had struck it rich with his Central

American import business, and then got out while the getting was good."

"Where was he? What was he doing?"

"Where was he? Who fucking knows? If I had asked, he probably would have lied. What was he up to? Yes, well that was the interesting part of the conversation."

"How so?"

"Well, we talked about the old days, and our dreams for taking this country back to greatness. He said he had begun formulating a plan to gain a new voice for our vision."

"A new voice?"

"Yeah, Berg said that the only people that got heard these days were the real asshole politicians, moon-faced cretin movie stars, journalists, and white evangelical Christian preachers. Unlike me, he has no political connections except those from his old Central American business, and those are definitely not viable for public viewing. Although charming and talented, he acknowledged he was too old to begin an attempt to break into show business—and as everyone knows, most of us engineers can barely write our names, so journalism was out too."

"Oh my, that leaves preaching?"

"Yeah, preaching, and why not? Here's what he said: 'Hey look, I am definitely white, and the word evangelical comes from the Greek word "euangelion," which means "good news" and that's what I am all about, baby, I feel like I've been preaching the good news my whole life, so the whole package, as crazy as it sounds, works really well for me.'

In a perverse way it made sense to me, too. Remarkable sense. Berg had always possessed the gift of persuasion and the analysis of his pathway options, and the best-fit solution was something perhaps only an engineer could really appreciate. Laurie and I spoke for a while longer. She asked if I was on Facebook or Instagram, and I told her I wasn't. She asked me to email her a photo of myself, which I did, and I have not heard from her since.

I read about Berg in the Austin American Statesman this spring during the first COVID surge. They had a photo of him. His face had changed somewhat with time, but it was not the awful descent mine had taken, and he looked quite good. I wasn't all that surprised. Berg had followed through with his idea. He was now a roaming evangelical preacher with a popular YouTube channel, and the story in the Statesman was about his upcoming visit to a Houston mega-church, despite the pandemic, to preach the good news. I found an email address on his website and wrote him a brief note, told him about my parents, my health, my life, my routines, and my despair. With a feeling of familiarity, I sent the email, didn't hold my breath and Berg didn't respond.

EIGHTEEN

THE END OF THE BEGINNING

Hisssssssssssss, bongo bongo, hisssssssss, bongo bongo. That cacophony of hissing and bongos may well be what keeps pulling me back to this bench and to this beyond-space-time reality. If I could only move to turn my head, I would have a look around, but the heat is like a lead weight now on my chest and shoulders, forcing my slow assimilation into this bench. The roar of a jet in the sky above briefly breaks the hypnosis, and I struggle to cock my head upwards towards the spiraling multi-colored contrails and the evil sulfurous sun and try desperately to stop thinking. I must have slipped again. Fog is rising off the river, hissing as it scuds along the creeping gelatin. I can barely breathe, the air is so thick.

"It's a hot motherfucker today, isn't it?"

My head turns slowly, involuntarily toward the voice. Berg. Berg is sitting next to me on the bench. He is wearing white linen pants, alligator loafers with no socks, a thin alligator skin belt, a pink Ermenegildo Zegna polo shirt with the collar turned up, and a gold Patek Philippe Grand Complications wristwatch with an alligator band.

He is trim and fit, the skin on his face quite tight as if maybe he had some work done. His hair is thick, and he has colored it reddish brown. His skin tone is a uniform bronze that looks lightly spray-tanned. He is not wearing a mask, and his New York accent, while not completely gone, is complemented by a slight, delicate and perhaps deliberate southern drawl. Berg looks like so many of my old domestic clients.

"Christopher, you look fucking terrible."

"Yes, I know. Berg, you are looking quite well."

"Thanks, I feel great! Life is good. Things are happening! You wouldn't believe all the young Christian ass I am getting!"

"Christian ass?"

"Yeah, no pussy, they save that for marriage, but the market for ass is wide open, get it, wide open? These evangelical girls have an interesting concept of virginity that doesn't extend to ass—and frankly that's fine with me.[1]"

"I saw you in the Statesman."

"Yeah, I know. I got your email."

"You didn't reply?"

"No, fuck that, I'm busy these days Christopher. But you told me your daily routine, and knowing you, you wouldn't deviate from it. I knew I would find you right here right now."

"You knew I would be here in this specific space, at this specific time?"

"Yes, motherfucker. Boy, it's hotter than hell, but it's great to see you and I wanted to thank you in person for changing my life."

"Changing your life?"

"Yeah, changing my whole fucking life and helping us to maybe make our dreams come true. That letter you sent me when I was offshore, about you delivering Stingers to those rag heads in Pakistan, that letter really got me thinking: hey, if Christopher can be a hero then I can too."

"Rag heads?"

"Yeah, it looks like in the end buddy you were actually on the wrong side, helping those terrorists kill Russians. But that's OK, not everyone can back the right horse or be in the right place at the right time."

"The wrong side?"

"Yeah, I got so fired up by your letter, I went off to help our freedom fighting brothers down in Central America and kill me some Sandinistas."

"Kill Sandinistas?"

"Yeah, I mean, what were we supposed to do, abandon our brothers in their quest to restore democracy to Nicaragua? Allow the Sandinistas to consolidate Soviet influence and incite Communist revolution throughout Latin America?"

"Soviet influence?"

"Yeah, Soviet, not Russian—those are two very different things, Christopher. The Russians are our friends. We can learn a lot from them about strong conservative governance."

"Friends?"

"You bet they are. Your letter helped me see that I had to support those brave men and women risking their lives for the restoration of democracy. I mean, what would have happened in 1776 if the French hadn't helped us out? It's kind of like now, where would we be if our friends the Russians hadn't helped us out in the 2016 election, right?"

"So, you helped brave men and women fight the Sandinistas? I never saw that."

"How could you have fucking seen it? Well, anyway, I was a little too late for that, so it never happened, but it's the thought that counts, right?"

"The thought?"

"Yeah, the intention, the desire, the fucking thought. I had the intention, and that's the important thing."

"Too late?"

"Yeah, I did what I could to support them from back here in the States in the late eighties, pretty mundane supply chain shit, you know, but by the time I really got hooked up internationally in the nineties, the fighting was all over. The thing is, like in all conflicts, war machinery gets left behind, some of it physical, some of it conceptual, but lots of it still quite useful. A few of us just kept one of the moneymaking machines operational for a while longer and we made ourselves a killing."

"A killing?"

"Yeah, made a financial killing with a war machine, kind of a double entendre, huh? I got in for about ten years, moved a mountain of flake, then got out. That's what old Zachary Swan used to say: in for ten—or was it twenty?—then out. I made beaucoup dineros, my friend, so much I can't keep them here in America. Not going to do it, wouldn't be prudent!" Berg wiggled his fingers at me and cackled.

"Beaucoup dineros?"

Berg is now off the bench, moving back and forth in front of me the way he used to move in college when he would engage with a hippy: smiling, smugly confident, eyes twinkling, punctuating with fingers, and gesturing like a Broadway actor, deliberately and effectively.

"Yeah, fucking beaucoup! So now what to do with all this fucking money, huh? Well, I say, let's change the world, and let's make America great again! When black trash gets mad, they burn down their neighborhood. When white trash gets mad, they burn down the whole fucking country, and that's what's happening right now my friend. A cultural political game-changing syzygy is starting to take place in America, and I intend to be part of it: aligning the cultural planets such that the walls come tumbling down. And our army will be the same country rubes who bought snake oil in the 1800s, McCarthy in the fifties, Vietnam in the sixties, leisure suits in the seventies, supplements in the eighties, Newt Gingrich in the nineties, Iraq in 2003, and my boy Trump in 2016. These people are suspicious and resentful of the lives and minds of intellectuals and they work very very fucking hard every single day to denigrate and minimize the value of that education, knowledge and disciplined thought they'll never have.[2] They aren't all clinically dumb, but more of them are dumb than one would expect—if one expects the normal distribution of a bell curve. I mean, they are definitely skewed towards the dumb end, from inbreeding in already shallow gene pools, poor nutrition, and pollution. A few of them are fucking geniuses, but they are really few and pretty far between, and they don't know what to do with their intellect down there in their hollers. The few that recognize their potential might make an escape and find a meaningful life elsewhere, but there are no significant examples of this phenomenon actually occurring. The important thing is that while they are not all idiots, they are all, every last one of them, fucking ignorant.

"Remember Christopher, Kant said that while all knowledge begins with experience, that experience requires reflection in order to convert it to useful knowledge. These people have a narrow bandwidth of life experiences that primarily consists of urination, defecation, masturbation, and fornication, and they don't reflect much on these experiences—as well they should not. Because of this deficit of experience and reflection, they are lacking in even the most fundamental knowledge of how the world actually works. They are so ignorant that they don't even know what they don't know. It's not that they actually like being ignorant, but they just can't help themselves. They lack education, they are frightened of the world beyond their small town, and when they do venture out on rare occasions, it's to visit other places that most closely resemble that small shitty town.

Because nature abhors a vacuum, filth and debris from TV and social media have cascaded into the pathetic emptiness of their minds. Their conspiracy theory websites and Christian talk radio provide them with a smug ersatz intellectualism that allows them to look you in the eye as they eat a turd and tell you that it's really grass-fed beef but ha ha ha you just don't understand. Respected scientists are ignorant elitists that are all—every single one of them—either stupid, or secretly collectively communicating, conspiring, and in cahoots to cover up the real truth. And Democrats are all pedophiles who cannibalize their child victims in the back rooms of pizza parlors. I mean, these are very special people who eat this shit, Christopher. And when it comes to Christian talk radio, the women are the real turd eaters—maybe that's why they are all so fucking fat. They are the monotonous and obsessive bible beaters, while the men are episodic bible-beating-wife beaters who usually beat those wives on a game day when their local team has lost. Hell, the Charleston Post and Courier won a Pulitzer Prize a couple of years ago for research connecting domestic violence in South Carolina with what these people believe the Bible says about how normal it is to beat your wife.[3] It's no wonder they divorce more than any other religious denomination.[4]

The men are infantile losers who live in a high school mirage of Springsteen's "Glory Days." They actually believe that they were all good-looking athletes and could have been something some day, when in fact most had severe acne and learning disabilities and never played sports. They've always been out of shape, and couldn't beg a date from the ugliest girl in the class. In spite of reality, these guys cannot shake the nostalgia for those amazing days when they were young, and they end up at forty trying to fuck any ugly skank they can in order to satisfy that fantasy. Oh, and the poor women, they had dreams, too, when they were young: of falling in love with a handsome prince on a white horse who would whisk them out of their family nightmare and away to his castle. They are different from the men in that they disposed of their fantasy a long time ago. Now they pray for the arrival of Jesus and the apocalypse he'll bring with him, so their pathetic lives can have some meaning. The middle-aged men are simple and just need a quick filthy piece of non-evangelical ass to temporarily satisfy their fantasy. The older guy needs something like a sixties vintage Nova to fix up. Or, lacking a Nova, he just needs to find a roadkill raccoon, take it home and skin it quickly and pretend he shot it, so everyone can see he hasn't lost his mojo. Simple shit. The women, on the other hand, are way more complex and require the whole fucking world as we know it to end in order to satisfy their fantasy, with only them and them alone whisked up to cuddle with Jesus in that big Motel 6 in the sky. Yeah, the women really have checked out on this life, and you would, too, Christopher. As kids, they prayed to god to stop their fathers from beating them, which god didn't do, so they married the first shithead that came along just to get out of the house. Ever since, they've been praying for god to stop their shithead husbands from using them as punching bags, and you know what? God still hasn't fucking listened, so this time they are looking to not only get out of the house but to get off this fucking planet.

Like I said, these are not necessarily dumb people, but they are pretty twisted and delightfully ignorant. They are tabula rasa, running purely on what they call country common sense, and they never stop being hungry for fast food and simple messages. And they have been in training:

stretching out, spending what's left of their hard-earned money on Paula White's prosperity prayer snake oil, buying Kenneth Copeland another jet, tithing to Joel Osteen so that he can lock them out of their own fucking church when they need shelter from a hurricane, and anything that's left over after these strategic investments they waste on twentieth century snake oil herbal supplements that do absolutely nothing for their bloated rotting bodies. Shit, remember the wall Mexico was going to build? Well, not only are these rubes paying for that fucker with their taxes, they gave additional snake oil wall money to old Steve Bannon, that filthy greasy messy motherfucker, which he and his cronies of course stole in order to buy yachts and cosmetic surgery and pussy instead of building a fucking wall. These real American folks are amazing! They are pro-life, but say kill them all and let Jesus sort them out when it comes to capital punishment and war. If a brown-skinned Jesus returned today preaching liberal peace and love and all that "share the wealth take care of the poor" bullshit, these motherfuckers would be the first in line to call for his crucifixion. They have voluntarily severed their connection with objective reality and, just like the Marines recruit killers from urban gangs, I want to recruit these wonderful little fucknuts. All you have to do is talk their language. Tell them they are not the ignorant cretins that they in fact are. Tell them that they are special. Tell them that you love them. Then watch as they fall slobbering at your feet. Ronald and Donald, and I don't mean those two fucking cartoon ducks, they figured all of this out, and so have I, Christopher, and I am starting to rock and roll just like they did. If you were smart, you'd get on board."

"But Berg, what do you know about religion, how are you going to speak to their dogma?"

"It's all simple mathematics Christopher, so it's actually a piece of cake. Look, the Bible is about 800,000 words total.

The Old Testament is 600,000 words. The New Testament is 200,000—of which Jesus speaks only about 1,000 unique words that I can fit on five typed pages. It's totally manageable. These evangelical y'all Qaeda women love to focus on the Old Testament because it helps them justify their husbands beating them and fucking around on them. Anyway, the Old Testament is filled with tons of that King David kind of shit, which is good. But the thing is so fucking long, so that's bad. But these women have been collecting all the good hateful shit for years, and its easily accessible, like Casey Kasem's top forty, so that's good. What I do in my YouTube videos is throw them some of their familiar rotten red Old Testament meat, and then I head to the New Testament and interpret things through my visionary eyes and soul and simply set those things within an appropriately fucked up context that is fit for their consumption, just like Hannity does with the news. This is not new stuff, Christopher. Martin Luther pulled this off four hundred years ago. He was the original religious trash talker. These Protestants have a natural proclivity for ignorance and violence couched in foul terms. My style is based upon the established historical and observed current demand. These people are extremely easy to read. They just want plain talk that they can understand, and it doesn't necessarily have to be in the Duck Don-nasty tone that seems to be the vogue these days. The same ignorant violent racist message elegantly packaged and delivered by yours truly using their sixth-grade vocabulary seems to delight them even more.

And style is almost everything, because the kids are my real targets: the Facebook, Instagram, TikTok, YouTube generation, the spawn of these mutant simians. Hitler said, whoever has the youth has the future,[5] and he was right. And who are these kids? Their fathers are the plumbers and electricians who come into your house and fuck the whole place up. There are nine of these blue-collar morons out there for every one real craftsman, and the real craftsmen will testify to that, my friend. They are underskilled and overpaid, somehow managing to earn more than one hundred thousand dollars a year despite their mental disabilities. These kids are not growing up poor. They are growing up with infantilizing morons for parents, lots of devices, and plenty of free time to jerk off and watch me. These lemmings don't believe in all the things their parents don't believe in, like science and fact, and because they have watched their idiot fathers pull down one hundred K a year with no education or real skills or the ability to even post a photo to Instagram, they believe that, also lacking education or training or skills, they are obviously worth a lot more. And I will support them in this fantasy, and I will show them the way to the land of good and plenty or whatever. These kids are the heirs to a moronic ethos, and they will inherit their father's guns, and I will leverage both of those things. The soft, overweight, undereducated, incapable, opiate-addicted children are the ones who I will inspire to march with me in a twenty first century crusade against the liberal, intellectual elite who want to spoil everything by increasing school funding for these, my army of violent little chimps."

Spots dance before my eyes. I feel dizzy and nauseous. I still can't get a deep enough breath to completely latch on to this space-time. "Berg, I thought the dreams of our youth meant something. I am having a hard time these days with almost everything, but some of it has to do with those dreams. Laurie tells me that helping corporations pollute our air and water in order to make more money for fewer people is a patriotic element of our dreams. Then I listen to you. Your delivery is what I remember of the old Berg, and I have paid attention to you now as I always did years ago. But what you say to me now doesn't make sense the way it used to.

Now you tell me that helping the mujahideen fight the Russians was wrong because the Russians are our friends now and they really always have been and the mujahideen who were our friends and comrades were really just terrorists all along. And you tell me that building an army of the most profoundly ignorant with which to take over our country and destroy democracy will fulfill our dreams. You assure me that you can twist the words of Jesus to satisfy the violent urges of damaged people and, because I know you Berg, I am confident that you can. Do you see why I am having a hard time with all this?"

Berg leans over, spits on the ground and laughs. "The dreams of our youth? You mean like limited government, free enterprise, fiscal restraint, and global leadership? Deregulating industry? Freedom to say whatever you want to whomever you want? Call a loser a loser and treat him appropriately, instead of throwing money at him? Those dreams?"

"Yes, about what it was like to be an American in the 1980's, when we rediscovered and once again stood for freedom, when we preserved the peace and reduced the number of nuclear weapons on earth by building strong defenses. Our national challenges have always been complex, but we Americans are decent hard-working people. As long as we remember our first principles and believe in ourselves, the future will always be ours."

"Shit Christopher, you sound like Ronald Reagan."

"That's probably because I'm paraphrasing his farewell speech. I found it meaningful."

"Well, those dreams belong to bygone days. They require people to have a rational ethos, to understand the costs associated with benefits, to pay attention like we did, to believe in hard facts. These people don't believe in anything that resembles reality. They don't believe in the teachings of that brown skinned Semitic guy Jesus from two thousand years ago, and instead have created their own fresh new pearly white, hard drinking, violent and vengeful machine gun Jesus who gleefully supports war and capital punishment. They love Israel and Jews, now that they have the Muslims to hate —and they reject the fact that Martin Luther was a raging anti-Semite—as were they until recently, when all of a sudden they weren't.

They don't believe in the evolution of anything, they don't believe the earth is more than six thousand years old, they don't believe the fossils you and I found on geology field trips in college are real, and instead believe they are simply tricks Satan's playing on us. So they reject in total the fundamental first principles of biology and geology. They don't believe in global warming—much less man-made global warming—so that means they don't believe in chemistry, physics, meteorology, and climatology or even simple fucking thermometers.

They've never left their shitty little towns, so they don't really believe there is in fact a world out there beyond the Dollar Store—but they do watch tons of anything on TV that speaks their language: Honey Boo Boo, Duck Dynasty, Swamp People, Yukon Men, Deadliest Catch, Fox News, especially ignorant dropouts like Sean Hannity whose only job in his entire life has been to run his mouth about whatever shit is bouncing around in his head at that particular time. Hannity is an asshole, but he's also a fucking genius when it comes to understanding these people—it comes naturally to him because he is one.

These people have never been schooled in anything close to critical thinking, and they don't fucking read, so even their ability to critically disbelieve is severely limited. They don't discriminate between magic tricks at a carnival and acid base reactions in a chemistry laboratory; it's all the same type of mystery to them. And it is no wonder that their favorite word is appropriately … wait for it … wait for it now… 'hoax.'"

"Berg, you are proposing to start a movement that is strategically lacking an informed ethos. Reagan also said that national pride or "new patriotism" is good, but doesn't count for much and won't last unless it's grounded in thoughtfulness and knowledge that ultimately results in an informed patriotism. I still believe in Reagan's dream of the shining city, built on rocks stronger than oceans, wind swept, God blessed, and teeming with people of all kinds living in harmony and peace—a city with free ports humming with commerce and creativity, and if there must be city walls, then the walls have doors, and the doors are open to anyone with the will and the heart to get here. What you are proposing, Berg, doesn't sound at all like Reagan's vision—in fact it sounds just the opposite, like it's simply a way for you to promote yourself, and that's it."

Berg sits down next to me on the bench again. He has worked up a sweat. He stretches out his linen legs, looks up at the sky, takes a deep breath and purses his lips. "You know Christopher, maybe you're right, maybe it is just a way to promote myself and acquire power. But what's wrong with that? All through history, great men have lied and killed for power because power provides you with everything. Hitler said the only goal in life is power—not to accomplish programs, because programs are for fucking intellectual assholes—but simply to have the power. While I think some of Adolph's methods were a bit unsound, undeniably he is one of history's most charismatic and effective leaders. He had the power of Alexander the Great, Atilla the Hun, Charlemagne, and Genghis Khan, and in the end that is what is important—that is what people remember, period. And you, at the end of the day, Christopher, you've managed to be on the wrong side of history so far and as a result you have been left with nothing, and it sounds to me like you're satisfied with nothing and you're going to keep steaming in that direction."

"Wrong side of history?"

"Yeah, dreaming about opening doors to your shining city for more Mexican rapists to walk through is bad enough, but how about helping those fucking Muslim rag head terrorists like you did back in the 80s—nothing personal you know, but that's some pretty fucked up shit you did, and that's just a fact."

"A fact?"

"Yeah, a fucking fact, Christopher, you blew it, big time then—but you don't have to blow it now. It's your choice. With or without you, I am going to change the world. It's up to you, Christopher. You are the master of your destiny."

Then the epiphany occurs, the moment of pure clarity, and I realize that Berg is right: I am the master of my reality, of my destiny, and like a dancer in a single graceful motion I inhale as I pull the Walther PPK 9mm from beneath my untucked sweat-soaked shirt, slide it under Berg's chin and into his neck until the backpressure stops me and then slowly and very deliberately let out my breath and squeeze the trigger. The back and top of his head explodes in a pink vapor that complements the sulfurous yellow air and my arm gracefully retracts, the pistol sliding back into its holster beneath my shirt. I surprise myself with the technical simplicity and the elegance with which I have executed this act. Berg's face is fully intact, although his mouth hangs open, and his body simply relaxes back into the bench and does not fall over. His fingers twitch a bit, his arms and legs moving ever so slightly as if he is listening to a private song in his head and moving to the rhythm. They say if you kill the head, the body will die—and it does, it just takes some time. I gaze at the purple rivers of gelatin and milky teal fog in front of me, the sulfur-spewing sun above me—the banging and hissing in my head is deafening now—and wonder just where my next stop in beyond-space-time will be. I relax back into the bench alongside Berg, expecting myself to slip. But something is different. Something is wrong. The noise in my head increases in intensity instead of fading, and far from feeling relaxed I instead feel claustrophobic, gagging as if I am being smothered. Like the closing iris of a camera, beginning at the perimeter of my vision Zilker Park begins to disappear and is slowly replaced by empty darkness.

Hissssssssssssss, bongo bongo, hissssssss, bongo bongo. The hiss and ping of the ICU is a symphony of near-death electronic instruments that only those at that threshold have the opportunity to hear. ICU nurses are remarkably effective at sedating patients into a plant-like state, so who knows what sounds actually penetrate into the minds of the intubated? Unlike the graceful awakening of a flower with the advent of the morning sun, my ICU awakening is clumsy and awkward as I regain consciousness, choking on the endotracheal tube taped firmly to my face. I think about yanking it out, but I can't move my arms. A nurse's face appears. It is uncomfortably close. Someone else in a gown and mask stands off to her side.

The nurse takes my fingers lightly in her gloved hand and speaks slowly, deliberately, and sweetly. "Hi honey, welcome back. I am nurse Carol, and you are in the Saint David Hospital ICU. If you understand me just squeeze my hand."

I squeeze as hard as I can.

"Good job! They found you passed out on a bench in Zilker Park. They brought you here. You have COVID and you can't breathe on your own right now. You are on a ventilator. Do you understand?"

I squeeze as hard as I can.

"Great! The most important thing for you to do now is rest and we will do our best to help you get better."

I squeeze as hard as I can.

"All right darling, you get some sleep, and we'll talk later."

I squeeze as hard as I can and close my eyes, working to ignore the machine that is choking me, breathing for me, killing me, and keeping me alive. The click-hiss-boom-boom of the ventilator and the beeping and whirring of monitors and machines fills my head, and I slip quickly away. I am back on the bench by the purple river under the burning yellow sky.

"Welcome back Christopher."

I turn my head and look into the smiling eyes of Berg. "Berg, what are you doing here?"

"Hanging out with you."

"I mean, how is it we are both here now in this space at this time? This isn't the past, and I don't think it's the present. I have never been to the future, so it's probably not that. Or is this something else?"

"It is what it is, I guess."

"Sorry, but I am just not used to slipping into a beyond-space-time like this."

"I don't know, Christopher, maybe you're like Schrödinger's Cat—until somebody checks on you in the ICU, then you're both alive and dead with me here in this beyond-space-time."

"I find this all a bit confusing, after all, I just killed you Berg."

"Really—you think I'm that easy to kill? All right, get ready, here's your beyond-space-time pop quiz: exactly where and when did you kill me? Was it when we might have been sitting here together in this space-time? Or was it in beyond-space-time when you were in the ambulance? Or maybe it was when you were in the hospital? Are you sure you didn't, in fact, kill me perhaps somewhere else, many years ago? You have five seconds to answer: five, four, three, two, one, bwaaaaaaaaaaaaaaaap—time's up!

"Well, now I am not exactly certain."

"Excellent—welcome to the Berg Uncertainty Principle, which says the less confident you are about our position and relationship in space and time, here and now, the less precisely you can understand past, or predict future, actions and interactions based upon our initial condition outside Kingsbury Hall at UNH back in 1976."

"All right, I agree, I have a significant degree of space-time uncertainty regarding the recent past right now, and we haven't physically seen each other in four decades, so my understanding of the distant past is uniquely dependent upon the slips I have made there recently, but what I am sure of is that I indeed had to stop you Berg, wherever and when-ever that may or may not have occurred. I know it is unfortunate for you and unkind of me, but of that need I remain certain."

"Really, you needed to stop me, your old friend Berg? Well, good buddy, this should be a wicked rich justification, so go ahead and let's hear your theory, shoot. Ha! Get it? 'Shoot!'"

"Berg, I had to stop you because you love your country so much."

"Let me get this straight, you thought you needed to shoot me in the fucking head because I love my country, because I am a patriot?"

"Exactly. You hear that annoying tripping hipster bongo player? He loves his country just as much as you love yours. But his reality and yours are not the same, so you don't share a common country."

"So why didn't you kill him, too?"

"For three reasons: one, because I respect you more than I respect him—you are way more dangerous."

"Explain?"

"You are inspirational, you are a leader—you always have been. You have the ability to create a compelling vision, even if it is a lie, and are able to transform that vision into a vivid picture of where you want people to follow you, even if that destination is a mirage. That hipster is too caught up in himself and his fresh wokeness. He's not in a position to make his own bed, much less lead anybody anywhere. He has no potential. He is not a threat."

"OK, fair enough. Call a winner a winner and a loser a loser. I like it, of course. What's the second reason?"

"You and that woke hipster are both tearing the fabric of what remains of an objective reality and our country apart. You at one end in your country with your army of mentally defective white cowards who possess the infantile expertise to hit pudding-soft targets and kill little kids in day care centers and old people worshiping in church. He and his unwashed friends at the other end in their country, calling for insurrection because a black kid had a bad day, robbed a store, then assaulted a cop and got shot. I can feel sympathy for that black kid, but I feel nothing but disgust for your white mob, and I love our country too much to simply sit here and watch it destroyed. You see, I love our country, not yours, and not his—ours: the one our founding fathers gave us. Benjamin Franklin said that what we have is a republic if we can keep it. Keeping it requires a collective jihad…a collective struggle."

"Yeah, not sure I totally agree with you on that one, except all the bad stuff about what that black kid did, but go ahead, number three?"

"You both have pathological optical properties. You filter, bend, and change reality to fit your preconceived notions of what you want it to be. Berg, your prism conflates country, which has permanence, with government, which is transient, and it conflates governing, which requires empathy, with power, which is an inherently selfish pursuit. Representatives may come and go every two years, the chief executive every four years, and senators every six. The country and its aspirations remain through it all. It is the country and those aspirations of liberty, justice, and deliberative democracy to which we owe our allegiance—not the government or the flag or a bumper sticker, but the country. Your love of the government requires you to see the Russians as our friends now—and for them to have always been our friends. You need the President to be a brilliant three-dimensional chess player instead of a checker-playing idiot. You need him to be a clever dealmaker and successful businessman instead of a jerk with a personality disorder and a trail of wrecked businesses and relationships in his wake. And you seek the most degenerate citizens, not the best, in order to enlist their worst tendencies in your quest for power.

That hipster over there has his own problems. He doesn't know enough to understand specifically why global warming is happening but he can deliver a sanctimonious sermon on why we should all go live in tents, not bathe, eat turnips, and smoke weed because of the impending climate apocalypse, while he buys clothes made on the other side of the planet, lives in an air conditioned McMansion with his parents, drives his Subaru the three blocks to Whole Foods instead of walking, and flies across the country to visit friends when he is feeling a little blue. His prism allows him to be a hypocritical woke jackass, but he is not in love with government or power. He and his friends love their country as they see it through their prisms, and they seek to defend it from fascism —which is, at the very least, a noble intent. Besides, my vision's pretty messed up with this thick fog and he's a moving target. I probably would have missed him."

A grimace creeps across Berg's face and he claps his hands slowly and deliberately. "All right Christopher, very impressive. You've analyzed me through your prism and catalogued me, you have shared your refractions and you may have even shot me, now please allow me to reciprocate, without the shooting part of course."

"Yes Berg, please go ahead."

"First of all, it appears you have used that hippy and me as dysfunctional boundary conditions of a patriot bell curve distribution with the inherent assumption that somewhere within two standard deviations on each side of the average of this distribution exists a state of preferred patriotic being within which you exist. Does this conceptual model sound about right to you so far?"

"Yes, I hadn't thought so much about the distribution and mathematics, but yes, I guess so, although I sound a bit narcissistic the way you put it."

"I agree—that's how you appear to me as well. Let's continue. In listening to you, I hear you propose the state of preferred patriotism originated in or resides within a time and space belonging primarily to a decade that existed between 1979 and 1989 or so, is that correct?"

"Yes, that's primarily where I find myself slipping back to: that time when we shared common values of honor and decency."

"Excellent Christopher, let's peel that apart a bit. My thesis is that these values of honor and decency that you speak of, and within which you frame your definition of patriotism, arise from somewhere other than the eighties zeitgeist you have pointed to and are in fact washed up anachronisms. My thesis is that by 1979 Emily Post had been dead for nineteen years and both she and honor and decency were all dried up mummies. By the 1980s, those people who still extended their metaphorical pinkies were freaks, representative of one boundary condition and maybe smelly old hippies on communes having sex with their barnyard animals were the other boundary condition. It is my position that average people during that decade were living a post-Post existence, their ethos reflected best by people we know like Wilbur Mills, Larry Flynt, Idi Amin, John Belushi, Hunter Thompson, Sid Vicious, Saddam Hussein, Oliver North, Don Henley, Dick Cheney, Carlos Lehder, Manuel Noriega, Newt Gingrich, Bill Clinton, Bill Cosby, Harvey Weinstein, and your buddy Osama Bin Laden.

Yeah, that's right. These people didn't extend their pinky finger when they had a drink and they didn't give a shit about anything, much less if people like you and Emily Post didn't approve of them. They did drugs, killed people, had people killed, lied, cheated, stole, fucked anything that moved, and pissed in trash cans. They all lived honest, transparent lives and were true to themselves. They are the progenitors of people like Roseanne Barr, Jeffrey Epstein, Paris Hilton, Charlie Sheen, Lindsay Lohan, Donald Trump, Kanye West, and Johnny Depp. My thesis is that this post-Post I have described is reflective of the average honor and decency of the 1980s distribution and in fact of our values as a society today. Look at that butt burglar Mike Pompeo and his buddy Ulrich Brechbuhl—a couple of baby high school weasels in 1979 that grew up to be corpulent high-caliber scumbags of the twenty-first century. These two made-in-China American flag pin-wearing Jabba-the-Hutts didn't just appear out of thin air. They are examples of the limbless creeping opaque waste products of iconoclastic giants they could never measure up to, but in whose moral dust trail they scavenged for turds and thrived."

"I am beginning to see your point, but most of those

people never talked about raising mutant armies with which to destroy their own country in the name of patriotism."

"Ah, I see. You believe that someone should be canceled simply for saying he has a dream that you disagree with? That's kind of what happened to Martin Luther King Jr., isn't it?"

"Yes, but Berg, Doctor King was killed by a vile racist for dreaming about a better world. That is a beautiful dream and one held by the majority of people in this country."

"Yes, well the majority might still have a slight edge on what you call that beautiful dream for the time being. But look, my thesis also states that an ugly dream held by the minority is even more sacred and deserving of protection. In this country, our country, my dream, my speech, is punishable only if a reasonable person understands it as a threat, regardless of my intent. If reasonable people think I am just a fucking lunatic and the only people who actually buy my bullshit are unreasonable, then my freedom to emit bullshit is protected. Check the case law on the topic if you like.[6] I think I was crystal clear with you that I was speaking in hyperbole to the unreasonable fucknuts of this country, was I not? And besides, I haven't said anything beyond what these other white Evangelical assholes say in their snide sneaky way every Sunday. I'm certainly way less violent than old Martin Luther—shit, I bet you would cap his ass too if he was around preaching his kill-the-Jews shit now, wouldn't you? Look, my position is that anybody that listens to the stuff I say on YouTube and buys it is by definition unreasonable, and therefore my freedom to say any fucking thing I want to say to them with impunity should be protected by law and protected from people like you."

"Yes Berg, but you said you intended to raise an army of these unreasonable people in order to do unreasonable things, that's my point."

"Yeah, blah, blah, blah. I said, I said, I said. Listen, I didn't threaten the crew of an airliner or point a loaded gun at anyone, did I? Hell, people said Reagan was a warmonger because he joked around about bombing the Soviet Union, even though for eight years he fought for global denuclearization. People said Obama was going to take away everyone's guns and put all the Republicans in Wal-Mart concentration camps because he said we needed to do something about mass shootings. He said, she said, people said. Should Obama have been cancelled because of something somebody said he said or was thinking about doing? People said that under Trump, the economy would collapse and there would be Russian tanks rolling around in what was left of our streets after North Korea nuked us. Call me crazy but, other than the global pandemic, things don't look all that bad right now, do they? I mean seriously, should anyone really have standing to intervene before observing an action or event? And even then, after making an observation, to whom is the job of hall monitor assigned? I mean, where does it end, Christopher? Shouldn't we simply let boys be boys, and if someone's behavior or opinion becomes unbearable, then do the honorable thing—either stand your ground and give them the finger or walk away—but don't blow their head off. Call me crazy, but I think maybe a little more trust in the wisdom of the universe and acceptance of its design for our fate, kismet, karma or whatever might be appropriate?"

"Well, maybe there is something to the Arab saying— insha' Allah—trusting in the will of Allah."

"Yeah, that's right. And finally, let's talk about engineering root cause analysis—what the Sufis call 'peeling the onion.' Ask the question 'why?' five times to find the true essence of the problem. Christopher, you really wimped out on this one—you never even asked 'why' once. So, let's start peeling the onion: you say you blew my head off because of something I said – why?"

"Why? Because weak-minded people will listen to the crazy things you say, and do terrible things."

"Why will they listen to my crazy shit, believe it, and then act?"

"Well, you actually made that very clear: because they are damaged and ignorant."

"Why are they damaged and ignorant?"

"For socioeconomic reasons—they are largely isolated in rural communities and cut off from the twenty-first century."

"Yes, and what else?"

"Maybe the education system has failed them as well—they certainly lack critical thinking skills."

"Excellent, we are getting closer to the center of the onion. And where is the culpability for this socioeconomic disconnection, for a loss of jobs, a decline in standard of living, shitty schools with ignorant teachers who were spawned and raised in the same polluted hellhole?"

"I don't know—globalization, offshoring of manufacturing, defunding the public school system?"

"Bravo. In five 'whys' you have started to peel the onion, and I say, 'started,' because there are always many layers left, no matter how many you peel. But what you have identified so far is very insightful, Christopher. It sounds to me like you have a problem with the federal government, going all the way back to NAFTA, the brainchild of your favorite president, Ronald Reagan, and his war on the newly formed Department of Education[7]. You are clearly passionate about this—did you ever write your state representative, your senator, or the president? Did you join any social change movements to work to fix these toxic root causes, volunteer in schools where you could share your superior intellect, education and experience, demonstrate in the streets and maybe burn your bra?"

"No. Quite frankly, I never even thought about any of those things, especially the bra part."

"Well, maybe next time you might consider a little self reflection, sacrifice, and social activism before you decide to go off and kill a friend, hmmm?"

"Berg, I am at a loss for words. You make a compelling argument that, regardless of how it conflicts with my preconceived conceptual model, possesses intellectual merit. So, while I still abhor your vision, I accept the logical thread in defense of it. I think I am a bit confused, because I have been so alone these last years and have not had anyone with whom to talk these things out. In retrospect, I believe I owe you an apology Berg."

"Well, I accept your apology, and it's very nice you had your epiphany, but according to you I'm still Humpty fucking Dumpty and all the king's horses and all that shit isn't going to put me back together again."

"Yes, well I am so sorry for that. I really felt you were an existential threat, not just to me, but also to our nation. I felt I had done due intellectual diligence and the factual basis upon which I built my opinion and decision was firm and not couched in conspiracy and superstition. But, regardless of those feelings, you are my friend, and I shouldn't have taken your life."

"Shit, don't worry about it. After all, it's just one miniscule life: a brief illusion in the immensity of beyond-space-time. You know, in a totally fucked up way a lot of what you said kind of made some sense to me too. Maybe we're both looking at the cosmos now from new vantage points that are no longer so far apart. Nonetheless, I still don't agree with all the nasty stuff you said about my man Trump. I love the guy, and you would too if, like me, you had grown up in New

York, read the tabloids, and listened to him on Howard Stern."

"Well, I still love Osama and you would too if, like me, you had hung out and gotten stoned with him in Pakistan, so maybe that kind of makes us even."

We both smile and sit silently, watching the vapors rise from the river, and the crystalline air forms, disintegrates, and reforms. We are content in our silence as only the closest of friends can be. I listen as the high-pitched whine of a cicada begins a monotonic call, the whine growing in intensity as others join in concert from the surrounding trees.

"Christopher, do you ever get off your ass and walk around this park at all?"

"Not really. It's usually a struggle for me just to get here and then back to my condominium. This summer heat really takes it out of me."

"Well, you know what I have to say about that? If you can't stand the heat, get off your bench and get out of the sun, you fucknut! Check it out, there's a grove of trees over there and a shady path – I bet we can find you a nice cool bench upon which to rot in there."

"Strange, I hadn't even noticed that path or those trees before."

"Well, my ass is going numb. Let's get off this stinking bench, stretch our legs, and go have a look? It reminds me a bit of New Hampshire."

I look at my bench and my immediate surroundings with which I have grown comfortable and then into the distance at the narrow path running through the grove of live oaks. From this vantage point, the leaves of the trees appear in shades of red, orange, and yellow, complementing the violet hued river and sulfurous sky behind me. A diffuse cool yellow gray light bathes the grove from which wispy fingers of clean, sweet earthy-scented air reach out to me. It is still daytime, but I can see a scattering of stars glittering down from the sky above.

"Yes, it looks appealing. Can I help you up, Berg?"

"Fuck off Christopher, what do I look like, an invalid?"

We rise from the bench and set off into the shade of the grove. There are no animals, or other people besides Berg and me, and the whine of the cicada slowly fades. It feels comforting to have no apparent destination. We walk. I am calm. I drink in the cool, clean air with familiar ease. I am satisfied. I am at peace.

"I love you, Berg."

"I love you too, Christopher."

"I sure wish we had a joint."

"Yeah, me too."

Some physicists say that reality is comprised solely of interactions—a magnificent interlocked system of systems—and that an independent untethered entity is effectively non-existent. Without relationships we are nothing. That, I believe, is how in the end we came through it all. Over the course of four decades, the two of us had bent, twisted, and peeled apart life through our prisms, each emerging with a divergent ethos. Yet many of our oldest and most personal cherished possessions—our fears and attractions, prejudices and naïve beliefs, our aspirations and wrecked dreams—remained intact and cradled within the arms of our inner selves, allowing us in the end to once again see the world and the stars, together.

NOTES

1. The Beginning of the End

1. Gramlich, J., What the data says (and doesn't say) about crime in the United States, Pew Research Center, November 10, 2020
2. Federal Bureau of Investigation, Uniform Crime Report, Hate Crime Statistics, 2019
3. Weinberg, R., The Blood Libel in Eastern Europe, Jewish History (2012) 26: 275–285
4. Gallagher, A., J. Davey, M. Hart, The Genesis of a Conspiracy Theory Key trends in QAnon activity since 2017, Institute for Strategic Dialogue, 2020
5. The Nielsen Total Audience Report, Q3 2018
6. Darwin, C. (1871). The Descent of Man. London: John Murray
7. Kruger, J., D. Dunning, Unskilled and unaware of it: how difficulties in recognizing one's own incompetence lead to inflated self-assessments, Journal of Personality and Social Psychology, 1999, Vol. 77, No. 6., 1121-1134
8. Bell, J.S., On the Einstein Podolsky Rosen Paradox, Physics Vol. 1, No. 3, pp. 195-290, 1964
9. Gross, D., 2005, Einstein and the search for unification, Current Science, 89, 2035-2040
10. Einstein, A., L. Infeld (1938). The Evolution of Physics. New York: Simon and Schuster
11. Hartmann, F. The Life of Paracelsus, Second Edition (no date - c. 1896). London: Kegan Paul, Trench, Turner & Co. Ltd.
12. Feynman, R., The Messenger Lectures, Lecture 6: Probability and Uncertainty in Quantum Mechanics, Cornell University, 1964
13. Dingman, S.L. (2002). Physical Hydrology, Second Edition. New Jersey: Prentice-Hall Inc. (pages 48-55); Shah, I. (1964). The Sufis. London: The Octagon Press (pages 258-260)
14. Haidt, J., The Happiness Hypothesis, Basic Books, 2006

2. The End of the Century

1. The Heritage Foundation, The North American Free Trade Agreement: Ronald Reagan's Vision Realized, November 23, 1993

3. Roots

1. Hujer, K, Christmas and The Stars, Popular Astronomy, Vol. 53 (1945) 486-489; Hijmans, S., Sol Invictus, the Winter Solstice, and the Origins of Christmas, Mouseion, Series III, Vol. 3 (2003) 377-398

2. Lindvall, T., M. Stroyeck, Holy Dung: Comic Signs of Consubstantiality in Martin Luther Films, Religions (2016), 7, 20; Skjelver, D.M., German Hercules: The Impact of Scatology on the Definition of Martin Luther as a Man 1483-1546, Pittsburgh Undergraduate Review, 14, No. 1, Summer 2009, pp. 30-78

3. Letter from Thomas Jefferson to Richard Price, January 8, 1789

4. Messenger, D.A. (2011). "Beyond War Crimes: Denazification, 'Obnoxious' Germans and US Policy in Franco's Spain after the Second World War." Contemporary European History 20.4, 455-478

5. Boehling, R., H-Diplo, Article Review, No. 683, 1 March 2017

6. Coates, M., Denazifying Germany: German Protestantism and the Response to Denazification in the American Zone, 1945-1948, University of York, Department of History, Master of Arts by Research, September 2014

7. Guilt by Association – Three Words in Search of a Meaning, The University of Chicago Law Review, 1949, 148 - 162

4. Berg

1. IR-2018-62, March 19, 2018, IRS 2018 'Dirty Dozen' tax scams: Abusive tax shelters make the list

2. Jewish Telegraphic Agency, Daily News Bulletin, Thursday, May 17, 1956, Vol. XXIII, No. 95

5. Laurie

1. Fordham University, Internet History Sourcebooks Project, Medieval Sourcebook: Martin Luther (1483-1546): The Jews and Their Lies, excerpts (1543) (https://sourcebooks.fordham.edu/source/_luther-jews.asp)

2. Wong, F.D., Christian Extremism as a Domestic Terror Threat, School of Advanced Military Studies, United States Army Command and General Staff College, Fort Leavenworth, Kansas, 2011

3. Tom Lehrer, National Brotherhood Week, That Was the Year That Was (1965), Reprise/Warner Brothers

6. Waste of 1980

1. Hickok, M.L., J.A. Padleschat, Strategic Considerations in Defending and Settling a Superfund Case, 19 Loy. L.A. L. Rev. 1213 (1986)

7. Stingers

1. Wood, R., Promoting democracy or pursuing hegemony? An analysis of U.S. involvement in the Middle East, Journal of Global Faultlines, 2019, Vol. 6, No. 2, 166-185
2. Kuperman, A.J., The Stinger missile and U.S. intervention in Afghanistan, Political Science Quarterly, 1999, Vol. 114, No. 2, 219 - 257

9. Karachi

1. Qur'an 3.45–49
2. Qur'an 3.49
3. Qur'an 3.55
4. Qur'an 3.57
5. *e.g.* Time Magazine, Letters, Monday, Nov. 12, 1945
6. Mason, P.Q., Sinners in the hands of an angry mob: Violence against religious outsiders in the U.S. South, 1865 – 1910, Ph.D. dissertation, University of Notre Dame, July 2005
7. Collins, J.J., Understanding War in Afghanistan, National Defense University Press, Washington, D.C., 2011; Laurence, J.H., Education Standards for Military Enlistment and the Search for Successful Recruits, Human Resources Research Organization, Prepared for: Office of the Assistant Secretary of Defense (Manpower, Installations, & Logistics), February 1984; Alexiev, A., Inside the Soviet Army in Afghanistan, Rand Corporation, Prepared for: Office of the Chief of Staff, HQ US Army, May 1988

11. Connections

1. Chouvy, P-A., Drug trafficking in and out of the Golden Triangle, An Atlas of Trafficking in Southeast Asia, The Illegal Trade in Arms, Drugs, People, Counterfeit Goods and Natural Resources in Mainland, IB Tauris, p. 1-32, 2013

12. Panama

1. Hearings Before the Permanent Subcommittee Investigations of the Committee on Governmental Affairs, United States Senate, One Hundred First Congress, First Session, Structure of International Drug Trafficking Organizations, September 12-13, 1989

2. United States Senate, Committee on Foreign Relations, Subcommittee on Terrorism, Narcotics and International Operations, Drugs, Law Enforcement and Foreign Policy, December 1988, e.g. page 41; Oliver North, Notebook Entry, August 9, 1985; Robert Owen (TC), Memo to Oliver North (BG), April 1, 1985

3. Drug Enforcement Administration, Worldwide Cocaine Situation Report 1992, Drug Intelligence Report

4. Cole, R.H., Operation Just Cause, The Planning and Execution of Joint Operations in Panama, February 1988 – January 1990, Joint History Office, Office of the Chairman of the Joint Chiefs of Staff, Washington, D.C. 1995

13. Perspectives

1. NSC, Oliver L. North Memorandum, "Release of American Hostages in Beirut," ("Diversion Memo"), Top Secret/Sensitive, April 4, 1986

2. Abshire, D.M., The Character of George Marshall, With Reflections on George Washington and Robert E. Lee, Institute for Honor, Washington and Lee University

   George C. Marshall Foundation Virginia Military Institute, In cooperation with: Center for the Study of the Presidency, Abshire-Inamori Leadership Academy, Center for Strategic and International Studies, February 25-26, 2005

3. NSC, National Security Planning Group Minutes, "Subject: Central America," Secret, June 25, 1984

4. Final Report of the Independent Counsel for Iran/Contra Matters, Volume I: Investigations and Prosecutions, Lawrence E. Walsh, Independent Counsel, August 4, 1993, Washington, D.C., United States Court of Appeals for the District of Columbia Circuit, Division for the Purpose of Appointing Independent Counsel, Division No. 86-6, Part IX Investigations of the White House 443, Chapter 28, George Bush, Bush Diary, 11/5/86, ALU 0140191

5. Proclamation 6518 - Grant of Executive Clemency

6. Nash, D., Fossilized Jews and Witnessing Dinosaurs at the Creation Museum: Public Remembering and Forgetting at a Young Earth Creationist "Memory Place", Studies in Christian-Jewish Relations (SCJR) 14, no. 1 (2019): 1-25

7. Crawford, E., Arrhenius' 1896 Model of the Greenhouse Effect in Context, Ambio, Vol. 26, No. 1, Arrhenius and the Greenhouse Gases (Feb., 1997), pp. 6-11

8. Kelly, H.A., Galileo's Non-Trial (1616), Pre-Trial (1632–1633), and Trial (May 10, 1633): A Review of Procedure, Featuring Routine Violations of the Forum of Conscience, Church History 85:4 (December 2016), 724–761

9. Sungenis, R.A., R.J. Bennett, Galileo Was Wrong: The Church Was Right, The Evidence from Modern Science, Twelfth edition, Catholic Apologetics International Publishing, Inc., 2017

10. https://archive.vn/20130416012531/http://www.unicalamus.org/status.htm; Sungenis, R.A., My Ph.D. from Calamus International University, January 28, 2007

11. Schwartz, J., New York Times, S. Fred Singer, a Leading Climate Change Contrarian, Dies at 95, April 11, 2020

14. The Witch is Dead

1. CNN. Timeline: Osama bin Laden over the years (http://edition.cnn.com/2011/WORLD/asiapcf/05/02/osama.timeline/index.html)

2. Gambetta, D., S. Hertog, Engineers of Jihad, Sociology Working Papers, Paper Number 2007-10, Department of Sociology, University of Oxford, 2007

3. Presidential Daily Briefing (PDB), Bin Laden Determined to Strike in US, August 6, 2001, Declassified and Approved for Release April 10, 2004

4. The Daily Collegian, Thousands celebrate in Beaver Canyon following Osama bin Laden's death, May 2, 2011

15. Engineering Death

1. Pedro De Cieza De Leon, The Second Part of the Chronicle of Peru, 1883, Translated and Edited by Clements R. Markham, London: Whiting and Company, Chapter V

2. Talalay, L.E., A Feminist Boomerang: The Great Goddess of Greek Prehistory, Gender & History, Vol.6 No.2 August 1994, pp. 165-183

3. Lazaridis, I., et al, Genetic origins of the Minoans and Mycenaeans, Nature, 2017 August 10; 548 (7666): 214–218

4. Taylor, R.M., The Longbow in English History, MA Thesis, Butler University, 1932; Loades, M., The Longbow, Osprey Publishing, 2013

5. Wilson, P.L., Pirate Utopias Moorish Corsairs & European Renegades, Second Edition, Autonomedia, 2003

6. Rajanthiran, R.S.P., The Hudud Controversy in Contemporary Malaysia: A Study of Its Proposed Implementation in Kelantan and Terengganu, Proc. of The Third Intl. Conf. On Advances In Economics, Social Science and Human Behaviour Study, 2015

7. Retief, F.P., L. Cilliers,The History and Pathology of Crucifixion, SAMJ, Vol. 93, No. 12, December 2003; Maslen, M.W., P.D. Mitchell, Medical theories on the cause of death in crucifixion, Journal of the Royal Society of Medicine, Vol. 99, April 2006

16. Those People

1. Card, D., G.B. Dahl, Family Violence and Football: The Effect of Unexpected Emotional Cues on Violent Behavior, The Quarterly Journal of Economics (2011) 126, 103–143; Peek-Asa, C., et al, Rural Disparity in Domestic Violence Prevalence and Access to Resources, Journal of Women's Health, Volume 20, Number 11, 2011

2. Office of the Historian, Bureau of Public Affairs, United States Department of State, Cuba, January 1961–September 1962 (Foreign Relations of the United States, 1961–1963, Volume X), iBook

3. Stephens, D., Coons, L.M., Landfill Performance Assessment at a Semiarid Site: Modeling and Validation, Ground Water Monitoring and Remediation, page 101 – 109, Winter 1994

4. https://www.mediamatters.org/alex-jones/alex-jones-boston-blasts-us-govt-prime-suspect

5. https://www.mediamatters.org/embed/clips/2016:11:29:51283:gcn-alexjones-20140314-shooting

17. A Changing Tide

1. Schiller, D., et al, Extinction during reconsolidation of threat memory diminishes prefrontal cortex involvement, Proceedings of the National Academy of Sciences, December 10, 2013, vol. 110, no. 50

18. The End of the Beginning

1. Ayers, D.J., Current Sexual Practices of Evangelical Teens and Young Adults, Institute for Family Studies, Research Brief, August 2019

2. Hofstadter, R., Anti-intellectualism in American Life, Alfred A. Knopf Inc., New York, 1963

3. Charleston Post and Courier, "Till Death Do Us Part," Pulitzer Prize, 2015

4. Glass, J., P. Levchak, Red States, Blue States, and Divorce: Understanding the Impact of Conservative Protestantism on Regional Variation in Divorce Rates, American Journal of Sociology, Vol. 119, No. 4 (January 2014), pp. 1002-1046

5. Kunzer, E., The Youth of Nazi Germany, The Journal of Educational Sociology, Vol. 11, No. 6, The Challenge of Youth (Feb., 1938), pp. 342-350

6. Watts v. United States, 394 U.S. 705 (1969)

7. Los Angeles Times, Education Dept. Won't Be Abolished: Reagan Backs Down, Citing Little Support for Killing Agency, January 29, 1985

ABOUT THE AUTHOR

Richard A. Greyson is a prolific writer who doesn't normally write books. A native New Yorker, he has lived most of his life elsewhere, rounding some – but not all - of the sharp edges of his lexicon.

Greyson is overeducated, never watches television, rarely wears a tie, and only wears socks when compelled to by the climate. He avoids the numbers zero and one but embraces those in between.

Greyson's work has taken him over and under the water, through jungles and deserts, and into dusty universities and shiny corporate conference rooms. He has delivered talks to audiences around the world on technical and not-so-technical topics and despite - or perhaps because of – this, Richard Greyson feels most comfortable alone in his library on the grey coast of New England.

Made in the USA
Coppell, TX
28 October 2021

64804124R00169